# Molly Moon

## And The Incredible Book Of Hypnotism

# Georgia Byng

MACMILLAN CHILDREN'S BOOKS

*To Marc with love for his encouragement
and support and for making me laugh*

First published 2002 by Macmillan Children's Books

This edition published 2016 by Macmillan Children's Books
an imprint of Pan Macmillan
20 New Wharf Road, London N1 9RR
Associated companies throughout the world
www.panmacmillan.com

ISBN 978-1-5098-2130-3

1 3 5 7 9 8 6 4 2

A CIP catalogue record for this book is available from the British Library.

Typeset by Intype Libra Ltd
Printed and bound by CPI Group (UK) Ltd, Croydon CR0 4YY

**www.mollymoonsworld.com**

# Chapter One

Molly Moon looked down at her pink, blotchy legs. It wasn't the bath water that was making them mottled like spam, they were always that colour. And so skinny. Maybe one day, like an ugly duckling turning into a swan, her knock-kneed legs might grow into the most beautiful legs in the world. Some hope.

Molly leaned back until her curly brown hair and her ears were under the water. She stared at the fluorescent strip light above her, at the fly-filled yellow paint that was peeling off the wall and at the damp patch on the ceiling where strange mushrooms grew. Water filled her ears and the world sounded foggy and far away.

Molly shut her eyes. It was an ordinary November evening, and she was in a shabby bathroom in a crumbling building called Hardwick House. She imagined flying over it like a bird, looking down at its grey slate roof and its bramble-filled garden. She imagined flying higher until she was looking down on the hillside where Hardwick village lay. Up and up she went until Hardwick House became tiny. She could see the whole of the town of Briersville beyond it. As Molly flew higher and higher, she saw the rest of the country and now the coastline too, with sea on all sides. Her mind rocketed upwards until she was flying in space, looking down at the earth. And there she hovered. Molly liked to fly away from the world in her imagination. It was relaxing. And often, when she was in this state, she'd feel different.

She had this special feeling tonight, as if something exciting or strange was about to happen to her. The last time she'd felt special, she'd found a half-eaten packet of sweets on the pavement in the village. The time before she'd got away with watching two hours of evening television instead of one. Molly wondered what surprise would greet her this time. Then she opened her eyes and was back in the bath. Molly looked at her distorted reflection in the underside of the chrome tap. Oh dear. Surely she wasn't as ugly as that? Was that pink lump of dough her face? Was that potato her nose? Were those small green lights her eyes?

Someone was hammering downstairs. That was strange, no one ever mended anything here. Then Molly realized that the hammering was someone banging on the bathroom door. Trouble. Molly shot up and hit her head on the tap. The banging outside was very loud now and with it came a fierce bark.

'Molly Moon, will you open this door *at once*! If you don't, I'll be forced to use a master key.'

Molly could hear keys rattling on a ring. She looked

at the level of her bath water and gasped. It was much too deep and well over the allowed level. She jumped up, pulling the plug out as she did so, and reached for her towel. Just in time. The door swung open. Miss Adderstone was in and darting like an adder to the bathtub, her scaly nose wrinkling as she discovered the deep, draining water. She rolled up her crimplene sleeve and pushed the plug back in.

'As I suspected,' she hissed. 'Intentional flouting of orphanage rules.'

Miss Adderstone's eyes glinted spitefully as she took a tape measure from her pocket. She pulled the metal strip out and, making excited slurping noises as she sucked on her loose false teeth, she measured how far Molly's bath had gone over the red line painted round the bottom of the tub. Molly's teeth chattered. Her knees were now turning *blue* and blotchy. Despite an icy draught that was coming through a crack in the window pane, the palms of her hands began sweating, as they always did whenever she was excited or nervous.

Miss Adderstone shook the tape measure, dried it on Molly's shirt, then snapped it shut. Molly braced herself to face the wiry spinster, who, with her short grey hair and her hairy face, looked more like a Mr than a Miss.

'Your bath is thirty centimetres deep,' Miss Adderstone announced. 'Allowing for the amount that has already been *deceitfully* run away, while I was knocking at the door, I calculate that your bath was actually *forty* centimetres deep. You know that baths are only supposed to be *ten* centimetres deep. Your bath was four times that deep, so you have, in effect, used up your next three baths. So, Molly, you are forbidden to have a bath for the next three weeks. As for a punishment . . .' Miss Adderstone picked up Molly's toothbrush. Molly's heart sank. She knew what was coming next: Miss Adderstone's favourite punishment.

Miss Adderstone glared at Molly with her dull, black eyes. Her face heaved in a monstrous way as her tongue dislodged her teeth and moved them around in her mouth before settling them back down on her gums. She thrust the toothbrush at Molly.

'This week you will be toilet monitor. I want the toilets spotless, Molly, and this is the brush you'll be using. And don't think you can get away with using the toilet brush, because I'll be watching you.'

Miss Adderstone gave one last, satisfied suck on her teeth, and left the room. Molly slumped down on to the side of the bath. So the something that she'd felt was going to happen tonight was simply trouble. She stared at her manky toothbrush, hoping that her friend Rocky would let her share his.

As she picked at a loose thread on her grey, balding, old towel, she wondered what it was like being wrapped up in a fluffy white towel like the ones in TV adverts.

'*Softness is the sign,*
*Everyone feels fine,*
*Wash your towels in . . .*
*Clou-oud Ni-i-n-e.*'

Molly loved adverts. They showed how comfortable life could be, lifting her out of her world into theirs. A lot of the ads were silly, but Molly had her favourites, which weren't. These ones were filled with her friends

– friends who were always happy to see Molly when she visited them in her mind.

*'Wrap yourself in luxury time*
*Clou-oud Ni-i-n-e.'*

Molly was shaken from her towel daydream as the evening assembly bell rang. Molly winced. She was late, as always. Always late, forever in trouble. Other kids called Molly 'Accident Zone', or 'Zono', because she was clumsy, uncoordinated and accident-prone. Her other nicknames were 'Drono', since people said Molly's voice made them want to fall asleep and 'Bogey Eyes', because her eyes were dark green and close together. Only Rocky, her best friend, and some of the younger orphans called her Molly.

'Molly! Molly!'

Across the corridor, which was now being stampeded by children rushing downstairs, Molly saw Rocky's dark-brown face, framed with black curls, beckoning her to hurry. Molly grabbed her toothbrush and ran to the bedroom which she shared with two girls called Hazel and Cynthia. As she crossed the corridor, two older boys, Roger Fibbin and Gordon Boils, ran into her and pushed her roughly aside.

'Get out of the way, Zono.'

'Move it, Drono.'

'Quick, Molly!' said Rocky, who was shoving his feet into his slippers. 'We can't be late again! Adderstone will have a fit . . . Mind you, then,' he added, 'she might choke on her false teeth.' He smiled encouragingly at Molly as she searched for her pyjamas. Rocky always knew how to cheer her up. He knew her well.

And this was how.

\*

5

Both Molly and Rocky had arrived at Hardwick House ten summers ago. A white baby and a black baby.

Molly had been found in a cardboard box on the doorstep by Miss Adderstone, whilst Rocky had been found in the top part of a pram in the car park behind Briersville police station. Found, because he'd been heard yelling at the top of his voice.

Miss Adderstone didn't like babies. To her, they were noisy, smelly, squelchy creatures and the idea of changing a nappy filled her with disgust. So Mrs Trinklebury, a shy widow from the town, who had helped with orphanage babies before, had been employed to look after Molly and Rocky. And because Mrs Trinklebury named children after the clothes or the carriers they arrived in – like Moses Wicker, who'd been found in a moses basket, or Satin Knight, who'd come dressed in a nightie with satin ribbons – Molly and Rocky were given exotic names too.

Molly's surname, Moon, had come from 'Moon's Marshmallows', which had been printed in pink and green on the sides of her cardboard box cradle. When Mrs Trinklebury found a lolly stick in the box, she called the baby Lolly Moon. And after Miss Adderstone forbade Lolly as a name, Lolly Moon became Molly Moon.

Rocky's name came directly from his red pram. On its hood had been written 'The Scarlet Rocker'. Rocky was solid in build, like a rock, and very calm. This calmness came from a dreamy quality he had – but it was different to Molly's. Molly daydreamed to escape, whereas Rocky's dreaminess was a sort of pondering, as he wondered about the odd world he saw about him. Even as a baby, he could often be found lying happily in his cot, thinking and humming to himself. His deep, husky voice, together with his good looks, made Mrs Trinklebury say that one day he'd be a rock star, singing love songs to the ladies. So, Rocky Scarlet, the name she had given him, turned out to suit him very well.

Mrs Trinklebury wasn't very clever, but her sweet centre made up for her simple nature. And it was very lucky that she *had* nannied Molly and Rocky because, with only bitter Miss Adderstone in charge, perhaps they would have grown up thinking the whole world was bad, and have turned bad themselves. Instead, they were bounced on fat Mrs Trinklebury's knee, and they fell asleep to her singing. From her they learned kindness. She made them laugh and wiped their eyes when they cried. And at night, if ever they asked why they had been doorstep babies, she told them that they were orphans because a naughty cuckoo had knocked them out of their nests. Then she'd sing them a mysterious lullaby. It went like this.

'*Forgive, little birds, that brown cuckoo*
*For pushing you out of your nests.*
*It's what mamma cuckoo taught it to do*
*She taught it that pushing is best.*'

If Molly or Rocky ever felt cross with their parents, whoever they were, for abandoning them, Mrs Trinklebury's song would make them feel better.

But Mrs Trinklebury didn't live at the orphanage any more. As soon as Molly and Rocky were out of nappies, she'd been sent away. Now she only came back once a week to help with the cleaning and laundry. Molly and Rocky wished for more doorstep babies to arrive, so that Mrs Trinklebury could return, but none ever came. Small children arrived, but walking and talking and, to save money, Miss Adderstone used Molly and Rocky as nannies for them. Now Ruby, the youngest child in the orphanage, was five, and she had stopped wearing nappies ages ago, even at night.

Night was drawing in.

In the distance Molly heard the muffled squawk of the cuckoo clock in Miss Adderstone's rooms striking six.

'We're *really* late,' she said, tearing her dressing gown from a hook on the door.

'She's going to have a tantrum,' Rocky agreed, as they sprinted down the passage. The two children sped expertly along the obstacle course that was the route downstairs; a journey they'd made thousands of times before. They skidded round a corner on the polished linoleum floor and long-jumped down the stairs. Quietly, and out of breath, they tiptoed across the chequered stone floor of the hall past the TV room and towards the oak-panelled assembly room. They slunk in.

Nine children, four of them under seven years old, were lined up along the walls. Molly and Rocky joined the end of a line, near two friendly five-year-olds, Ruby and Jinx, hoping that Miss Adderstone hadn't reached their names on the register yet. Molly glanced at some of the unfriendly, older faces opposite her. Hazel Hackersly, the meanest girl in the orphanage, narrowed her eyes at Molly. Gordon Boils made the motion of cutting his throat with an imaginary knife.

'Ruby Able?' read Miss Adderstone.

'Yes, Miss Adderstone,' piped up tiny Ruby beside Molly.

'Gordon Boils?'

'Here, Miss Adderstone,' said Gordon, making a face at Molly.

'Jinx Eames?'

Ruby prodded Jinx in the ribs. 'Yes, Miss Adderstone,' he answered.

'Roger Fibbin?'

'Here, Miss Adderstone,' said the tall, thin boy who stood next to Gordon, eyeing Molly maliciously.

'Hazel Hackersly?'

'Here, Miss Adderstone.'

Molly was relieved. Her name was next.

'Gerry Oakly?'

'Here, Miss Adderstone,' said seven-year-old Gerry, thrusting his hand into his pocket where he could feel his pet mouse trying to escape.

'Cynthia Redmon?'

'Here, Miss Adderstone,' said Cynthia, winking at Hazel.

Molly wondered when her own name would pop up.

'Craig Redmon?'

'Here, Miss Adderstone,' grunted Cynthia's twin. Miss Adderstone seemed to have forgotten Molly. She was relieved.

'Gemma Patel?'

'Here, Miss Adderstone.'

'Rocky Scarlet?'

'Here,' Rocky said, his voice wheezing.

Miss Adderstone slammed the register shut. 'As usual Molly Moon is not here.'

'I am here now, Miss Adderstone.' Molly could hardly believe it. Miss Adderstone must have read her name out first, to intentionally catch her out.

'Now doesn't count,' said Miss Adderstone, her lips twitching. 'You will be on washing-up duty tonight. Edna *will* be pleased to have the night off.'

Molly squeezed her eyes tight shut with regret. The idea that something special might happen to her tonight was fading fast. The evening was obviously going to be just like so many others, full of trouble.

Evening vespers began, as usual. This was when a hymn was sung and prayers were said. Normally, Rocky's voice boomed above everyone else's, but today he sang quietly, trying to get his breath back. Molly hoped he wasn't going to have a bad winter riddled with wheezing asthma attacks. And then the evening proceeded, as it always did, three hundred and sixty-five days a year.

After the last blessing prayer, the dinner gong sounded, and the heavy dining room door swung open. Girls and boys shuffled through it, welcomed tonight by a disgusting smell of old fish. They'd seen the fish often enough, lying in plastic crates in the alley outside the kitchen, scuttling with flies and beetles, smelling as if it had been there a week. And everyone knew that Edna, the orphanage cook, would have baked the fish in a thick, greasy, cheese-and-nut packet sauce to disguise its rotten taste; a trick that she'd learned in the navy.

There Edna stood now, broad and muscly, with her curly grey hair and her flattened nose, ready to make sure every child ate up. With a tattoo of a sailor on her thigh (although this was only a rumour), and her terrible language, Edna was like a grumpy pirate. Her temper lay like a sleepy dragon inside her, a temper that was fierce and fiery if woken up.

Every single child felt nervous and sick as they stood in a queue and made their excuses, while Edna slopped out smelly helpings.

'I'm allergic to fish, Edna.'

'Load a bleedin' codswallop,' came Edna's gruff reply, as she wiped her nose on her overall sleeve.

'It *is* cod's wallop,' Molly whispered to Rocky, looking down at her fish.

The ordinary evening was nearly over. All that was left before bed was Molly's washing-up punishment. As usual, Rocky offered to help her.

'We can make up a song about washing-up. Besides, upstairs I'd only have Gordon and Roger trying to bait me.'

'They're only jealous of you. Why don't you just go up and wallop them for once?' said Molly.

'Can't be bothered.'

'But you hate washing-up.'

'And so do you. You'll get it over quicker if I help you.'

So on this ever-so-ordinary night, the pair set off for the basement pantry. But Molly had been right. A strange thing *was* going to happen tonight, and it was about to take place.

It was cold in the basement, with dripping pipes over-head and vents in the wall that let in mouldy-smelling cold air and mice.

Molly turned on the tap, which spluttered lukewarm

11

water, whilst Rocky went to fetch the washing-up liquid. Molly could hear Edna's grumbling in the passage as she trundled the trolley load of eleven fishy plates down the tunnelled slope towards the pantry.

Molly crossed her fingers that Edna would just leave the crockery trolley and go, although it was more likely that she would come into the pantry and get cross. That was more Edna's style. Rocky arrived with the washing-up liquid. He squirted some into the sink, pretending he was in one of their favourite TV adverts.

'Oh *mamma*!' he said to Molly. 'Why are your hands *so* soft?'

Molly and Rocky often acted out the adverts from the telly, and could do scores of them word for word. Pretending to be the advert people made them laugh.

'So soft?' Molly replied whimsically. 'It's becus I use thus wushing-up luquid, darling. Other brands are simply murderous. Only *Bubblealot* is kind.'

Suddenly, Edna's dinosaur hand came down on Molly's, shattering their make-believe world. Molly shied sideways, expecting an earful of insults. But instead a sickly sweet voice said in her ear, 'I'll do that, dearie. Off you go now and play.'

*Dearie*? Molly didn't think she could have heard Edna right. Edna had never *ever* spoken nicely to her. Normally, Edna was plain horrid and grisly. But now she was smiling an unnatural, snaggly-toothed smile.

'But Miss Adder—'

'Don't worry about that,' said Edna, 'You just go and relax . . . Go and watch the lovely blasted telly or something.'

Molly looked at Rocky, who was looking just as confused. They both looked at Edna. The change in her was amazing. As amazing as tulips growing out of the top of her head would have been.

And that was the first strange thing that happened that week.

# Chapter Two

Sometimes when bad luck comes your way, you
think it will never end. Molly Moon often felt
this way about her luck, which wasn't surprising since
she was so often in trouble. If only she'd known that
her luck was about to change, she might have enjoyed
the following day, for by the end of it Molly would feel
that all sorts of wonderful things were going to happen
to her. But that morning, from the moment she opened
her eyes after a sound sleep on her lumpy orphanage
mattress, Molly's day started to go wrong. This is how
it happened.

She was woken with a shock by a bell ringing loudly in
her ear. Big-boned Hazel, Miss Adderstone's pet, liked
to wake Molly up as violently as possible. Hazel had
her shoulder-length black hair neatly scraped back
under a hairband and had already squeezed her
athletic body into her tight-fitting, blue school uniform.
   'It's the cross-country races at school today,

Bogey Eyes, and that fifty-word spelling test,' she announced. She walked away, swinging her bell happily, delighted to have ruined Molly's morning.

Molly quickly dressed and went into the bedroom that Rocky shared with Gordon. Gordon threw a soggy paper cup at her to welcome her in. Rocky was singing to himself, oblivious of everything around him.

'Rock,' said Molly, 'did you remember the spelling test today?'

They tried to catch up over breakfast, only to have their homework books confiscated by Miss Adderstone. Then Miss Adderstone took great delight in watching Molly clean a loo with her toothbrush. By eight-thirty, Molly was feeling sick.

The morning didn't improve on the way to school either.

Their school, Briersville Junior, another grey stone building, was a fifteen-minute downhill walk from the orphanage. On the road, one of the village boys threw a water bomb at Hazel. When she ducked, the water bomb hit Molly, exploding on impact and soaking her. Hazel and her acolytes, the four other older orphanage kids, thought this was very funny.

As a result, school started with Molly and Rocky missing assembly, trying to dry Molly's cardigan and shirt on the radiator in the girls' cloakroom. They knew they were going to be late for the first lesson, which was an unwise move.

'Late!' Mrs Toadley, the form teacher shouted as they entered the classroom. 'And you missed assembly. I shall give you punishments later. Aaa tishu ooo!' Mrs Toadley had a small sneezing fit, which was what always happened whenever she got worked up.

15

Molly sighed. More punishments.

Mrs Toadley's punishments were imaginative. And, of course, Molly knew about them first hand. For instance, when Molly had been caught chewing paper for the tenth time, Mrs Toadley had made her sit in the corner of the classroom and eat a pile of computer paper. It had taken Molly two hours and was particularly unpleasant. It's very difficult to pretend pulpy paper is actually a ketchup sandwich or a doughnut – it just tastes of paper.

Molly hated Mrs Toadley, and she was glad that she looked so repulsive – blubbery-faced and half-bald, with a stomach like a water-filled rubber bag. Her appearance served her right. Molly might have pitied Mrs Toadley for her noisy, gurgling insides, for being allergic to everything, and so sneezy. But as it was she hated her.

Mrs Toadley's sneezing fits were usually useful for cheating, but cheating together in today's spelling test was out of the question as neither Rocky nor Molly knew the answers. They sat down at two worm-eaten desks in the front row of the class.

It was a test from the land of Gobbledygook. Not only did the class have to spell the words but they also had to give their meanings. Molly and Rocky blundered through it, guessing the answers.

When they had finished, Mrs Toadley collected the spelling tests and set the class an English comprehension exercise as she set to work marking them. She started with Molly's. Within minutes, Mrs Toadley's squealy, high-pitched voice whistled through the classroom, followed by a succession of loud sneezes. Molly's stomach went tight as yet another telling-off

16

began. Her strength began to crack. After all, a person can only take so much battering. She put on her best anti-tell-off armour and switched off. She had to, to stop Mrs Toadley's cruel tongue hurting her. In her mind, she floated away from the classroom until Mrs Toadley's ghastly tones were tiny and distant, as if coming down a telephone line, and the squirly pattern on her stretchy skirt became a purplish-orange blur.

'*You got NOTORIOUS wrong too,*' came her squeaky voice. '*Aaatishuooo . . . It actually means "famous, but in a bad way", and I must say that's you all over, isn't it, Molly? EH? . . . EH? . . . EH?*'

Molly sat up.

'Molly Moon! Will you listen to me for once, you useless girl!'

'I am sorry if I have disappointed you, Mrs Toadley. I'll try harder next time.'

Mrs Toadley snorted and sneezed and sat down, her veins throbbing with adrenalin.

Molly gave the morning ten out of ten for dreadfulness. But in the afternoon something much worse happened and it was nothing to do with the teachers.

After lunch, Molly's class changed for the cross-country running race. It was pouring with rain and the paths that led up the hill, away from the school and into the woods, were muddy. Droplets of rain ran down the cloakroom windows as Molly searched for her lost gym shoe. By the time she'd found it, and she and Rocky had stepped out into the rain, the others were a long way ahead. Rocky wanted to catch up, but the slippery ground made progress difficult. After running through the sludgy woods, Molly needed a break, and Rocky was beginning to wheeze. So they sat down on a bench under a tree for a little rest. Their gym shoes were sodden, and their legs were cold and wet, but their plastic anoraks made them feel hot. Rocky took his off and wrapped it round his waist.

'Come on,' he said. 'Let's start again, otherwise we'll be way behind.'

'Or why don't we just go back?' suggested Molly.

'Molly,' said Rocky irritatedly, 'do you *want* to get into trouble? You're mad.'

'I'm not mad, I just don't like running.'

'Oh, come on, Molly, let's keep going.'

'No, I just don't . . . feel like it.'

Rocky tilted his head and looked searchingly at her. He'd spent the last ten minutes helping her find her shoe, which had made him late too, and now Molly wanted to get them into even more trouble.

'Molly,' he said exasperatedly, 'if you don't come, they'll probably make us go round twice. Why don't you just *try*?'

'Because I'm no good at it and I don't want to.'

Rocky stared at her. 'You could be good at running, you know, if you tried. If you got better at running you'd like it, but you won't even try.' Rocky looked up at the rain clouds above him. 'It's the same with lots of things we do. If you're not good at things, you just give up. And then you're not good at things more, and so you don't try more, and so then you're even *worse* at things and then . . .'

'Oh, shut up, Rocky.' Molly was tired and the last thing she wanted was a lecture from her best friend. In fact, she was shocked that Rocky should bother. He was normally so easygoing and tolerant. If anything annoyed him he'd normally just ignore it, or wander away from it. 'And then,' continued Rocky, 'you get into *trouble*.' He took a big, fed-up, wheezy breath. 'And you know what? I'm sick of you being in trouble. It's as if you like it. It's as if you *want* to get yourself more and more unpopular.'

Molly's heart jolted in amazement as his unexpected words stung her. Rocky *never* criticized her. Molly was furious. 'You're not so popular yourself, Rock Scarlet,' she retorted.

'That's because I'm usually with you,' Rocky said, matter-of-factly.

'Maybe actually it's because no one likes *you* much either,' Molly snapped. 'I mean, you're not perfect. You're so dreamy, it's like you live on a different planet. In fact, communicating with you is like trying to get through to an alien. And you're not exactly reliable. Sometimes I have to wait *hours* for you to turn up. Like yesterday, I waited *ages* for you by the school lockers. And finally you wandered up as if you were on time. And you're so secretive you're almost sneaky. I mean, where were you yesterday after school? Recently, you've been disappearing *all* the time. People may think *I'm* weird, but they think you're just as strange. You're like a weird wandering minstrel.'

'Still, they like me more than they like you, that's for sure,' said Rocky truthfully, turning away.

'What did you say?'

'I said,' said Rocky loudly, 'they like me *more* than they like you.'

Molly stood up, giving Rocky the filthiest look she could.

'I'm going,' she said, 'now I know you think you're so much better than me. And you know what, Rocky?

You can run on and catch the others up. Go and make yourself more popular. Don't let me hold you back.'

'Oh, don't get so worked up. I was only trying to help you,' said Rocky, frowning. But Molly was enraged. It was as if something inside her had suddenly broken. She knew she was less popular than Rocky, but she didn't want to hear it. It was true that everyone bullied her, and no one ever bullied Rocky. He was untouchable, confident, difficult to upset and happy to daydream. Hazel and her gang steered clear of him, and he had plenty of friends at school. Other children secretly wanted to be like him. Molly hated him now for betraying her. She glared at him and he puffed his cheeks out at her in an 'Oh-you-drive-me-crazy' way.

'Same to you, too. And you look like a *stupid* blowfish like that. Perhaps some of your new friends will find it clever.' As she stamped away from him, she yelled, 'I hate this place, in fact I can't think of a *worse* place to be in the world. My life is just *HORRIBLE*.'

Molly stormed off through the bushes. She wasn't going to do the cross-country race, nor was she going back to that miserable school today. She was going to her special place, her secret place, and they could all whine and moan and shout till they were blue in the face.

# Chapter Three

Molly blasted her way through the school woods, the wet, ferny undergrowth slapping at her legs. She picked up a willowy stick and thrashed the plants. The first hairy fern she came to was Miss Adderstone. SHWIPPP. The cane zipped through the air and cut off her head. 'Old cow!' Molly muttered.

A dark-green creeper was Edna. SHWIPPP. 'Filthy old bag!'

She came to the base of an old yew tree. Poisonous red berries were rotting on the ground around it and a huge, yellow fungus was growing revoltingly on its trunk. 'Ah! Mrs Toadley!'

THWACK! THWACK! Molly felt a little better once she had sliced Mrs Toadley into smelly bits. 'Notorious yourself,' she said under her breath.

Sitting down on a tree stump, Molly kicked at a nettle and thought about what Rocky had said. The nettle bounced back and stung her ankle. As Molly found a dock leaf and rubbed it on the nettle sting, she thought that maybe Rocky had been right – a bit – but she still felt cross with him. After all, she never nagged *him*. Sometimes, if he was singing one of his songs, she had to shake him to get his attention. She, however, didn't expect him to change his habits. Molly had thought Rocky liked her exactly as she was, so it was a big shock to discover that he disliked even a part of her – a bigger shock to see him side with the others. She wondered how often he'd been resentful of her without saying anything. He'd been wandering off a lot lately. Had he been avoiding her? Molly's mind burned. What had he said? That she never tried at anything? But she did adverts with him brilliantly. She tried at those. Maybe she should find something else to be good at. That would show him. Inside, Molly was a stew of anger and worry.

Molly strode on through the woods, feeling very sorry for herself and taking deep breaths to calm down. The trees cleared, and she stood in the wind on the bare hillside, looking down on the small town of Briersville. There was the school, and past it the high street, the town hall, civic buildings and houses. All glistened from the afternoon rain. Cars that looked the size of guinea pigs beetled through its snaking streets. Molly wished that one of those cars was coming to pick her up, to drive her home to a cosy house. She thought how lucky other children at school were; however bad their day, they always had a friendly home to return to.

Molly diverted her thoughts to the giant billboard that stood on the edge of the town, displaying a different advert every month. Today the message beaming into everyone's lives was, 'BE COOL,

DRINK QUBE'. The picture on the huge hoarding was of a man on a beach, wearing sunglasses, drinking a can of Qube. The famous Qube can flashed its gold-and-orange stripes, as if Qube, not the sun, lit up the world. Molly liked the way it was hot-looking, and yet had a cool drink inside. Beautiful beach people crowded adoringly round the man who was drinking. They all had wonderful white teeth but the whitest teeth of all belonged to the guy with the can of Qube.

Molly loved the Qube ads. She felt she'd practically walked on the white, sandy beach where this one was set, and knew the glamorous people who played there. How Molly longed to be transported to their fantastic world. She knew they were actors and that the scene was fabricated, but Molly also trusted that this world of theirs existed. One day she'd escape from the misery of Hardwick House to begin a new life. A fun-filled life like the lives of the people in her favourite adverts – but it would be real.

Molly had tasted Qube once, when Mrs Trinklebury had brought in a few cans of it. But the cans had been shared and so she'd only had a few mouthfuls. With its minty, fruity taste, it certainly was different.

As Molly walked down into the town she thought how great it would be if simply drinking one can of Qube could make a person popular. She'd love to be popular like the glossy people on the poster. How Molly wished she was rich and beautiful too. As it was, she was poor, weird-looking, and unpopular. A nobody.

Down the hill Molly walked, towards the town library.

She was very fond of the old, disorganized library. It was peaceful, and its thick photographic books gave

Molly faraway places to dream about. Both Rocky and Molly loved it there. The librarian was always too busy reading or sorting books to bother them. In fact, it was the one place where Molly wasn't the butt of a telling-off. And she could relax in her secret place.

She climbed the granite steps and passed the stone lions at the top, going into the foyer. The sweet smell of the wooden floor polish made Molly instantly feel ten times calmer. She wiped her feet and padded over to the library notice board where there were messages from the outside world. This week there was somebody trying to sell a water-bed and someone else trying to find homes for kittens. There were notices about yoga courses, tango lessons, cooking classes and sponsored walks. The biggest notice of all was for the Briersville Talent Competition the following week. This reminded her of Rocky, since he was entering with one of the songs he'd written. Molly hoped he'd win but then, remembering that she was still cross with him, she stopped herself hoping at once.

Quietly, she opened the door of the library itself. The librarian was sitting at her desk, reading a book. She glanced up at Molly and smiled.

'Ah, hello,' she said, her kind blue eyes twinkling through her glasses. 'When I saw your school anorak through the doors, I thought it was your friend. He's been in here a lot lately. It's nice to see you again.'

Molly smiled back. 'Thanks,' she said.

The librarian's friendliness made her feel funny. Molly wasn't used to grown-ups being kind to her. Awkwardly, she turned away from the woman's gaze and started to read the pamphlets that were stacked in front of the newspaper table, where an old lady was reading a magazine called *Dog Show*, her pink-rinsed hairdo glued into shape with spray.

So it was the library where Rocky had been secretly sloping off to. Molly wondered again if it was because he was trying to avoid her. Then she decided to quit worrying, and she turned to look about the library. She walked towards the rows of bookshelves, borrowing a cushion from a nearby chair on her way.

Molly passed along the tall aisles of books. A to C, D to F. The shelves were crammed with books, often two deep. Some books, Molly thought, hadn't been looked at for decades. She passed the G to I books, then the J to Ls. M to P, Q to S.

T to W

and X to Z.

Z. Molly's favourite place. The X to Z section was right at the far end of the library where the room narrowed and there was only space for a short shelf. In between the shelf and the wall was a snug place warmed by an underfloor pipe and lit by its own lightbulb. The carpet was less worn out as hardly anyone ever went there, because there weren't many authors or subjects that started with X, Y or Z. Occasionally people would come to that aisle for Zoology, or books by an author whose name began with Z. But not very often. Molly took off her anorak and lay down, her head by Y and her feet by Z, propping her head up with the cushion. The floor was warm and the distant, rhythmical thudding of the building's boiler along with the librarian's soothing voice on the phone helped Molly start to breathe peacefully, and soon she was lying on the floor imagining herself floating in space again. Then she drifted off.

A rumpus woke her up. She had slept for about half an hour. Someone – a man with an American accent – was in a terrible temper, and his gruff voice was getting louder and louder by the second.

'I cannot believe this,' the speaker bellowed. 'I mean this is unbelievable. I made a deal with you a few days ago on the phone. I wired you the money to rent the book, then I fly over from Chicago to get it. Three *thousand* miles I've come, and you, meanwhile – you go and *lose* it. I mean, what kind of badly run institution is this?'

This was a very strange sensation for Molly. Someone else was getting a telling-off. The librarian's wren-like voice piped up nervously.

'I'm sorry, Professor Nockman, I really can't think what could have happened to it. I saw the book with my own eyes last week. I can only assume it's been taken out by another member of the public . . . Although it's always been in the restricted section, so that shouldn't have . . . oh, dear . . . Let me look in the files.'

Molly raised herself up to peep through the shelves to see who was making this fuss. At the main desk, the librarian was frantically flicking through a box file, staring beseechingly at the cards, begging one of them to explain where the missing book had gone. Molly knew what she felt like.

'It's by Logam, you said?' she asked in a worried voice.

'*Logan*,' the cross voice corrected her. 'And the title begins with "H".'

Molly got on to her knees to peer through a higher shelf to see what this man looked like. There was his middle, a barrel-like stomach in a Hawaiian shirt with palm trees and pineapples on it. Molly moved up a level. The shirt was short-sleeved and on his hairy arm the man wore an expensive-looking gold watch. His hands were small, fat and hairy, whilst his fingernails were disgustingly long. He strummed the desk impatiently.

Molly moved up one more shelf.

His nose was upturned and his face was round with a double chin. His black greasy hair started halfway back across his head and hung down to his shoulders. His beard was a small, sharp, black triangle just under his bottom lip, and his moustache was clipped and oiled. His eyes were bulbous and his face was sunburnt. In all, he looked like a very ugly sea lion, and, Molly thought, very unlike how she'd imagined a professor should look.

'So?' he asked belligerently. 'Have you found it yet?'

'Er, well no, I'm terribly sorry, Professor Nockman, it seems that it hasn't been lent out. Oh, my goodness. Oh, this really is very embarrassing.' The librarian's words tumbled nervously out of her mouth. She started to scrabble around in her drawer. 'Professor Nockman, perhaps for now you ought to take your cheque back.'

'I DON'T WANT TO TAKE MY CHEQUE BACK,' boomed the ugly man. 'WHAT SORT OF LOUSY LIBRARIAN ARE YOU, LOSING BOOKS!'

Professor Nockman started to rant with fury. 'I want that book. I paid for that book. I'll *have* that book!' He stormed over to the G to I aisle. 'Some idiot probably put it away in the wrong place.'

The librarian shifted nervously in her seat, whilst the man waddled through the aisles, huffing and sweating. Molly could hear his angry breath. Now he was just the other side of her bookshelf, so close that Molly could have touched him. He smelt of old chip fat and fish and tobacco. Round his rashy neck, on a gold chain, hung a scorpion medallion which nestled in his hairy chest. The golden scorpion had a diamond for an eye, which caught the light and winked at Molly. The Professor's pudgy, taloned finger ran menacingly along the top of the T to W books.

'Right,' he suddenly announced. 'Right. It's obviously not here, so what we're gonna do is this. You,' he said, marching over to the desk, pointing aggressively so that his fingernail almost poked the librarian between the eyes, 'you are going to check with your colleague and find out what happened to my book. As soon as you know you'll call me.' The warthoggy man pulled a snakeskin wallet from his back pocket and out of that, a business card. He wrote something on the back of it.

'I'm staying at the Briersville Hotel. You will telephone me and keep me updated. And you will get that book back in here as a matter of priority. I need this book for very important scientific research. My museum will be *horrified* to hear how it has been mislaid. Although they shan't hear of this, of course, if you find it. Have I made myself clear?'

'Yes, Professor.'

The Professor then picked up a sheepskin coat and, grunting angrily, left the library.

The librarian bit her lip and then started adjusting the pins in her bun. Outside, the main doors banged shut. Molly leaned back on her knees. In front of her a big Y denoted the beginning of the Y shelves. Y Y. Why?

Why was that ugly man so keen to get that book? He had said that he had paid to rent it out, even though it was a book from the Not-to-Be-Lent-Out section. And he'd come a long way for it. It must be a very interesting book. More interesting, Molly supposed, than Yachting or Yodelling or Ypnotism. Ypnotism? Molly looked at the book in front of her. Its cover had been ripped so that the first letter of the title had been removed. In a blinding flash, Molly realized that the missing letter had been an H!

Quickly, she pulled the heavy, leather-bound book from the shelf and, checking furtively that no one was watching, she opened the cover.

There in old-fashioned type were the words:

# HYPNOTISM
## An Ancient Art Explained
by
Doctor H. Logan
Published by Arkwright and Sons
1908

Molly didn't need to look any further. She quietly shut the book, wrapped it in her anorak, and while the librarian was reaching under the desk in a cupboard, Molly left the library too.

And *that* was the second strange happening of the week.

# Chapter Four

With growing excitement, Molly walked back through the outer streets of Briersville, and across the uphill fields to the orphanage. It had stopped raining, but even so, she had the hypnotism book wrapped tightly in her anorak. It was only teatime but already the grey November light was fading. Pheasants chirruped loudly in the woods as they settled to roost, and rabbits darted for cover as Molly walked by.

When she arrived at Hardwick House, the windows of the stone building were already aglow from lights within. Behind the thin curtain in a first-floor window, Molly could make out the wizened silhouette of Miss Adderstone as she petted her bad-tempered pug dog, Petula.

Molly smiled to herself and pushed open the iron gates. As she walked quietly across the gravel, the side door of the orphanage opened. It was Mrs Trinklebury. She threw her plump arms around Molly and hugged her.

'Oh, h-hello, Molly, poppet! You're back. At least I didn't m-miss you completely. H-how are you? All right?'

'Yeah, just about,' said Molly, giving her a hug back. Molly would have loved to tell Mrs Trinklebury about the book, but she decided it was better not to. 'How are you?'

'Oh, good as ever. Bit of trouble with H-hazel just now, but what's new? Look, I saved you a cake.' Mrs Trinklebury reached into her flowery knitting bag and rummaged about. 'Here you go,' she said, passing Molly a grease-proof paper package. 'It's a ch-choco-late fairy cake. Made some last night.' The glass in her spectacles flashed as they caught the light coming from the hall. 'B-but don't let Miss You-know-who catch you with it.'

'Oh, thank you,' said Molly appreciatively.

'M-must be going now, dear,' she said, pulling her old crotcheted coat tightly around her, doing up its flowery buttons and kissing Molly. 'Keep warm, chuck. See you in a week.' With that, Mrs Trinklebury set off for the road into town, and Molly went inside.

She nipped up to her bedroom, and since everyone else was at tea, had time to hide the book and the fairy cake carefully under her mattress. Then she went down to the dining room and sat by herself at the small table by the fireplace.

Molly usually had tea with Rocky, but this time he wasn't there to ward off trouble. She ate her bread and margarine, warily watching Hazel at the large table on the other side of the room. She was showing off because she'd won the cross-country race. Hazel's beefy legs were covered in mud, her big face was still

31

red from all the exertion and she'd stuck a leafy twig into her black hair, like a feather.

Molly knew that when Hazel saw Molly alone a bullying session would begin. And the usual escalation of nastiness would take place. Hazel would make a few vicious comments, Molly would pretend not to care. Hazel's taunts would become more malicious until she pierced Molly's shell. Molly might blush or her face might twitch, or worse, she might get a lump in her throat and her eyes might water. It was very difficult for Molly not to let her confidence crack when Hazel and her cronies ganged up on her. Quickly, Molly stuffed the last of her bread into her mouth and prepared to leave. But she was too late.

Hazel spotted her and shouted coarsely, 'Look everybody, Zono's finally made it. Did you fall in a puddle, Drono? Or was there a frog in the path that frightened you? Or did your weird spammy legs snap?'

Molly smiled sarcastically, trying to shake the insults off.

'Is that supposed to be a cool smile?' asked Hazel with a sneer. 'Look everybody, Bogey Eyes is trying to look cool.'

Molly hated Hazel – although she hadn't always. She'd felt sorry for her to start with.

Hazel had arrived at the orphanage four years ago, aged six. Her bankrupt parents had been killed in a car crash, leaving her nothing, not even relations. And so, alone and destitute, she'd been sent to Hardwick House. Molly had done her best to make Hazel feel welcome, but very soon she'd realized that Hazel didn't want her friendship. Hazel had pushed Molly up against a wall and explained to her that she was better than her. *She* had known a wonderful family life and she remembered her parents. *She* hadn't been dropped like rubbish on the doorstep. She'd come there because a tragic twist of fate had killed her loving parents. With lots of stories about her fancy past, Hazel was a glamorous figure amongst the other children. But to Molly and Rocky she was hard and poisonous. For four years, Hazel had teased, taunted and bullied Molly. For some reason Hazel hated Molly. And now Molly loathed Hazel back.

'I said, is that supposed to be a *cool* smile?' repeated Hazel.

The four big children near Hazel sniggered. Cynthia and Craig, the podgy twins, and Gordon Boils and Roger Fibbin, who were Hazel's special sidekicks, were all weak characters, too weak to ever stand up to their leader. They loved to watch her bully Molly.

Greasy-haired Gordon Boils sat on Hazel's left, wearing his bandanna and clenching his fists. Since he had tattooed each of his fingers, using a compass and ink, the fingers on his left fist read, 'G O R D', and the fingers on his right fist read 'K I N G'. From where she was sitting, Molly could just read 'KING GORD'. As Gordon took a bite of his teacake, Molly was reminded of his trademark trick of taking a fresh slice of bread and blowing his nose in it, making what he called a snot sandwich, which he'd then eat. He had a revolting imagination and if paid would do just about *anything*. He was Hazel's little spaniel.

On Hazel's right was the ear-whisperer, Roger Fibbin. He was Hazel's informant; her spy. As Molly looked at him, in his crisp, white shirt and with his tidy hair, she thought how much he looked like a shrunken adult. His sharp nose and cold, spying eyes were sinister. Rocky and Molly called him 'the Sneak'. And they called Cynthia and Craig, 'the Clones'.

The nastier the things Hazel said, the more her pack tittered and encouraged her. Gemma and Gerry, friendly seven- and six-year-olds who were quietly sitting on another small table by the dining room door, started to look uneasy. They hated to see Molly bullied, but were too young to be able to help her.

'Or did a farmer attack you because you look like a bogey-eyed rat?' suggested skinny Roger.

'Or did a rat attack you because your sweaty hands stink?' piped up muscly Gordon.

'Or did Rocky and you sit in the bushes planning your wedding?' jibed Hazel.

All at once Molly smiled. It was a smile that suddenly came from an excitement deep inside her, and from the hopes that the hypnotism book had kindled in her. Already, she had daydreamed about what she would be able to do if she learned to hypnotize people. Hazel and her posse just better watch out. Without a word, Molly stood up and left the room. She couldn't wait to look at her book. But it was a while before she got a chance.

After tea, all the children had to rest on their beds, except for those who were allowed to practise their acts for the Briersville Talent Competition. Molly was itching to start reading the hypnotism book but couldn't risk it, as Cynthia was reading a comic on her bed beside her.

The minutes crawled by. Molly listened to singing drifting up the stairs. She heard Rocky's husky voice and again hoped he'd win the contest, but she still felt moody about what he'd said, so she didn't go down-stairs and see him. Then came homework hour. It felt like homework year.

Miss Adderstone's cuckoo clock struck six. At vespers, Molly did her best to avoid Rocky and so Rocky ignored Molly. After singing a hymn, to tape-recorded organ music, Miss Adderstone, with her spoilt, over-fed pug dog yapping under her arm, made some announcements. The first was that Molly would be on Hoovering duty for a week since she had failed to complete the cross-country race. The second was that some American visitors were coming the next day.

'They will be arriving at four o'clock. May I remind you that they are interested in adopting one of you, strangely enough. If you remember, the last Americans to come here left empty-handed. Do not let me down this time. I'd like to get rid of one of you, at least. They won't be interested in adopting dirty, flea-bitten rat runts.' Miss Adderstone's eyes hovered on Molly. 'So clean up. Only a respectable child will be chosen. Some of you, of course, don't need to be told this.'

Every child in the room felt excited when they heard this news. Molly even detected a glimmer of hope in Hazel's eyes.

At supper Molly sat on her own, eating a bruised apple.

Finally, when Molly thought she was about to explode from curiosity, she found a moment when her bedroom was empty. Quickly taking the book and the squashed fairy cake from under her mattress, she hid them in her laundry bag, and set off to find a place to read.

'Hades' means Hell in Greek. This was the orphan-age name for the infrequently visited laundry rooms that were deep in the bowels of the building. Molly made her way down to them now, looking as if she was off to do some washing.

The washing cellars were dark, with low ceilings. The walls were lined with rusty pipes that hung with drying clothes so the cellars were warm at least. At the far end were some old porcelain sinks with limescale-covered plug-holes where the children washed their laundry. Molly found a warm spot under a light-bulb, below some drying pipes, and, bursting with anticipation, she reached inside her laundry bag.

All her life she'd yearned to be special. She'd fantasized that she *was* special and that one day, something miraculous would happen to her. Deep down inside, she felt that, one day, a brilliant Molly Moon would burst out and show everyone at Hardwick House that she really was a somebody. Yesterday, she'd thought something important was going to happen. Maybe the important thing was a day late.

All evening Molly had wondered whether this book was going to make her dreams come true and her mind had raced about what it might teach her. Perhaps Molly's imagination had stretched a little too far. It was with trepidation and a timid hand that she slowly lifted the dry, leather cover of the old book. It opened with a creak.

There was the first page again.

# HYPNOTISM
## An Ancient Art Explained

Molly turned to the second page. What she read made her tingle from head to toe.

'Dear Reader,

Welcome to the Wonderful World of Hypnotism and congratulations for making the wise decision to open this book. You are about to depart on an incredible journey. If you put into practice the following nuggets of wisdom, you will find that the world is full of golden opportunities! Bon voyage and bon chance!

Signed,

Doctor H. Logan,

Briersville,

February 3rd 1908.'

Molly noticed with amazement that Doctor Logan had come from Briersville. This was extraordinary, as sleepy Briersville didn't have many interesting people to boast of. She eagerly turned the page.

'INTRODUCTION

'You have probably heard often enough of the ancient art of Hypnotism. Perhaps you have seen a performing hypnotist in a travelling fair, hypnotizing members of the audience, getting them to behave in peculiar ways, and amusing spectators. Maybe you have read statements of how people have been hypnotized for operations so that they feel no pain.

Hypnotism is a great art form. And like other art forms, hypnotism is something that most people can learn, if they are patient and practise hard. A few students of hypnotism will have a natural talent. Even fewer will have a real gift. Will you be one of the gifted few? Read on.'

Molly's hands began to sweat.

'HYPNOTISM', the book read, 'was given its name by the Ancient Greeks. "HYPNOS" means sleep in Greek. Hypnotists have practised since the earliest of times. Hypnotism is also known as "MESMERISM", a word that comes from the name of a doctor called Franz Mesmer. He was born in 1734 and died in 1815, and his chief pursuit in life was the art of hypnotism.

'When a person is under the powers of a hypnotist, they are in a TRANCE. People go into trances all the time without realizing it. When you put your pen down, for instance, and one minute later can't remember where you put it, you can't remember because you were in a small trance.

'Daydreaming is another form of entering a trance. People daydreaming are in a world of their own and when they come out of their daydream trance, they often don't know what people around them have been saying or doing. In trances, people's thoughts float away from the noisy world into quieter places of the mind.'

Molly thought of the trick she had learnt; of drifting off into space and looking down at the world, of turning herself off when people were shouting at her. Maybe, without knowing it, she had been putting herself into a trance. The book continued.

'Our minds like to relax in this way, as a rest from thinking. Trances are very normal things.'

When Molly read the next sentence, her heart skipped a beat.

*'If you are good at going into trances, the chances are you will be very good at hypnotism.'*

Hungrily, she read on.

*'What a hypnotist does is bring people into trances and then keep them there by talking to them in a hypnotic way. When the person is in a deep trance, a sort of wide-awake sleep, the hypnotist can then suggest things that the person should think or do. For instance, the hypnotist might say, "When you wake up you will not want to smoke another pipe." Or, "When you wake up you will no longer feel afraid of riding in automobiles."'*

Molly put the book down for a moment. 'Or,' she thought aloud, 'when you wake up you will think you are a monkey.'

Molly smiled as ideas began to jostle through her head. Then a shiver of suspicion stopped her in her tracks. Was this book for real or was it written by a madman? Molly considered this as she flicked through the pages.

The book was peppered with drawings of people in Victorian clothes, showing examples of positions for hypnosis. There was a picture of a woman lying flat with only a chair under her head and her feet. She was called 'The Human Plank'. There were lots of strange diagrams of a man making all sorts of faces, one a puffed-up blowfish face, another where his eyes were turned upwards, showing their whites. 'Yuk, disgusting!' Molly thought. As she turned the thick pages of the heavy, old book, Molly came to the end of Chapter Six and realized it was immediately followed by Chapter Nine. Two chapters, Chapter Seven, 'Hypnotizing Using the Voice Alone', and Chapter Eight, 'Long-Distance Hypnosis', had been carefully removed. Molly wondered who'd taken the pages and whether they'd gone missing years ago or only recently. It was impossible to tell.

Then she remembered the warthoggy man in the library. He said he'd travelled all the way from *America* just to find this book. The Professor must believe that the secrets contained between its covers were extremely valuable. It must be very, very special. Perhaps – Molly thought to herself – perhaps she'd chanced upon a real treasure!

Near the end of the book were some pages of brownish photographs. One was of a man with curly hair and glasses and a bulbous nose.

*'Doctor Logan. The World's Most Famous Hypnotist,'* it said underneath. Molly was relieved to see that you obviously didn't need to be a great beauty to be a good hypnotist. Eagerly, she flicked back to the first chapter, 'Practise on Yourself'.

The first heading was *'VOICE'*. It read: *'A hypnotist's*

*voice must be gentle, calm, lulling. Like a mother's hand rocking a baby to sleep, so the hypnotist's voice must lull the subject into a trance.'*

This sounded too good to be true. Molly had been labelled with the nickname 'Drono', because people said her voice made them want to go to sleep. Now, this ability, instead of being something to be ashamed of, felt like a talent to boast about. The book went on: *'Here are some exercises which must be said slowly and steadily. Practise them.'*

Molly read the sentences out loud. 'I HAVE A WON-DER-FUL CALM VOICE. I AM CALM AND PER-SUAS-IVE. MY VOICE IS VER-Y . . .'

All of a sudden she heard loud steps. She shut the book quickly, slipped it into her laundry bag, and pulled out her squashed chocolate fairy cake.

Hazel was coming into Hades. She stamped noisily into the pipe room with her tap shoes still on.

'Urgh,' she said, 'what are you doing hanging out in here, weirdo? I heard you trying to sing. Give up. Your voice is flat.'

'Just singing while I find my socks,' said Molly.

'More like you're down here thinking about how everyone dislikes you.' Hazel collected her hockey kit from a high pipe and turned to look at Molly. 'You're like a sock, aren't you, Drono? A worn-out, stinking, unwanted, weird sock. Why don't you enter the talent competition as a sock? Or better still, enter as the ugliest person in the world.' And shuddering, she added, 'Urgh, I bet your parents were ugly, Bogey Eyes.'

When Molly didn't react, Hazel added, 'Oh, and by the way, you missed your dimwit stinking Trinklebury

41

today.' With a satisfied smirk, she turned and walked away.

Molly watched her. She smiled to herself and took a nibble of her fairy cake. Under her breath she said, 'Just you wait, Hazel Hackersly, just you wait.'

# Chapter Five

The next day was Friday. Molly woke, at six in the morning, smiling from a dream that she was a world-famous hypnotist. Since then, she had been concocting a daring plan.

She had no intention of going to school. She couldn't possibly go and sit in dire, dishwater Toadley's lessons whilst the book, with all its secrets waiting to be learned, lay under her mattress. Besides, she couldn't leave the book unguarded. Snoopy Miss Adderstone might find it. And if she took it to school, Hazel would snatch it.

When the morning bell went, she pretended not to wake up and kept her eyes shut, even when Rocky came to visit her. When Hazel rang the bell in Molly's ear for the second time, pulling her covers off, Molly just lay listlessly in her bed.

'Brain not working again, Bogey?' Hazel jeered.

'I don't feel very well,' Molly moaned.

Molly missed breakfast. When she was sure

everyone was downstairs, she hurriedly swung into action. Jumping out of bed, she opened the bedroom window, and with a pair of scissors scraped some green mildew off the stone wall into a plastic soap dish. Then she carefully mashed the chunks of green mould into a fine powder. She applied the powder to her face, giving her skin a very realistic sickly green tinge. Afterwards, she wiped the dish and put it back by the basin.

Next, she crept along to the sick room. There was a kettle, which Molly switched on. A moment later, she had filled a glass half-full with boiling water, and hidden it under a low armchair. Then she grabbed the metal sick bowl and placed it high up on top of a cupboard in front of the chair.

Back in the bedroom, Molly rifled through her satchel and found a packet of emergency ketchup which she'd saved for sandwiches. With this in her pyjama pocket she got back into bed, her trap set.

People started to return from breakfast. Gordon Boils plodded into Molly's room. 'Sick? Some hope,' he said. Molly heard something flicked, and felt something small, nasty and damp land on her neck before Gordon left. Then Molly recognized the voices of Gerry and Gemma, as they came to see her.

'Bet she caught a cold. Maybe she *did* fall in a puddle yesterday,' whispered Gemma.

'Poor Molly. She's probably sick because the big kids are nasty to 'er,' said Gerry.

'Mmn. Shall we go and feed your mouse?'

Finally, Miss Adderstone stomped in.

'Sick, I hear,' she said unsympathetically. 'Well, you'd better come to the sick room.' Miss Adderstone shook her.

44

Molly pretended to wake up and, acting as head-achy and fluey as possible, followed Miss Adderstone down the shabby corridor, and past other children who'd come out of their rooms to stare at her. Miss Adderstone made Molly sit on the sick room armchair. And taking a key from the metal chatelaine that hung round her waist, she opened a drawer, found the thermometer, and jabbed it into Molly's mouth. Molly's sweaty fingers were crossed tightly behind her back as she hoped madly for Miss Adderstone to leave the room. Seconds later her wish was granted.

'I'll be back in five minutes. We'll see if you're sick.' Sucking her false teeth, Miss Adderstone marched out.

As soon as she was safely away, Molly found her glass of water – once boiling, now very hot – and put the thermometer in it. She watched anxiously, her heart beating fast, as the mercury rose up the stalk. That was high enough, a temperature of forty-two degrees should convince Miss Adderstone that she was unwell. But, to be sure, Molly tore open the ketchup sachet before putting it back in her pocket. Now her nerves started to set in, making Molly feel very jittery as she waited to accomplish the final part of her plan.

In another minute, she heard sucking noises and Miss Adderstone's clipped steps coming back. Molly hung her head, trying to look as ill as she could. Miss Adderstone entered and without speaking, roughly pulled the thermometer from Molly's mouth.

Molly took a deep breath. As Miss Adderstone pushed her glasses up the ridge of her nose to inspect the thermometer, Molly started to grimace. 'Miss Adderstone,' she groaned, making heaving movements with her body, 'I think I'm going to be *sick*.'

Miss Adderstone looked as though she thought she was about to be sprayed by a skunk. Urgently, she turned to get the sick bowl. 'Where's the . . .?' she began to ask. Then she saw it high up on the cupboard.

Molly was making retching noises, 'Uuueeuughhh uuurgh,' and whilst Miss Adderstone stood on a stool to reach the bowl, Molly squirted some of the ketchup into her mouth and took a mouthful of water too. When Miss Adderstone stepped down, with the sick bowl in her hand, Molly was ready.

She seized the bowl. 'Blaaauuuuuuurgh.' The fake pink sick splattered on to the steel. After a few more retches, 'Uuuuurgh, uuuuuuuuargh,' Molly felt satisfied that the performance had been very convincing.

'Sorry, Miss Adderstone,' she said feebly.

Miss Adderstone looked appalled. Taking a step back she consulted the thermometer again. 'Collect your things at once, dressing gown, toothbru . . .' Miss Adderstone faltered. 'Get your belongings. Then go to the sanatorium. You've got a temperature of forty-two degrees. Trust you. I hope we don't all catch it. And wash that filthy bowl. Take it upstairs with you.'

Molly felt like running and punching the air, so thrilled was she to have fooled Miss Adderstone, but she didn't show it. She shuffled dolefully back to the bedroom, put on her thin dressing gown and her slippers, took a cardigan from her drawer as well as her laundry bag which, of course, held the hypnotism book. Then she made her way up the bottle-green linoleum staircase that led to the sanatorium.

It wasn't a proper sanatorium with lots of rooms and beds. It was just one room, up in the attic of

Hardwick House, far away from the bedrooms and immediately above Miss Adderstone's apartment. Molly passed Miss Adderstone's landing, with its heavy mahogany furniture and its severe portrait of her. Petula's purple cushion lay on the floor below a brown sideboard and next to it sat a collection of small flint stones and pieces of gravel. It was Petula's particular habit to suck stones and spit them out. Beside the stones was a saucer full of chocolate biscuits.

Up the stairs Molly went to the sanatorium room. She opened the door and, since the November day was a sunny one, found it was warm inside. Dust motes danced in the shafts of light that poured through the window and dead flies lay at the bottom of the window pane. A brass bed stood against the yellow wall. Molly took the horrible plastic bottom sheet off its mattress, since she wasn't planning to wet the bed, and remade it with its cotton sheets and two blankets. Then she settled down to read.

Molly decided to skip Chapter One, 'Practise on Yourself', as she was impatient and she reckoned that she'd already spent years learning how to dream and going into trances. She turned instead to Chapter Two.

'How to Hypnotize Animals.
'Now you have mastered the art of entering a trance, you may be ready to hypnotize an animal. Hypnotizing animals is a difficult art – more difficult than hypnotizing human beings. But if you achieve what I call the "Fusion Feeling" when you are hypnotizing animals, you will recognise the "Fusion Feeling" later when you are hypnotizing people, and that will be very useful to you.

47

*'If you don't get the "Fusion Feeling", animals and people are not properly hypnotized.*

*'Step One:     Go into a trance yourself.*

*'Step Two:     In your trance, think of the animal (dog, cat, lion) that you are going to hypnotize. Think about the essence of that animal. Try to become that animal.'*

Molly shut the book and put it under her covers. She stared at the light that played on the yellow wall and she started to transport herself into a trance, up a sort of misty slope, away from the world, and into her mind. She could easily feel distant and floaty and soon her surroundings looked like a blur, except for the light on the wall. Then Molly shut her eyes and, following the book's instructions, she thought of her animal. Petula, Miss Adderstone's pet dog, was the only animal in the orphanage. She would have to be Molly's subject.

*'Think about the essence of that animal. Try to become that animal.'* Doctor Logan's words drifted through Molly's mind.

The essence of Petula. Molly concentrated on the velvety-furred pug. She was a bad-tempered dog, spoilt and cossetted, over-fed and lazy. How had she become so bad-tempered? She was the only dog Molly had ever met that was always bad-tempered. Molly saw her in her mind – her solid, black-haired frame, her crooked front legs that were bent because of her fat, overweight body, her turned-up tail, her squashed face, the white mark on her forehead, her snarl, her bad breath, her bulging eyes. In her trance, Molly stared into Petula's dull, watery, squinty eyes. Closer

48

and closer she got, until Petula's eyes were the size of black snooker balls, then black basketballs, then huge, black medicine balls. And then, as Petula's eyes seemed to blow up to the size of two black hot-air balloons, Molly's mind slipped under them into Petula's doggy mind.

She found herself feeling doggy. In her imagination, she felt her four sturdy legs, her ears, her highly sensitive nose. Molly smelled the chocolate biscuits on the floor beside her, she smelled the musty velvet cushion underneath her. This was amazing. She was actually smelling Petula's hairy cushion. Then she felt her tummy, swollen and over-stuffed. She felt sick – from all the chocolate biscuits that Miss Adderstone fed her. Ow! It really hurt. Molly knew just how Petula felt and even found herself making a whining, growling noise in sympathy. 'Ggrrrrr.'

In the distance, Molly heard Miss Adderstone's cuckoo clock strike eight, and she opened her eyes. So, *that* was why Petula was such a grumpy, unfriendly dog. She had a tummy ache from eating too many biscuits.

Molly felt as though a door had suddenly been opened in her head. She was stunned that she'd so easily understood Petula. And she wondered what other latent skills lay inside her. Skills that Mr Logan's lessons would enable her to use. If Molly learned every lesson in the book as quickly as this, she'd soon be an expert.

For a moment, Molly faltered. Actually, she hadn't done anything yet. Maybe she'd made up Petula's feelings. Eagerly Molly opened the book again. She'd soon see if hypnotizing Petula were really possible. All she had to do was follow Step Three.

# Chapter Six

When everyone had left for school, Molly heard Miss Adderstone's clipped steps as she grudgingly made her way up to the sick room. Miss Adderstone was relieved to find that Molly was asleep. Holding her nose, she crossed the room and left a note on Molly's table.

'Since you are most likely infectious, you will stay out of the company of others until you are better. When you can keep foods down, go down to the kitchen passage and call Edna. On no account are you to go into the kitchen and breathe over the food.

'Here is a thermometer. When you are better and your temperature has reduced to a normal 37.5 degrees, you must return to your bedroom and assume your normal schedule. I will expect you then to make up for the cleaning duties that you have missed.

Miss Adderstone'

50

Sucking on her dentures, Miss Adderstone went down to her apartment for her morning glass of sherry. The day had been particularly tiresome so far, she felt, so she poured herself two. Not long afterwards, Molly heard her feet crunching across the gravel outside. As the iron gates swung creakily open, Molly looked out of the window in time to see Miss Adderstone tottering towards her minibus. She was going somewhere, but without Petula. Now was Molly's chance to experiment! Molly speedily finished reading Step Three in the Hypnotizing Animals chapter.

*'Finding the essence of your animal may take you weeks, but do not give up. Find the "voice" that fits your animal.'*

Well, Molly had already instinctively done that. She'd growled exactly like Petula.

*'Step Four. Face your animal, slowly approaching it if necessary. Think of the animal's "voice" and now perform it slowly and calmly. Repeat the animal's voice, in a lulling way, until the animal becomes rocked into a trance. A pendulum may be used. (All students of hypnotism should aquire a pendulum and study Chapter Four.) Once the animal is in a trance, you will know it from the "Fusion Feeling".'*

Molly shut the book and went to the attic landing. She looked over the banister and could just see Petula snoring noisily on her velvet cushion. Molly quietly slipped down the stairs until she was three metres away from Petula. Half-closing her eyes and concentrating on Petula in her mind, until the growl came out of her mouth again, Molly tailored the growl, so that it was slower and more rhythmical.

'Ggrrrr – grrrrr – grrrrrrr,' she went. For a moment she felt silly, but then, seeing Petula's ears prick up and her eyes open, Molly concentrated seriously.

The little dog saw Molly on the top stair and heard her making a familiar noise. Petula listened and cocked her head to one side. Normally she would have growled, since a child approaching usually meant there was a risk of her being picked up. And *how* Petula *hated* being picked up. It always made her tummy hurt. The stupid boss was always picking her up and how painful it was. But this child was sympathetic. The noises this child was making were comforting. Petula saw that the child was getting closer, but she didn't mind. In fact, Petula wanted her close, so that she could look into her lovely green eyes. She liked the way the child's voice was making her feel relaxed.

Soon, Molly was only a foot away from Petula. Petula's black eyes stared straight at her.

'GRRRR – grrrrr – GGRRRR – grrrrr.' Molly growled her essence-of-Petula growl, hoping and longing for the hypnotism to work. And all of a sudden Petula's eyes glazed over, as if a pair of curtains had been shut behind her eyes, while they were still open. It was a peculiar thing to watch. And whilst she watched, Molly felt a warm, fuzzy feeling rising from her toes all the way up her body to the roots of the hair on her head. It was the fusion feeling that Doctor Logan had described. Molly stopped making her noises. Petula sat, like a stuffed dog, staring into space. Molly had done it! She could hardly believe it. This was amazing! She'd actually hypnotized an animal.

Now, thought Molly, she could 'suggest' things to Petula, but then she realized with annoyance that this would be difficult since she didn't speak 'dog'. How she'd *love* to tell Petula to dribble in Miss Adderstone's sherry glass, or to bite her ankles, or to roll in a cow pat and then sleep on Miss Adderstone's bed. Suddenly Molly thought of the best thing she could do for Petula. She would put her off the chocolate biscuits that Miss Adderstone constantly fed her. Petula ate the biscuits out of habit and greed, not realizing they were making her feel ill and bad-tempered. Molly reached in her pocket for her half-used ketchup sachet.

Petula looked up at the girl in front of her, who was the nicest, most sympathetic person she'd ever met. The girl was holding one of Petula's chocolate biscuits and was squirting something disgusting on it. Something red. Petula knew it must be revolting because the girl was making horrid faces at the red stuff. And it was all over one of Petula's biscuits. The biscuit seemed very unappetizing now. And the girl thought so too. She was making retching noises. And Petula trusted the girl. In her doggy mind she knew that she must remember what this nice girl was showing her. Chocolate biscuits were bad, bad, *bad*.

Then the girl stroked Petula's head and Petula liked her even more. The girl started to make soft growling noises again and as she moved away she uttered a sharp bark. This snapped Petula out of her trance.

Petula shook her floppy ears with a puzzled expression on her face. She didn't remember what had happened in the last ten minutes, but she felt different. For some reason, a new feeling had come over her; that she didn't like chocolate biscuits any more. But she very much liked the person sitting on the stairs.

Molly waved at Petula. 'Good girl,' she said.

Petula still had a tummy ache, but she liked this girl so much that she made her way up the stairs for a stroke. She wagged her tail, which was a lovely sensation, because she hadn't wagged it for *weeks*.

Molly patted Petula and felt very satisfied. Then she went to the loo and flushed the ketchup-covered chocolate biscuit away.

Although Molly's stomach rumbled a lot that day from hunger, she didn't care. She was devouring the hypnotism book. At lunchtime, smells of baked eel – Miss Adderstone and Edna's lunch – wafted upstairs. Molly nipped down to Petula's landing and was very pleased to see that she hadn't touched any of her biscuits. Molly had chocolate biscuits for lunch, then went back to her book.

At four o'clock Molly heard everyone arriving back from school and Miss Adderstone filling Petula's biscuit bowl. When everyone was at tea, Molly took three of the biscuits. Half an hour later, she heard a car outside. Molly peered from her window to see the American visitors arrive – a thin, bearded man and a woman in a pink headscarf. Miss Adderstone, in her turquoise crimplene suit and on her best behaviour, was squawking, 'Welcome, come in.' For a moment, Molly felt a pang of longing. If only it might be *her* who was chosen and taken away. Whisked away like Satin Knight and Moses Wicker had been. But she knew that adoption was a rare thing, and that if anyone was chosen today, *she* definitely wouldn't be. And anyway, when she thought of her book, life at the orphanage didn't seem quite so bad.

Twice more that day the biscuit bowl was filled. Each time, Molly sneaked downstairs to help herself and this way she was able to keep her hunger at bay.

Molly read late into the night, concentrating hard on Dr Logan's lessons. When she finally turned the light off, she had the warm, comfortable feeling that time was on her side. She could be ill for at least another day before Miss Adderstone came to investigate. Molly could survive on Petula's biscuits, and absorb Dr Logan's wisdom at her leisure. In a few days, Molly should have the secrets of the book well and truly stowed away in her head. It was annoying that two of the chapters had been torn out, but she could learn everything from the other seven. She couldn't wait to tell Rocky about her find. Their argument now seemed petty beside the powerful secrets of the hypnotism book. Molly lay in bed, wondering where she could find a chain and a pendulum.

The image of the bad-tempered professor in the library crossed her mind. Molly felt slightly guilty. This must be the *best* textbook about hypnotism in existence, written by one of the world's most famous hypnotists. The poor professor's research would be incomplete without Logan's thoughts upon the subject and he had come thousands of miles for it. No wonder he was so fraught. His museum would be very angry that money had been wasted on expensive airfares. Well, Molly thought, she'd put the book back after she'd finished with it. Then they could pore over it for years. And with her conscience appeased, she drifted off to sleep.

She didn't give the professor another thought. And *that* was her big mistake.

# Chapter Seven

The next day was a Saturday. Molly was woken from a deep sleep by Petula trying to jump on her bed. When Molly looked down, Petula dropped a stone on to the floor as a present. She seemed much chirpier. Molly pulled her up and scrunched her ears.

'I'm the one who should be thanking you, Petula. You've really helped me, you know.'

Petula tapped Molly's chest with her paw as if to say, 'No, *you're* the one who's helped *me*.'

So, they were friends.

Molly swung her legs out of the bed and went to the window. Over the slated village roofs, she could just make out the church clock. The other children were already out on the Saturday morning walk.

Miss Adderstone liked to drive the children in the mini-bus to the bottom of a hill called St Bartholomew's Hump, ten miles away. Dropping them there, she expected them to walk up the Hump and back over hilly countryside to the orphanage. This gave Miss Adderstone three and a half hours to herself, which she always spent in town. Molly knew she often went to the foot doctor to have her corns clipped and her bunions seen to, and then perhaps somewhere for a couple of glasses of sherry.

Which meant that Molly had roughly three hours until everyone returned.

Wasting no time, she put on her dressing gown and left the room. It was lovely to be able to slide down the banister with no one around. Petula bounded after her, rushing into Miss Adderstone's apartment through her dog flap, and out again with her lead in her mouth. She followed Molly down to the ground floor. Molly walked through the hall, then skidded across the polished floor of the assembly room and quietly entered the dining room. Down to the kitchens they went, down the slope past the cutlery drawers and the plate racks. Edna could be heard clanking metal saucepans as she started to prepare lunch. Molly walked stealthily on, in her head turning over the lessons she had learnt from Chapter Three, 'Hypnotizing Others', and Chapter Four, 'Pendulum Hypnosis'.

In the attic room, Molly had already made an imaginary journey into Edna's head. There she'd found a disgruntled person, full of resentment, bored by life and tired of working. Molly thought she knew how to hypnotize Edna. It shouldn't be too difficult. After all, grunting Edna was very like an animal. She took a deep breath as a wave of nervousness flickered through her. But if it all went wrong, Edna would just think she was strange. Molly walked into the old-fashioned kitchen with its cracked white-tile walls, its broken sinks, its two gas ovens and its flagstone floor. Petula followed.

Edna was taking chicken heads out of a bag and putting them into a huge saucepan of boiling water.

'Er, hello, Edna,' Molly said. 'That smells nice.'

Edna jumped and then shot Molly a dirty look. 'You're bleedin' creepy, you are, creepin' about like that,' she said. Edna obviously wasn't in that freakish good mood of the other night. Molly tried again.

'What's that you're making?'

'Bloody soup, of course,' grunted Edna, pulling a feather off one of the chicken heads. For once Edna's language was correct; the soup really was bloody with all the chicken heads in it.

'Yum,' said Molly, her stomach turning. 'A navy recipe?'

''Spect you've come for something to blasted eat. Better not be bleedin' infectious.'

'You look bleedin' uncomfortable,' said Molly suddenly.

''Course I *look* bleedin' uncomfortable,' Edna retorted, 'I *am* flippin' uncomfortable. This kitchen's too 'ot.' She pulled at her white overall and flapped her arms, reminding Molly of a big, fat turkey.

'Why don't you sit down,' suggested Molly. 'I'll stir the blasted soup, and you can make yourself comfortable. Come on, Edna. You bleedin' deserve it.'

Edna looked suspiciously at Molly. But something in Molly's words made her feel at ease.

'If you sit down, you'll feel more comfortable,' Molly coaxed.

And, lazy as Edna was, she agreed. 'Yeah, I can't see

why not. After all, you've been in blasted bed for two days, whilst I've been slaving away down 'ere.'

She sat down in the kitchen armchair, her legs splayed out like a doll.

'I bet that feels more comfortable,' Molly said, taking the spoon from Edna. 'You must be bleedin' exhausted.'

Edna nodded 'I am . . . phew.' She leaned back and exhaled noisily.

'You're doing the right thing,' said Molly, looking at Edna calmly. 'Taking breaths like that, deep breaths, will make you feel much – more – relaxed.'

'Mmn, I s'pose you're right,' agreed Edna, puffing out a grumbly breath.

Molly's voice slowed subtly. 'If you – take a – few – breaths – you'll see – how relaxed – you feel . . . and how much – you needed – to sit down.'

'Yes,' said Edna, 'I *did* bloomin' well need to sit down.' But then she opened her eyes. ''Ang on a minute, you're bleedin' infectious. I shouldn't be letting you near that food.'

This was annoying. Molly realized that maybe hypnotizing Edna wasn't going to be such a breeze. Maybe she should have brought some sort of pendulum with her to focus Edna's mind.

'It's all right, the boil-ing of the blood-y soup will kill – any – germs,' said Molly. And in an inspired move, she began to stir the soup slowly and rhythmically. The wooden spoon circled to the rhythm of her words. Edna watched the spoon. 'Don't – you – think,' said Molly, 'the boiling soup will kill – the – germs? Nothing – to – worry – about.' Molly concentrated hard as she spoke and stirred. Edna seemed about to

60

say something, but her eyes were overcome by the movement of the stirring spoon, and her laziness got the better of her.

'Mmmnnn, I s'pose you're bleedin' right,' she sighed, and sat back again.

'I ex-pect – your – shoul-ders – and back – are feeling – much – more – comfort-able,' said Molly.

'Mmmn,' agreed Edna, 'they are.' Then she said, 'Molly, you've got very big eyes, you know.'

'Thank you,' said Molly, turning her green eyes on Edna's. '*Your* eyes – probably – feel – ver-y – heav-y – now – you – see – how – much – you – need-ed – to relax.'

Edna's eyes started to flutter as she looked at Molly's eyes and watched Molly stir.

'And this – room – is – so – warm – and – comfort-able – if – you – just – sit – there – and – I'll – stir – the – soup – round – and – round – and – round – and – round.' Molly stirred, trying not to look at the simmering chicken heads bobbing about in the pot.

'Round – and – round – I'll – stir – and – Ed-na – you – should – just – re-lax – and – to – re-lax – even – more – per-haps – you – should – shut – your – eyes . . .'

Edna did not shut her eyes but she did look very distant and dreamy. Inside, Molly was so excited that she wanted to shout, 'Yes! I've nearly done it,' but instead she said calmly, 'I – will – count – backwards from – twenty, and you – will – feel – more – and more – relaxed – as – I – count – back-wards.' Molly stirred and really concentrated on her most sooth-ing voice. 'Twenty . . . nineteen,' Edna's frown disappeared. 'Eighteen . . . seventeen,' Edna's eyelids

61

hovered. 'Sixteen . . . fifteen . . . fourteen . . . thirteen . . .'

At thirteen, Edna's eyelids suddenly clamped shut, and all at once the fuzzy, tingling feeling started to creep up Molly's body.

'The fusion feeling!' Molly gasped. Then, noticing that this made Edna's eyes flutter again, she counted more. 'Eleven . . . ten . . . nine . . . Now – Edna – you – are – so – deeply – relaxed – that – you – are – in – a – trance . . . Eight . . . so relaxed . . . Seven . . . deeply relaxed.'

Molly stopped stirring the soup and walked over to Edna. 'Six,' she said, only a foot from her. 'Five . . . and as I count down now, you, Edna, will be more and more in a trance until, when I get to zero, you will be completely willing to do as I say . . . four . . . three . . . two . . . one . . . zero . . . Good,' said Molly as she looked at Edna sitting quietly in the armchair. She had done it! She could hardly believe it. The low, steady voice that had given her the name Drono was obviously the perfect voice for hypnotism. Perhaps her eyes had something to do with it too. They felt as if they were glowing.

For a moment, Molly was lost for words. She'd been concentrating so hard on *how* to hypnotize Edna that she hadn't thought about what to tell her to do. So she said the first thing that came into her mind.

'From now on, Edna, you will be really, really, really nice to me, Molly Moon. You will defend me if anyone tells me off, or punishes or bullies me.' That was definitely a good start. 'And when I come into the kitchen you will let me make tomato ketchup sandwiches . . . You will buy me delicious things to eat from

62

the town, because you like me so much, and . . . and . . . you will stop making cheese-and-nut-sauce fish. In fact, you will refuse to make fish *any more* unless it is *fresh* that day, and,' Molly hesitated, then added recklessly, 'and you will become *very* interested in . . . Italian cooking. You will get Italian cookery books and try your hardest to become the *best* Italian chef in . . . in the world . . . and you will cook lovely Italian food from now on. Except for Miss Adderstone, who you will give her normal food – but make it much, much spicier. Also, without knowing it, you will make Hazel Hackersly's food very spicy too, and Gordon Boil's and Roger Fibbin's . . . Is that clear?'

Edna nodded robotically. It was a wonderful sight. Molly wanted to laugh, but then her stomach gave a loud rumble and she said firmly, 'And now, Edna, you will drive me to town and buy me a proper breakfast, and you will remain under my command.'

Edna nodded and stood up, and with her eyes still closed walked straight into the door.

'But obviously, Edna,' said Molly quickly, 'you have to open your eyes to walk and to drive.'

Edna opened her eyes and nodded. Her expression was distant and glazed, just as Petula's had been.

'OK, Edna. Let's go.'

So Edna, dressed in a white overall, a chef's hat and white clogs, walked out of the building like a zombie. On the way, Molly picked up a coat to cover her pyjamas, and outside, Petula picked up a piece of gravel to suck.

Driving with Edna wasn't a good experience at the best of times. When she stamped down on the accelerator, making the back wheels of her Mini kick up gravel, Molly put her safety belt on. Edna was not altogether 'there', it seemed. On the way down to Briersville she drove with a very peculiar expression on her face – as if someone had just dropped an ice cube down her dress. She drove down the main road in zig-zaggy jerks, nearly hitting an oncoming truck. Then she shot two red lights and drove through a flower-bed in a pedestrian-only park. Finally, she stopped the car on the pavement outside a café and, staring blankly ahead of her, she led Molly and Petula inside. From the door, Molly worriedly checked the street, very relieved to see that no policeman had spotted them.

Inside the café, two builders looked up from their bacon sandwiches and studied Edna. In her white outfit, she looked odd anyway. On top of this she was moving like a clockwork doll. Quickly Molly encouraged Edna to sit down.

'Can I help?' asked a chirpy waiter, who had a carnation in his buttonhole.

'Er, yes please,' said Molly, since Edna was staring straight at the salt cellar with a surprised look on her face and was beginning to dribble. 'I'll have four tomato ketchup sandwiches, not too much butter, and a half glass of orange squash concentrate, with no water added.' Molly's mouth watered. It was lovely to be able to order her favourite things.

The waiter looked bemused. 'Shall I bring some water for you to mix with it?'

'No thanks,' said Molly. 'But a bowl of water for our dog would be great.' Petula sat at her feet loyally, cocking her head to one side as Edna blew a raspberry.

'And for the lady?' asked the waiter.

'I love bleedin' Italy,' said Edna, sucking a fork.

'It's nice to be out of the hospital for the day, isn't it?' Molly said to Edna kindly, as if she was on an outing from a loony bin. The waiter smiled sympathetically.

Twenty minutes later, after the most embarrassing breakfast of Molly's life, they were driving back to the orphanage. Past the town shops. Past Shoot It, the camera shop, past a bicycle shop called Spokes, past the antiques shop with its curly painted name, Mouldy Old Gold. Molly thought of things she'd always wanted and felt on top of the world. Miss Adderstone probably had *mountains* of orphanage money stacked up in her bank account. All Molly had to do was hypnotize Adderstone into taking her shopping. Molly looked across at Edna, who was smiling like an idiot with her mouth wide open. She was completely under Molly's spell. Would everyone be as easy to hypnotize as Edna? So far, Molly seemed to be a natural.

'Edna,' said Molly. 'When we get back, you will walk down to the kitchen, and as soon as you pass the door, you will wake up. You will forget about our trip to town. You will not know that I hypnotized you. You will tell Miss Adderstone that I came downstairs for a headache pill and that you think I'm still very ill. Do you understand?'

Edna nodded.

'And, from now on, whenever you hear me clap once, you will go straight into a trance again, during which you will always do as I say. And whenever I clap twice, you will come out of a trance, not remembering anything that happened. Is that clear?'

Edna nodded again, her mouth hanging open like a

puppet. Then, slamming her foot down hard on the accelerator and her hand on the horn, she urged the car up the hill.

Professor Nockman was woken from a frenzied sleep full of pendulums and swirling motifs by a car screeching and beeping loudly in the street outside his room in the Briersville Hotel. He rubbed his eyes and ran his tongue along his plaque-covered teeth. 'It's noisier than Chicago here,' he grumbled to himself as he untangled the scorpion medallion from the mesh of his string vest, and reached for a glass of water.

After his frustrating experience at the library, the professor had extended his stay in Briersville. He decided that if he badgered that pathetic librarian often enough, she'd find the hypnotism book. Or, he hoped, he might see someone reading it. Briersville was a small enough town.

Since Thursday, he'd been prowling its streets, stalking people carrying books. Mothers with small children had crossed the road to avoid him and one group of teenagers had called him a weirdo, but he didn't care. He was determined to get hold of Dr Logan's book.

He had particular reasons of his own for needing the secrets contained in it, and they had nothing to do with museum research.

Professor Nockman knew a great deal about the life of the famous hypnotist. He had read how Logan had grown up in Briersville and travelled to America, where he became rich and famous with his hypnotism show. Nockman had studied yellowing, old press cuttings describing the amazing feats of hypnotism performed by the Doctor in the show that had made him one of the greatest celebrities of his time. He had visited Hypnos Hall, the palatial mansion that Logan had built with money made from his career as a show-man.

But he had become especially fascinated when he learnt about a book that Dr Logan had written, which, it seemed, contained everything he knew about hypnotism and how to do it. Very few copies of this book had been printed and it was extremely rare. But, Professor Nockman had discovered, one of the only surviving copies of it was owned by the library at Briersville. From that moment, he'd been absolutely determined to acquire that book for himself. He'd almost got it too, until that stupid librarian had lost it.

Thinking of that librarian now made Nockman quake with rage. He imagined throttling her skinny neck and the blood rushed to his head. Puce in the face, he reached for the phone.

'Room service,' he said angrily, 'bring me a pot of librarian . . . I mean coffee.'

He was desperate for that book. He had never wanted anything as much. Nothing in his dishonest life had been quite as attractive and he had big plans that depended on his finding it. *Nobody* was going to stop him having it and he wouldn't return to the States until he had that book safely in his oily, fat hands.

# Chapter Eight

Edna and Molly arrived back at the orphanage in a swirl of flying gravel. The place was empty and quiet since Miss Adderstone was still out and the other children had not yet returned from their walk. Petula slipped outside to explore the garden and Molly went back up to the attic room, feeling very pleased with herself. She sat down on the bed to think about the extraordinary thing she had just done. Hypnotizing Edna seemed almost as though it had been a dream. Music from the kitchen radio drifted faintly up the stairs as Molly marvelled at her new power. Her eyes felt tired. Something odd had definitely happened to them when she'd hypnotized Edna. They'd felt as if they'd been glowing, and now they felt dull and heavy. Molly flicked through the hypnotism book to see if there was anything about glowing or tired eyes. In the 'How to Hypnotize a Crowd' chapter, there was a part that read, *'It's All in the Eyes'*.

*'To hypnotize a large crowd, you must learn to hypnotize using only the eyes. This is very tiring for the eyes. Practise these exercises.'*

The book had diagrams of an eye. An eye looking left. An eye looking right. An eye looking at objects close and far. Then Molly came to something called 'The Looking Glass Exercise'.

*'Stand in front of a looking glass and stare straight into your own eyes. Try not to blink. Soon your face will change shape. Do not be alarmed. Your eyes will feel as if they are glowing. This glowing feeling is the feeling you must have to hypnotize people with your eyes only. And this is the trick you need to hypnotize a crowd.'*

So had Molly hypnotized Edna using just her eyes? Molly was sure she'd used the spoon, like a pendulum, and her voice, too. She went to the mirror and stared at herself. There was her pink, blotchy face and her potato nose. She stared at her closely set eyes. Her eyes glared back, green and intense. Ten seconds, twenty seconds, thirty seconds, she stared. Her eyes quivered, and then seemed to get bigger and bigger and bigger. The music downstairs sounded very distant. Molly concentrated on her eyes and tried not to blink, trying to make her eyes feel as if they were glowing again. Then, suddenly, something peculiar happened. Molly lost her own face entirely, and, as if by magic, a *different* face began to grow where Molly's real face had been. Molly's hair turned orange and spiky. A big safety pin grew out of the side of her nose and her eyelids were covered with blue-and-white make-up. She was staring at herself as a punk. Molly's legs felt all tingly, and her eyes felt as though they were throbbing, glowing and throbbing, switching on and off like the beam of a lighthouse. And this, the book said, was the eye trick for hypnotizing crowds. Molly blinked hard. She was relieved to see her normal face in the mirror. *That* had been very strange. Had the looking glass exercise made her hypnotize herself? Perhaps the book would explain what had happened.

Molly scanned the section entitled 'The Looking Glass Exercise'. There was a paragraph called 'Hypnotizing Yourself'.

> *'Imagine forms of yourself that you would like to be,'* suggested the book. *'For instance, if you would like to be kinder, or bolder, imagine yourself as being kinder or bolder, and in the looking glass, you will see an alternative you.'*

Molly sat back feeling puzzled. She hadn't imagined herself as a punk, yet the vision had just leapt out of the mirror. It was as if her unconscious mind had wanted her to be like a punk and had – through hypnosis – shown her a different identity. What were punks? She had always thought of them as being rebellious people. Molly certainly wanted to rebel. Yes, it seemed that her unconscious mind was one step ahead of her, showing her how, deep down, she wanted to be.

Sliding the hypnotism book safely under her mattress, she sat down to wonder what *other* Mollys could be conjured up. Then, still wondering about this, she took a pencil, and began to bore a hole through a piece of soap from the basin. She unravelled a piece of cord from the bedcover's fringe, snapped it off and threaded it through the soap. Now she had a home-made pendulum. It wasn't a very good one, but it would have to do, and though she was tired, there was time to try it out on Edna before everyone else arrived back. So, putting her dressing gown on, she went downstairs.

On the way she passed Petula, who trotted happily along after her. Down the swooping staircase Molly went until she was standing on the chequered stone floor of the hall. Molly heard music again, coming from the TV room and, to her surprise, she heard Hazel Hackersly's whiny singing voice. Hazel must have somehow evaded the Saturday morning walk.

Molly crept up the passage and peeped through the common room door. She saw Hazel dressed in a cat outfit, wearing a white leotard, white tights, white tap shoes and white fluffy ears on a hair band. It was her talent competition outfit. In her hand she swung a white tail, and whilst she danced, she sang.

'*I'm sorry I chased those pigeons,*
*I'm sorry I killed that rat,*
*I'm sorry I like to steal the milk,*
*It's just I am a cat . . . Miaoww Miaoww.*'

Molly watched Hazel tap dancing round the room, opening her eyes very wide, fluttering her eyelids and looking really stupid. Molly wished she had a camera. Then she had another idea. When Hazel was curtsying, Molly took a deep breath and went in.

'Oh, not *you*, Drono . . . *and* you're with smelly Petula. Not *better*, are you?' moaned Hazel. Petula growled at her.

'Yes, a bit better, thank you,' said Molly, taking the

soap pendulum out of her pocket. She sat down in front of Hazel and began to swing the soap pendulum as if she was just playing with it.

'What's that?' said Hazel. 'Soap you have to carry around because your hands sweat so much?'

Molly held the pendulum in front of her face and swung it rhythmically from side to side.

'What are you doing?'

'Just re-lax-ing,' said Molly.

'No you're not. You're trying to hypnotize me,' snapped Hazel. 'Typical of a weirdo like you to think that hypnotism is something real.'

Molly stopped swinging the soap. 'No I'm not,' she said quickly.

'You're so weird,' sneered Hazel, and Molly realized that she had approached Hazel too clumsily. Her previous successes had made her overconfident. Hazel was now too alert for Molly to hypnotize.

'I wasn't trying to hypnotize you. This isn't a pendulum, it's a . . . soap-on-a-string, so that I won't lose it in the bath.'

'I hope you're not planning to have a *bath*,' said Hazel nastily, rewinding her cassette, 'because Adderstone would not be pleased to hear you'd ignored her punishment. If you're covered in sick you'll just have to stay that way. No bath for *four* weeks, wasn't it?'

'Yup,' said Molly. 'I'm just preparing myself.'

Hazel looked at Molly in disgust. 'Prize weirdo,' she said. Then, as Molly was leaving the room, Hazel said slyly, 'By the way, have you heard?'

'Heard what?'

'Rocky's found a family.'

The words walloped Molly. It was as if a cascade of icy water had drenched her from head to foot. She found it hard to speak. 'Wh . . . when?'

Hazel smiled spitefully. 'That American couple that came yesterday. Amazingly, they liked him . . . *Weird* couple. Anyway, he left last night. Didn't say goodbye to you, did he? That's because, well, he told me he's gone right off you. Said it was like eating too much of something. He said he's kind of overdosed on you . . . Said he'd drop you a line.'

'You're joking . . . or anyway, making it up,' said Molly.

'No, no, not joking, although I s'pose it is funny,' Hazel replied coldly.

Molly stared at Hazel's mean face. 'Liar,' she said, turning away. But inside, fierce emotions scorched her. Rocky leaving? The idea was horrific. Molly couldn't believe it. The thought of losing Rocky was devastating, like losing your arm or your leg or your whole family all at once, because he was all the family Molly had. Hazel must be lying. Rocky would *never* have left without consulting Molly. In fact, he wouldn't leave unless she was adopted *with* him. That had always been their pact. If they went, they'd go together. Hazel's bullying had simply reached a new level.

Yet a dreadful suspicion filled Molly – that Hazel wasn't lying. As Molly left the room and headed for the stairs, a growing fear chilled her heart. Her clammy hands began to sweat but she felt intensely cold. On the first floor landing, the light coming from the boys' bedroom doorway lit the passage, familiar and friendly. Seeing this, Molly knew Rocky's possessions would wink at her as soon as she entered his room. She would feel a fool for falling for Hazel's story. But with every step she took her head became more numb. Then the ghastly truth hit her as undeniably as a thump in the face.

Rocky's bed was stripped of its sheets, its three blankets were folded into neat rectangles, and its pillow was without a cover. His bedside table stood bare of comics. The wardrobe was open and his clothes were gone.

Molly could hardly breathe. An invisible terror seemed to have gripped her neck and her brain so that she couldn't use her lungs. She fell against the door post, staring at the anonymous corner and the ownerless bed.

'How could you?' she whispered. Molly slopped across the room and sat on Rocky's old mattress. It was a little while before she could breathe normally and think logically. In her heart she felt sure that Rocky wouldn't leave without saying goodbye unless he had a very good reason. They'd had an argument but it wasn't *that* serious, and although Rocky had been extra-secretive lately, Molly didn't believe that he was sick of her. That part of the idea was Hazel's vicious imagination. But what could explain his sudden disappearance? He had always been unreliable and a bit of a wanderer but Molly didn't think that his faults could actually make him *forget* to say goodbye to her. They were like brother and sister. He couldn't have been *that* vague. It was all too strange.

With Rocky gone, Molly had no one. No one except Petula. The younger kids were OK but they were too young to be her friends. Living here without Rocky was inconceivable. She must find out where he was and talk to him.

But as she dragged herself upstairs to her attic room, Molly was confused and lost. In a daze, she turned the basin tap on to wash her face. She felt very muddled, upset and disorientated. She glanced up at herself in the mirror. There were her closely set eyes, burning with tears. She stared intently at her reflection, remembering what had happened when she'd practised the looking glass exercise before. Perhaps if she imagined herself feeling good now, she could hypnotize herself into happiness.

As she stared her features disappeared. The miaowing music for Hazel's tap dance floated upstairs, and Molly imagined that she didn't feel so bad. In a moment her face changed. Her cheeks became rounder and rosier, her hair, softer, blonder and curlier. Ribbons grew in it. She looked pretty! Like a child star. It was incredible! Molly started to feel a tingling sensation, like the fusion feeling, creeping up her body again. Her depression peeled away from her like a crusty old cocoon and optimism took its place. Once more, through the mirror, Molly's unconscious mind was telling her how she wanted to be and how she could change.

As Molly's unfamiliar glossy self stared back at her, the idea hit her. A huge and stunning idea.

She had this eye trick under her belt. And the eye trick was the hypnotism trick used on *crowds*. There would be an audience – a *crowd* of watching people – at the town talent competition in a few days' time. *Somebody* had to win that competition, with its huge cash prize. Why shouldn't that somebody be Molly?

Molly blinked – and was herself again. But now she was feeling hopeful. She refused to believe that Rocky hated her, even if he had gone.

She made up her mind on the spot. She'd discover where he was, she'd work out a way to leave Hardwick House, and then join him. It might be difficult but, Molly promised herself, she'd use every ounce of her energy and talent to find Rocky and she wouldn't give up until they were together again.

# Chapter Nine

By Saturday evening, Molly was up and about. Although she felt better than before, she missed Rocky. All through evening vespers, as other children whispered excitedly about his adoption, Molly felt sad and bereft of his voice. She longed to look at him, at his black, shiny hair with its tight curls, at his smooth, black skin, at his soft, dark eyes. She missed his patchy jeans, which every week had new holes in them, and his hands that were more often than not covered in biro doodles. But most of all she missed his reassuring smile. As she mouthed the words of the hymn she felt her loss as a frightening chasm of emptiness, deep inside her. Then she toughened herself up, and she turned her attention to the delicious smells that were coming from the dining room. As Miss Adderstone made her evening announcements, Molly's mouth watered.

'The first announcement is this. Gemma and Gerry, you will both have window-cleaning duties every afternoon next week, since you have been gossiping all the way through vespers. Rocky Scarlet's departure may be of great interest to you but it is not to me. There must always be silence at vespers.' Miss Adderstone sniffed and Gemma and Gerry looked at each other glumly.

Miss Adderstone steam-rolled on. 'The second announcement. Tomorrow is the Briersville Talent Competition. I believe some of you will be entering. You will walk from school to the town Guildhall to arrive for the competition by one o'clock. The prize money is, as you know, a ridiculous £3,000, and if any of you win, you are expected to donate your winnings to the orphanage funds. Is that clear?'

'Yes, Miss Adderstone.'

'After supper we will be having a brief preview.' Miss Adderstone looked at Hazel and smiled her false teeth smile. Then the smile left her face. 'Molly Moon, I see you are well again. You will sit on a solitary table at supper as I cannot have other children catching what you had.'

'Yes, Miss Adderstone.'

Molly followed the others through to the dining room. Nobody talked to her, but she didn't care. Inside, the different-sized tables were laid with napkins and candles and Edna was standing triumphantly beside a large pot of steaming spaghetti with peas and green vegetables in it. It smelled really tasty.

'Spaghetti primavera,' Edna declared dramatically. 'Justa lika my mamma maka.' And holding up some oily bread with olives in it she added proudly, 'And my very own home-made ciabatta bread.' The bread had a red, white and green Italian flag stuck into it, as did

78

all the other loaves of bread. Behind Edna on the wall was a map of Italy.

'Have you gone mad, Edna?' asked Miss Adderstone coldly.

'No,' retorted Edna. 'I happen to have a love of Italy, deep down in my soul, and sometimes it comes out.'

'It's never come out before.'

'Never come out in front of you before,' said Edna, 'but there's always a first time for everything . . .'

'Well, I hope you've made me my normal food . . . I don't want any of this Italian muck.'

'Certainly, Miss Adderstone.'

Unimpressed, Miss Adderstone made her way to her table with a plate of liver and kidney pie. As this cooled down she poured herself a glass of sherry which she sipped greedily whilst the children queued up for their meal. Molly noticed that Edna gave Hazel, Gordon and Roger special plates of spaghetti. Extra hot, chillied spaghetti, she hoped. It seemed Edna had remembered all Molly's instructions. Very impressed, Molly took her place at a small, solitary table by the window. From there, she had a really good view of everyone else.

Edna's vegetable spaghetti was fantastic. Molly looked at the small children's faces as they tasted it. Gemma, Gerry, Ruby and Jinx were gobbling it up as if it might be snatched away from them before they'd finished it. It was, without doubt, the best thing that Edna had ever cooked. But not for Hazel, Roger and Gordon. They all gasped and spluttered after a mouthful of theirs.

'Pass me the water,' Hazel croaked. Gordon Boils

forgot about Hazel being the boss. He filled his glass first and glugged it back.

'Gordon!' Hazel snapped. He poured some water for Hazel and then Roger snatched the jug.

'That . . . is . . . horrible,' said Hazel, gagging and pointing at her spaghetti.

And from four tables away, Edna's voice boomed, '*What* did you say?' Edna's food had improved but Edna had not, and her temper was as fierce as ever. She came marching over and children shrank in their seats. 'What did you bleedin' say about my food, 'Azel bleedin' 'Ackersly?'

'Well, it's too spicy for me,' said Hazel in a wormy voice. She wasn't used to being told off.

'Spicy? Are you blasted barmy? You're eatin' spaghetti bleedin' primavera. It's *Italian*, 'Azel 'Ackersly . . . from the land of olive groves and opera. If you can't taste the finesse and the warmth of the 'ills in my pasta, if you think the summer sun in my food is too 'ot, then you, I'm afraid, are a complete and utter blinkin' *moron*, an' bogs' swill to you.'

Hazel looked at her plate and her eyebrows went up and down. Edna seemed to have gone mad.

'It's delicious, Edna,' said Molly loudly. Hazel shot her a dagger look.

Edna smiled appreciatively. 'Thank you, Molly,' she beamed.

'Molly Moon,' Miss Adderstone shouted across the dining room. 'However much you like Edna's food, you know it is against the orphanage rules to shout across the *deening* room. You will come to my office later for a punishment.' Then she drank her glass of sherry in one and let out a drunken burp.

Perfect, thought Molly, looking at Edna and wondering whether she had remembered Molly's other instructions. Edna was staring at Miss Adderstone with a look of outrage. A blush of red was beginning to flush her cheeks and her face was twisting into angry contortions.

'Is there something wrong, Edna?' Miss Adderstone asked crisply.

Edna's face grew redder and redder and redder like the centre of a molten volcano. Then she exploded.

'Wrong . . . *Wrong*? Molly Moon just complimented my food, Agnes Adderstone . . .'

Miss Adderstone's mouth opened in astonishment, and a small piece of kidney fell out of it. Never had Edna answered her back or called her by her first name in front of the children.

'. . . She complimented my spaghetti primavera . . . maybe loudly, but I like her compliments loud, and what's more, I like 'er. *I like 'er an awful lot.* I like 'er *more* than I like Italian cooking, which I like more than anything else in the world, and you, YOU TOLD HER OFF!' Edna pointed one of the Italian flags at Miss Adderstone and roared, 'You are *not* bleedin' well punishing Molly Moon later . . . Over my stinkin' dead body!'

Miss Adderstone put her knife and fork down and stood up. 'Edna, I think maybe you need a little holiday.'

'A little 'oliday? You must be joking. My work's just startin'. I've got a blasted mountain to climb. I've got the whole of Italian cookin' to learn.' Edna now put the Italian flag to her chest as if swearing an oath, and to everyone's amazement she stepped on to a chair and then on to a table. 'Because *I* am going to become the *best* Italian chef in the *world*.'

Everyone stared. Gordon Boils couldn't resist looking up her skirt to try and see the legendary tattoo on her thigh. Miss Adderstone walked unsteadily towards the dining room door.

'Edna,' she said sternly, 'I would like to talk to you later.'

'Aren't you going to finish your supper?' said Edna from her lofty heights.

'No. I too found my dinner too spicy.'

As Miss Adderstone went, Edna said under her breath, 'Old cow. She should 'ave tried my spaghetti.'

# Chapter Ten

After supper, Molly went obediently to the door of Miss Adderstone's apartment, and knocked. Miss Adderstone opened the door and promptly put a handkerchief over her mouth when she saw Molly.

Miss Adderstone's parlour was a dark room, panelled with chocolate-brown painted wood and furnished with prune-coloured chairs. A patterned grey carpet covered the floor and the whole place smelled of mothballs, sherry and on top of this a hint of antiseptic mouthwash. There were two small tables with lacy cloths on them, but no photographs in frames, as Miss Adderstone had no family or friends. Three lamps with fringes lit the room, just illuminating the pictures on the walls. All the pictures were of dark woods, dark rivers and dark caves. As Molly was thinking how spooky it was, Petula bounded up to her, dropped a stone at her feet and licked her knee. Molly gave her a pat.

'Control yourself, Petula,' Miss Adderstone said.

Then, 'Sit.' Both Molly and Petula sat down at once. Molly on a hard stool by the unlit fireplace. For a moment, the room was silent except for the sound of Miss Adderstone sucking on her false teeth and, Molly was sure, the sound of her own heart beating. She was feeling extremely nervous. Miss Adderstone was her biggest challenge so far, and there was a horrible chance that this might all go wrong, especially since she didn't have a wooden spoon or any sort of pendulum object to focus Miss Adderstone's mind. But her nerves were steeled by her hatred for Miss Adderstone, who, she realized, must have knowingly and therefore, callously, let Rocky leave without saying goodbye to her.

The cuckoo clock on the wall broke the silence with its rusty, hollow chime, 'Cuckoo!' Molly jumped. Miss Adderstone sneered. For another six chimes the clock cuckooed. Molly watched the dusty wooden bird with its broken beak shoot in and out of the cuckoo house on its spring, until it finally disappeared into its hole. Miss Adderstone turned to look out of the window, and spoke to Molly.

'As you know, Rocky has left. He was responsible for many house duties that will now need doing by someone else. I have decided to give them all to you as you are the sort of child that will learn a lot from hard labour. That display of yours in the dining room which provoked Edna was very vulgar. I hold you entirely to blame.'

When Miss Adderstone turned, Molly was looking down.

'Have the courtesy to pay attention when I'm speaking to you.'

84

Molly gritted her teeth and glanced up. She had summoned up the special eye sensation and now, as she looked into Miss Adderstone's joyless, dreary eyes, her new power, like a trained laser beam, shot to the very core of her mind. Miss Adderstone turned away. She felt oddly unstable. 'Thank you, that's more like it,' she managed to say as normally as she could. She twitched, wondering whether this odd feeling was her heart palpitating again. After a sip of sherry, she felt better.

'As I was saying . . .' Miss Adderstone's cold eyes found Molly's again, drawn to them like a moth is drawn towards light. She was powerless to stop herself looking, so she looked. And as she did, a peculiar thing happened.

All Miss Adderstone's anger drained away from her and all her thoughts too. She couldn't remember what she was going to say. All she knew was that Molly's green eyes were very, very relaxing and she was experiencing a warm, yawny feeling inside. And then, Miss Adderstone was, all of a sudden . . . gone. Molly's eyes throbbed and the fusion feeling shot through her body. As Miss Adderstone's head tilted sideways and her tongue lolled out of her mouth, pushing her false teeth forwards, Molly's nerves lifted. It was obvious that she was now in complete control. When Molly began talking, her voice sounded like an angel's to Miss Adderstone.

'Agnes – Adderstone – listen – to – me. You are now – under my – command.' Molly's voice sounded like waves lapping a shore. Miss Adderstone nodded. 'From now on, I can do nothing wrong, do you understand? You will like me now as much as Edna does . . .

which is a ten-ton amount . . . Anything I ask for, you will give me.' Miss Adderstone nodded feebly. 'And the first thing I want is Rocky's telephone number. Give it to me now.'

Miss Adderstone shook her head. And in a monotonous, robotic voice she said, 'I – have – no – record – I – destroyed – the – number.' Molly was shocked. Miss Adderstone was obviously not as hypnotized as she looked. She must be only half-hypnotized. Molly pumped up her eye power.

'Miss Adderstone, you *must* give me the number,' she said forcefully.

'I'm telling – the truth,' said the robot Adderstone. 'I – never – keep records . . . I always – destroy – records of – children once they've left. It's always good – to see the – back of them . . . I wish they'd all – leave here and leave me – alone, except for you, Molly . . .' Miss Adderstone whined, 'Don't you go, Molly.'

Molly ignored her. So, Adderstone always threw records of children away! How completely horrible!

'You *must* remember the town he's gone to,' Molly ordered harshly, 'or the family's name. I *want* you to *remember.*'

Miss Adderstone obediently looked into the depths of her cobwebby mind. 'The family name – was . . . Alabaster, the town was . . . was . . . I can't remember . . . It was a long – address in America – near New York.'

'You *must* remember!' Molly nearly jolted Miss Adderstone awake. She pumped her eye power again. 'You must remember the town.' Miss Adderstone stood dumbly, her eyes rolling in her head. 'Come on,' she demanded. 'Think!'

'Polchester, Pilchester, Porchester,' growled Miss Adderstone. 'Something like – that.'

'Where are the records kept?' demanded Molly. 'Show me. You can't have thrown everything about Rocky away. I don't believe you.'

Miss Adderstone meekly opened a grey filing cabinet in the corner of the room. 'Here,' she gestured, 'here – are all – the files.'

Molly nudged Miss Adderstone out of the way and hungrily flicked through the drawer. Rocky's file was not there. Instead, Molly saw her own name on a folder. She pulled it out.

As Miss Adderstone stood like a sentry by the desk, Molly opened her folder. Inside was a passport and one sheet of paper. 'Is this all you have on me? No reports . . . nothing else?'

'That's it,' confirmed Miss Adderstone.

Molly read the sheet in front of her and froze.

| Name | Molly Moon |
|------|------------|
| Date of Birth | ? |
| Place of Birth | ? |
| Parents | ? |
| How came to Hardwick House | Doorstep Drop |
| Description of Child | ? |

And in Miss Adderstone's crabby hand was written: 'A plain child. Unremarkable. An outsider. Not likeable.' And that was it.

Molly stared at the piece of paper. She felt more of a nobody than ever in her life before. She opened her passport, which she'd never seen although she remembered having her picture taken for it. Miss

Adderstone always kept the children's passports up to date, so that if some foreigners came to adopt, they could fly home immediately with the child they'd chosen. A six-year-old Molly Moon smiled excitedly out of the little book. Molly remembered how keen she'd been to have her picture taken, and how Miss Adderstone had scolded her for smiling when the camera flashed. Molly felt enormously protective of the little girl in the picture. Looking hatefully at the stiff spinster in front of her, she wondered how a person could be so utterly without kindness. Then, as she cast her eyes about the chilly room she was suddenly filled with curiosity. She wondered what Miss Adderstone's own file would contain if she had one? So she asked her.

Miss Adderstone's reply made the gloomy room seem even colder and darker.

'My mother – went into a lunatic asylum – after I was born. My father was a drunk. I went to – live with my – aunt. She was – cruel. She – beat me. My uncle beat – me too. They were – very, very strict.'

Molly hadn't expected this. For a second, she felt a wave of sympathy for Miss Adderstone. It seemed she'd had it worse than Molly. But Molly checked herself immediately, and cleared all compassionate thoughts from her head. She took the paper with her own sad record from her folder along with her passport and stuffed them into her pocket. Then, she wiped her sweaty hands on her skirt and concentrated again.

'Right. Now, Miss Adderstone, I'm going to take you into a deeper – trance – and – you – will – obey – everything – I say.'

Miss Adderstone nodded like a clockwork toy, and Molly licked her lips. All Molly's life, she had been the target of Miss Adderstone's beastliness. Now it was time for revenge.

Twenty minutes later, Molly left Miss Adderstone's rooms with Petula trotting beside her. She felt more powerful than she'd ever felt before.

The dress rehearsal for the talent show was at eight o'clock in the hall. Molly sat on the eighth step of the stairs, so that she could see well. When Miss Adderstone stepped on to the makeshift stage, in front of the empty fireplace, Molly sat back and sighed a deep, satisfied sigh. For Miss Adderstone had dressed herself up. She was wearing a pink frilly nightie, and Wellington boots. On her head she wore a bra and round her neck, on a string, hung her false teeth.

'Good evening, everybody,' she said in a sing-songy voice, her mouth a rubbery cave without her teeth. Then she lifted up her nightie and showed everyone her knickers. 'Woopsie Daisy!'

All the children watching went quiet and stared aghast at Miss Adderstone's white, wrinkly legs. The change in her was so dramatic and strange that it was as if a Martian had landed in the room.

'On with the show!' Miss Adderstone announced flamboyantly. Clicking her false teeth in the air like Spanish castanets, she stamped her Wellington boots and with a flamenco flourish stepped off the stage and sat down on a chair at the side of the hall.

A few stifled, nervous giggles came from here and there. Then Miss Adderstone screeched in her usual crabby way, 'Gordon Boils! Spit that gum *out*.'

Gordon Boils shrunk in his chair. He'd preferred being told off by the old Adderstone. This Adderstone was creepy.

'Sorry, Miss Adderstone,' he said in a tiny voice, spitting out his gum and putting it in his pocket.

Molly stepped on to the stage.

Cynthia and Craig booed in unison, 'Eurgh, get off, Drone Zone.'

Molly stared at her shoes, concentrating on the eye sensation, very, very hard. She was going to try to hypnotize everyone using only her eyes.

'What's the matter . . . forgotten the tune of your drone?'

'That's enough of *that*,' snapped Miss Adderstone, clacking her false-teeth castanets, and biting the air with them. 'Anyone who makes trouble will get the *nip*.'

Everyone went quiet. Then Molly slowly lifted her eyes to the audience. They beamed out into the small crowd, like a searchlight. And each and every person out there was caught, stunned like a rabbit in head-lights. Molly felt as if she was playing a computer game. Every time a person locked on to her eyes, she felt their defences fall. She worked through the rows. Gemma, Gerry, Ruby and Jinx were the easiest, but even the older ones were a walkover. All the eyes that normally held scorn and dislike for Molly were now blankly expressionless. Gordon, Roger . . . Then some-one tapped Molly's shoulder.

'I think I'm first,' came Hazel's mean whine. Molly turned and cast her look upon Hazel. Hazel's slit eyes challenged Molly's. Then her face twitched oddly.

Hazel's eyes felt funny. She was looking at Molly –

ugly, unpopular Molly, whom she normally wouldn't look at for long, but for some reason now her eyes felt magnetized. Hazel tried to look away, but she couldn't. And, like a person clinging to a river-bank, being pulled away by a strong current of water, Hazel, too weak to hold on any longer, let go.

The room was quiet. Everyone sat wide-eyed and thunderstruck. Molly looked around, satisfied, and very impressed with herself that she hadn't needed to use her voice at all.

'In a minute I will sit down. When I do, I will clap my hands. When you hear me clap, you will all snap out of your trances and you won't remember that I hypnotized you at all . . . And from now on, whenever you remember nasty things you have said or done to Molly Moon, you will hit yourselves over the head with whatever you are carrying.'

Molly left the stage and sat down. She clapped sharply once. She hadn't hypnotized everyone to love her. She didn't need to do that now. She just wanted to be sure she could manage a crowd, and she could. As the room came to life around her, Molly reached into her pocket, pulled out the sheet of paper that she'd found in Adderstone's files and ripped it up.

So far in life, Molly had drawn a short straw. Now she was going to get what was due to her. A life like the world of Molly's favourite adverts. It might be just around the corner. Molly shivered with anticipation as she thought of all the lovely things she'd always wanted but never had. She'd line her pockets with the talent competition prize money, but that would just be for starters. She felt sure that with hypnotism under her belt, she'd never be short of money again. And as for people, Molly decided there and then that from now on, *no one* would push her or pinch her or boss her or bully her or ignore her. She was going to be a somebody now and the world ought to watch out, because a new, shiny Molly Moon was about to burst through the ether and dazzle it.

# Chapter Eleven

The next morning, the orphanage awoke to the lovely smell of fresh croissants and pizza bread, and the aroma of baking matched Molly's sunny mood.

Edna's Italian theme was going over the top in the dining room. She'd brought her hi-fi in, and opera was playing loudly. Laid out on the tables were books on Italy.

'Been to the library, Edna?' Molly asked, taking a crunchy croissant and a sweet bun from a plate.

'Yes, you see I'm a fan of Italy,' Edna explained politely, as if Molly didn't know. 'I love Italy, Italian cooking in particular. The Italians really bleedin' know 'ow to live.' She poured Molly a hot chocolate.

'Let me do that, Edna,' said Miss Adderstone with a toothless smile, tugging the chocolate jug from Edna's stubborn grip. 'Molly, my dear, where would you like to sit?'

She led Molly across to the window as if she were royalty. Children whispered as Miss Adderstone swept past, her false teeth necklace swinging with every step. This morning she had a huge pair of knickers on her head. She was wearing her crimplene suit, except that it had been snipped maniacally, all over, and was full of cuts and slashes. It looked like the mad creation of some crazy fashion designer.

'I like your suit,' said Molly.

'Oh, thank you, thank you, Molly. I did it myself last night with a pair of scissors.'

Behind them, someone screamed. Miss Adderstone turned with her usual foul expression (for nothing had changed in the way that she felt towards other children) and looked horrified. Hazel Hackersly had hit herself with her mug and tipped hot chocolate all over her head.

'*What* do you think you are doing, Hazel?' Miss Adderstone said furiously. 'Excuse me, Molly.'

There was another yell as Roger chucked milk all over his hair. Miss Adderstone snapped her false-teeth castanets and descended upon him like a bad-tempered lobster. 'That's it, Roger Fibbin. For that, you get a nip.' And, click-clacking her way towards the quaking Roger, she gave him a nasty nip on the arm.

'Eeeooooww,' Roger cried out, his eyes wide with alarm.

Molly winced. She hadn't hypnotized Miss Adderstone to be quite *that* fierce.

Edna, who had come over to Molly's side, whispered in her ear, 'I think Agnes 'as gone a bit bleedin' funny in the 'ead.'

When Molly left the dining room, she noticed Gordon Boils hitting himself on the head with a croissant. She looked at him in a concerned way.

Molly missed Sunday school. Instead, all morning, Edna and Miss Adderstone were at her disposal. Edna made her delicious snacks and Miss Adderstone gave Molly a foot massage whilst Petula sat on her lap. By twelve noon, Molly was feeling wonderfully relaxed and ready for the afternoon's challenge.

The other children left on foot, but Edna escorted Molly down to the minibus, carrying her rucksack and opening the back door for her. Then she climbed into the front seat with Miss Adderstone. Molly, with Petula on her lap, was chauffeured to the Briersville Guildhall.

The hall was a Victorian stone building with a copper-green pepper-pot roof. Its steps fanned out in two directions like a moustache on the front of the building. And today its steps were covered with children. Children dressed up in all sorts of outfits. In sequinned suits, in top hats and tails. Some were dressed to sing and dance, some were dressed to do magic, some were dressed to act a part, and some were dressed to do a comedy routine. All were prepared for the talent competition. And each child was accompanied by a parent. Molly found it difficult to pass. There were parents tying back hair, parents stitching last-minute hems and parents giving pep talks.

'Just belt it out, Jimmy . . . Show 'em what you're made of.'

'Sally, don't forget to smile when you sing.'

'Remember, Angelica, it's all in the eyes.'

'It certainly is,' thought Molly, as she made her way up the steps.

No one noticed the plain, gangly girl who squeezed past. No one noticed the minibus parked on the road that waited for her return.

Clutching her rucksack, with the hypnotism book safely in it, Molly made her way to a desk in the front hall.

'Name?' asked a lady with rhinestone-rimmed spectacles.

'Molly Moon.'

'Address?'

'Hardwick House Orphanage.'

The woman handed Molly a card with her name on it. 'Make sure you're backstage when the show starts and you'll be told when you're on. Good luck,' she said with a kind smile.

'Thanks, I need it.'

Molly walked down a parquet-floored passage, to the tall-ceilinged Grand Hall, where hundreds of metal chairs with red canvas seats were lined up in rows, some already occupied. Molly saw a low platform in the middle of the room with six chairs on it. These were for the judges.

The passages around Molly echoed with voices singing musical scales, as contestants warmed up. She walked on past Hazel and Cynthia, who both made a face at her, and entered the backstage room. This was like stepping into a cage of brightly coloured birds, all squawking and clucking. Mothers and fathers fussed over their children, children fussed over their costumes. Last-minute nerves filled the air with tension. The sight of these family groups gave Molly a pang of envy. She turned away and sat down in the corner in front of a television which was on with the sound turned off. Molly felt that it was only fair that she should win the talent competition. These other kids had had it easy all their lives compared to her. But

Molly's confidence was slipping. She watched the TV, hoping it would calm her, and stop her palms from sweating.

A commercial break was showing the Qube ad. The same man from the Qube poster on the billboard overlooking Briersville was now on the television tipping back a can of Qube. Molly felt very at home, and her concentration focused on the familiar advert. 'Oooh you're so cute, can I sip your Qube?' Molly spoke the lines of the woman in the sparkly swimming costume. Then she echoed the thoughts of the hero of the ad. 'Hey, the world really looks better with a can of Qube in my hand.' Now Molly knew a deep voice over the top of the scene was saying, 'Qube . . . It'll quench more than your thirst!'

Molly watched and felt homesick for Rocky. They always laughed together when they acted out the Qube ad. She wished they were both on that paradisiacal beach now. But at that moment, Mrs Toadley walked into the waiting room. The teacher's explosive sneezing shook Molly from her thoughts.

'Aaaaaatishshshoooooo. Oh,' she said disdainfully, wiping her nose with a hanky, 'I'm surprised to see you here. I didn't know you had any particular *talents*.'

'You'd be surprised,' said Molly coolly.

'I'm a judge, you know,' declared Mrs Toadley with another sneeze.

'I know, and I'm *really* looking forward to performing for you,' said Molly cheerfully, as Mrs Toadley waddled away.

After five more minutes, a man with a shiny red waistcoat came in and began handing out cards with numbers on.

'May I go last?' Molly asked politely.

'Certainly.' The man gave her a card with the number thirty-two on it, and took Molly's card with her name on it.

The competition began. Molly left the changing room when two boys began fighting over a magic wand. She stepped up to the wings of the stage and waited, next to the woman who sat on a stool in charge of the curtains. From there, Molly had a side view of the stage. After every act, the woman pulled a cord and the heavy velvet curtains swung shut, with a swish of musty air. The compère, the man in the red waistcoat, then hopped in front of the curtain and announced each performance.

Molly watched the other contestants go before her. Tap dancers, jugglers, mime artists, ballet dancers, a boy with a drum-kit who did a five-minute drum solo and a girl who did impersonations of TV stars. Some children took sheets of music up with them, for a pianist who sat at a white piano on the side of the stage. She watched ventriloquists, singers, musicians, comedians, and a few who were overcome with stage fright. Each time an act finished, the performer went down the front steps to sit in the audience. Each time, Molly's stomach fluttered with nerves.

She peeped through a hole in the curtain to see what the audience looked like. In the front row, she saw fat Mrs Trinklebury, staring up happily. But Molly could only see the front few rows lit up by the stage spotlight. The rest of the audience was in *darkness*. This made her panic. If she couldn't see the audience's *eyes*, how could she be sure that they were looking at her? If a mother in the back row was fishing about in her handbag, or a judge was doing up a shoelace, they might not look at Molly's eyes. If they weren't hypnotized her secret would be out. Molly didn't know how to hypnotize a whole audience with just her voice. The chapter on 'Hypnotizing People Using the Voice Alone' had been ripped out of her book. This was terrible.

'Number twenty-seven, Hazel Hackersly,' announced the compère.

Hazel bustled on to the stage. Molly should have enjoyed this delicious moment. The night before, she had had a 'meeting' with Hazel. But instead, Molly was worrying about how to see her audience.

Hazel's dance began. A dance? Really it was more of a stamping about the stage. Hazel jumped and stomped as if she was hammering nails into the floor. She sang, or rather shouted, her cat song, the words of which had changed. Now it went:

*'I'm sorry I can't dance*
*I'm sorry I'm a brat*
*I'm sorry I'm a bully*
*It's just I am a* prat.'

When she came off stage smiling, as if she'd just given an Oscar-winning performance, there was a shocked silence, before a few people began to clap half-heartedly.

'Oh dear,' said the lady on the stool, 'I don't think that'll win.'

'Number twenty-eight,' announced the compère, and Molly's stomach cramped painfully, confidence draining out of her. The darkness in the audience was terrifying. She sat down, trying to compose herself, trying to get the feeling in her eyes, but doubts kept buffeting her, knocking her concentration. This was dreadful. And then, Molly's desperate mind had a brainwave. She hoped it would work.

'Number thirty, said the compère. Molly stared and stared at the floor.

Number thirty was a boy who did bird impressions, and made the audience ooh and aah. Number thirty-one, a girl dressed as a Greek goddess, went on. While she sang her song, Molly struggled to pull herself together. It was now or never.

She focused her eyes and tapped the compère on the shoulder. When he looked round, her eyes locked on to his. Then Molly turned to the curtain puller and looked into her eyes too. Number thirty-one finished. The jolly man went back on stage.

'And now, last but not least,' he said, 'we have number thirty-two . . . Miss Molly Moon.'

Molly walked on to the stage, her hands more sweaty than they had ever been in her life. The curtain opened and the hot spotlight hit her face. Molly walked up to the microphone, her stomach twisting with nerves. She was suddenly filled with a fear that she couldn't remember how to hypnotize *anything*, let alone a whole audience full of Briersvillians. She looked out into the black hole of the hall, and could feel the people out there all looking at her. The air was thick with anticipation. There was silence except for a few coughs and a sneezing fit from Mrs Toadley.

'Good afternoon, ladies and gentlemen,' she said nervously. 'I am Molly Moon, and this afternoon I'm going to show you the talent that I have for reading minds.'

She heard a murmur of interested noises.

'For this, I have to be able to see you, so ladies and

gentlemen, er, boys and girls, the hall lights will now go on.'

Shielding her eyes from the spotlight, Molly looked upwards. 'Light controller, please could we have the spotlight off and the audience lights on.'

In two switches, the stage spotlight went off and the gang of lights above the audience came on. There were lots of people out there. In the front row Molly noticed Hazel hitting herself with her cat's tail.

'Hello, everybody,' Molly said, feeling calmer. 'Now, ladies and gentlemen, I can show you what I can do, if you'll let me for a moment concentrate and think. Soon I will start to get telepathic thoughts . . . *your* thoughts, and I will tell you what you're thinking.'

Molly stared at the floor.

From the audience's viewpoint, this girl looked the part. There she stood, concentrating in a very theatrical way. Of course, all this mind-reading business was an act, but the girl was pretending very well. It would be interesting to see how she read their minds. Perhaps she had some 'plants' in the audience, who'd act as if they'd never met her before.

Then, to their surprise, when the girl looked up again, each person in the hall thought how, on a second glance, this girl was much more *special* than they had first thought. The wafer-thin, plain child was really rather enchanting. The longer the audience studied Molly, wondering why they hadn't seen her charm before, the more and more ensnared they became by her mesmerizing gaze.

'It won't take long now,' Molly said as she went methodically through the rows of gaping faces, checking each person's eyes. A second was all it took to check, and to feel the fusion feeling getting stronger and stronger. Molly was amazed that most of the audience had fallen under her spell immediately, the judges included. Mrs Toadley looked like an old toad, with her mouth hanging open. Mrs Trinklebury looked as if she was about to have a fit of giggles.

The only problem was a woman in the sixth row. 'Madam, yes, you in the sixth row, with the sunglasses, please could you take them off.'

When the woman removed her glasses, Molly found that she was already in a trance. A boy who had been to the loo almost slipped through Molly's net, but she caught him on the way back to his seat. And as he sat down glazy-eyed, Molly was confident that every single person there was well and truly in the palm of her hand, sweaty as it was. She'd even eye-balled the light operator. 'Now, dim the audience lights again,' Molly told him.

Under the shiny beam of the spotlight, she began to talk to her audience.

'You . . . are all under my command,' she began. 'You will all forget that I came on to the stage to read minds. Instead, you will think that I came on stage and . . .' Molly's clear instructions reverberated through the Guildhall.

Molly's act began. All the people sat back in awe. This Molly Moon's song-and-dance routine was so good, so accomplished, so entertaining, that they felt they were witnessing a star being born. The girl was breathtakingly talented, charismatic and funny, with an adorable face. She danced so gracefully that her feet didn't seem to touch the ground. She sang like an angel, and then she told jokes. Such funny jokes! Jokes that made them laugh until they thought their sides would split.

In reality, Molly was simply standing on the stage, describing to the audience what they *thought* they were seeing and hearing. Before she finished, Molly had a special word with Mrs Toadley.

'From now on you will tell everyone you meet what a horrid, bullying teacher you are,' Molly told her, and Mrs Toadley opened and shut her mouth like a fat goldfish to show that she agreed.

Then Molly clapped her hands, and instantaneously brought everyone out of their trances. The whole audience erupted into loud applause, cheers and wolf whistles. Number thirty-two, Molly Moon. She was obviously and undisputedly the winner. She had more talent in her little toenail than all the others put together. And there she stood, dressed in a very ordinary skirt and top. It just went to show that all those fancy outfits really weren't necessary. Why, that Molly Moon had such stage presence that she didn't need a costume or make-up. There was something extra-special about this girl. She was just so – *likeable*. She definitely had that special magic that people call 'Star Quality'.

The audience clapped until their hands hurt. Molly stood there, smiling and bowing. She liked this applause and adoration. At last she went to sit down in the front row. People near her congratulated her profusely.

'M-molly, that was m-marvellous,' stuttered Mrs Trinklebury. Even Hazel Hackersly was smiling at her doe-eyed, which Molly found a revolting experience.

Then the judges walked up the aisle and on to the

stage. Mrs Toadley was second in line after the mayor. 'I'm a horrible, bullying teacher, you know,' Molly heard her tell the man behind her.

'I know,' he said, 'I've got a child in your class.'

As the mayor announced Molly as the outstanding winner, the other judges nodded their heads like those nodding toys you see on the back shelves of cars.

'. . . quite simply the most talented child this town has ever had the pleasure to watch. So please put your hands together once again for our very own, home-grown, Molly Moon.'

Molly stepped up to receive her prize money. She could hardly believe she'd done it. Her fervent wish on the hill above Briersville as she'd gazed at the Qube poster had been to become rich, popular and good-looking. And now, with a flash of her eyes those wishes had been granted.

'Thank you very much,' she said coyly.

As she clutched the fat envelope, full of crisp, new bank notes, she was seized by a strong feeling of wanting to leave the scene of her crime as quickly as possible. So, after posing for a few pictures, she left the stage and walked swiftly out of the building. Before anyone realized she was leaving, she'd walked down the Guildhall steps and climbed into the back of her chauffeur-driven minibus.

'To the Briersville Hotel,' she ordered.

Edna turned to smile at her, Petula jumped on her lap and Miss Adderstone looked at her obediently. 'Yes, madam.'

With a screech of rubber tyres on the road, the car sped away.

# Chapter Twelve

Everything was going according to plan. Molly and Petula spent the afternoon in a room in the Briersville Hotel. And while it was far from being the best hotel in the world – its beds were old and lopsided and its oak furniture was scratched and worn out – it was a good place for Molly to catch her breath, and Petula found the armchair comfortable.

Molly instructed Miss Adderstone and Edna to wait for her in the minibus, whilst she started on the next phase of her plans. She picked up the telephone and rang the international operator.

'The name's Alabaster. They live in America,' Molly explained.

'I'm afraid you'll have to be a bit more precise than that,' the operator replied. 'Which state and what's the town?'

'Polchester, or Pilchester or Porchester. It's some-where near New York.'

'I'm sorry, but this is just too vague,' the lady said.

'There are thousands of Alabasters in the United States . . . It would take me all night to go through them.'

'Are – you – feeling – relaxed?' Molly said slowly.

'Sorry?' said the operator. 'If this is some sort of prank, you can hang up now.'

'No, er, thanks for your help,' said Molly. She was very disappointed to learn that Rocky was going to be a lot more difficult to find than she'd expected.

Still, Molly was excited to be in the hotel room. She switched the television on and sat down to count her prize money. Inside the envelope, the money was in a bundle held together by a flat piece of paper. Molly ripped the paper off and fanned the cash out like a pack of cards. Molly had never held a ten-pound note, and never even seen a fifty-pound note, let alone *sixty* fifty-pound notes! £3,000 looked good, smelled good and felt good. The money made Molly feel powerful and free. She could go anywhere in the world with £3,000. Australia, India or China. She could just buy a ticket and go. Or she could spend it all on sweets. Lorryfuls of sweets.

Molly didn't want sweets, but there were a few things that she did want. So, putting the money into her pocket, and her hypnotism book under her anorak, she and Petula went shopping.

Ten minutes later, they were walking down Briersville High Street. Molly was carrying a travelling basket for Petula, which she had bought in Animal Love, the pet shop. Petula was looking proud and perky, with a brand new red collar round her neck.

Molly stopped at the optician's and, on a whim, stepped inside. Five minutes later, she came out again, in a pair of dark glasses. She'd always wanted a pair and now, she felt, they might also be useful to disguise her. She didn't want people recognizing her from the show. Then, she continued on round the bend in the road and paused in front of the wooden-framed window of the antique shop, Mouldy Old Gold.

The window display was an eccentric collection of interesting bits and pieces. Mirrored glass balls, cut-glass crystal goblets, silver boxes with secret compartments, a parasol with a parrot handle, magnifying glasses, a corset, a huge ostrich egg, a bowl of wax fruit, a sword and a pair of Victorian riding boots. And then, on a small, velvet platform at the back of the display, a golden disc caught Molly's eye. On its surface was etched a dark spiral which seemed to pull Molly's eyes towards it. It was beautiful and, though Molly's breath had steamed up the window, she was sure she could see that it was on a chain. To Molly, it looked exactly like a pendulum should look.

Molly took off her sunglasses, pushed open the shop door and stepped inside. An old-fashioned bell rang over the top of the door, alerting the shopkeeper, Mr Mould, who was at the back polishing a pair of antique spectacles. He briskly licked his fingers, tweaked his bushy eyebrows, and scurried to the front to greet the customer. When he saw a scruffy child with a pug dog his eagerness faded.

'Good afternoon,' he said, adjusting his collar.

'Afternoon,' said Molly, looking up from a display case full of jewellery and fancy hairpins.

'Can I help?' asked Mr Mould.

'Yes please. I'd like to have a look at the pendulum from your window display, please.' Molly had decided to treat herself. She needed a proper, heavy pendulum and it would be the perfect present for herself to celebrate her achievements in hypnotism.

'A pendulum . . . hmm . . .' hummed the shopkeeper.

He went to the window and reached inside. Then he brought out a tray and put it on the glass counter between him and Molly.

'I think there may be a pendulum sort of thing in here.'

Molly looked inside the drawer. It was full of coloured bead necklaces, chains, lockets, and pendants, but the pendulum she'd fancied wasn't there.

'Ah. The one I'm talking about is the golden one on the velvet at the back of the window,' she explained.

'Hmm,' coughed Mr Mould, 'I'm afraid that pendant will be beyond what you can afford, young lady.' He fetched the antique pendulum on its chain and let Molly admire it as he turned it over in his hand. Close up it was even better-looking than it had seemed before. Its gold was worn but not dented and the spiral on it was perfectly etched.

'How much is it?'

'Well . . . hmm . . . £550. It's solid twenty-two carat gold and rather old. Perhaps this one would be more suited to your purse.' Mr Mould picked up a pewter necklace with a dull brown stone in it. Molly ignored the pewter piece and studied the golden pendulum. Its spiral seemed to turn as Molly looked at it. She found it irresistible. She had to have it. Molly was sick of not being able to afford things. From now on, she'd buy whatever she wanted! With an extravagant gesture, she reached inside her pocket and pulled out her wad of cash. 'I'll take the gold pendulum,' she said politely, and she counted out eleven fifty-pound notes.

Mr Mould stared. 'You must have been lucky at the races!'

'No, lucky at the talent competition,' Molly explained.

'Oh! So you're the girl who won! My grand-daughter rang me and told me about you. She said you were fabulous!' The old man couldn't disguise his amazement. He was astonished that a girl as ordinary-looking, as ugly even as Molly could be thought of as 'cute', 'gorgeous' and 'lovely' – which was how his granddaughter had described her. 'Let me shake your hand then,' he said. 'Congratulations.'

He shook Molly's clammy palm. 'So, you had them all cracking their ribs, laughing,' he said, half-hoping that Molly would do an impersonation for him or tell him a joke.

'Mmmnnn,' Molly said, smiling enigmatically.

'So you're buying yourself a present.' The shop-keeper pressed the button on the till, making it open with a ting, and slipped the £550 into its drawer.

'Yup.'

'And where did you learn to perform like that?'

Molly was so happy and excited that she didn't mind telling him. 'From a very old book,' she said mysteriously, tapping the big, heavy shape under her anorak.

'You're joking!'

'No, I'm not. It's a very special book.'

'Which is why you're carrying it about with you,' said the shopkeeper.

'You got it,' said Molly.

The shopkeeper wrapped Molly's purchase. 'Thank you, and enjoy your pendant.'

'Thank you. Goodbye.'

'Goodbye.'

As Molly tucked the parcel into her pocket and turned to leave, the bell above the shop door rang, and another customer came in. In a cloud of cigarello smoke, he bustled past Molly, knocking her slightly.

Molly stepped out of the shop, pulling up the collar of her scruffy blue anorak and putting her new dark glasses on again. Mr Mould gazed after her.

The new customer blocked his view. 'Let me have another look at the pair of glasses you showed me this morning,' he demanded.

'Ah yes, Professor Nockman,' said Mr Mould, shaken from his daze, pulling the spectacles that he'd been polishing earlier out of his top pocket and putting them on the counter. 'You'd never guess it but that girl out there has just won the town talent competition!'

His impatient, short, fat customer wasn't at all concerned with modern Briersville life. But he did have an interest in Briersville life a hundred years ago. He'd been into Mr Mould's shop several times since he'd discovered that the elderly antique dealer knew the story of the town's famous Dr Logan and that Mr Mould had even bought and sold artefacts that had been used in Logan's travelling hypnotism show.

Today, Professor Nockman was back in the shop because of the pair of antique spectacles that were on the counter now. They had black lenses with a white swirling pattern on them and were said to have once belonged to Dr Mesmer himself.

'Supposed to be protection against hypnotic eyes,'

110

Mr Mould had explained. 'Fun but foolish. But, I should think,' he had added hopefully, 'very appropriate for your museum collection.'

The spectacles were expensive and Professor Nockman hadn't decided whether to buy them or not. He picked them up and scratched at his oiled moustache with a plump, long-nailed finger. Mr Mould continued to stare down the high street at Molly and Petula, who were strolling along, looking in shop windows.

'Are you absolutely sure you haven't had this book by Dr Logan pass through?' said Nockman. 'Because my museum would pay over the odds for it for the hypnotism exhibition that I'm organizing.'

'No . . . no, definitely not,' said the shopkeeper, dragging his gaze away from Molly. 'Apparently she can dance like Ginger Rogers. My granddaughter thought she was beautiful! She looks quite plain to me. Well, I suppose it's all in the eyes of the beholder.'

'Yeah, whatever,' said the professor, trying the strange spectacles on and looking up at the ceiling.

'She bought herself a beautiful gold pendant, although she called it a pendulum. A funny thing for a child to buy. I hope she doesn't fritter all that prize money away.'

'A *pendulum*?' said Professor Nockman, suddenly giving the shopkeeper his full attention. He turned his swirly spectacle-clad eyes upon him. 'How much money did she win?'

'£3,000 I believe. It's amazing, isn't it? She looks so ordinary. Well, you know what they say, "Don't judge your book by its cover". And talking of books, when I asked her where she learned to perform like that, she said, "From a very special, old book." What an eccentric child!'

'What book?' demanded Nockman, his nose twitching, like a dog's that had just picked up a scent.

'Some book she's carrying.'

Professor Nockman hurriedly took off the antique spectacles and, at last, looked out into the street at the girl. She was reading the notices outside the newsagent and, held awkwardly in the crook of her arm, under her blue anorak, was the hard-edged shape of a large, rectangular object. Nockman was struck so powerfully by the feeling that he'd just struck a bullseye that he gasped. He'd been stalking Briersville looking for people carrying his book *all* weekend, longing for a vision like this. He'd hit the jackpot. He was sure of it. His mind raced as he thought about what Mr Mould had been saying about her. She'd bought a pendulum, won a whole load of money, everyone thought she was gorgeous, but she wasn't, and the secret of her success lay in a special, old book. This book she obviously didn't want anyone to see since she was hiding it under her jacket. Nockman's gut instinct surged up inside him and told him that the shape under the odd-looking girl's anorak was, without any shadow of a doubt, *his* hypnotism book.

Molly and Petula were now disappearing round the corner. The professor lunged for the door handle, then he remembered the spectacles.

'I'll take the glasses,' he said. 'How much did you say they were?'

'They're absolutely unique,' said Mr Mould shrewdly. '£450.' He handed the silver-rimmed spectacles over.

Nockman's mind was galloping. He knew the shop-keeper was charging too much and he didn't like it, but if they were really effective anti-hypnotism glasses, he might need them and he didn't have time to bargain.

'I'll take them.' Professor Nockman put the money out on the desk. 'Don't bother wrapping them,' he said. 'And if you get *anything* else on hypnotism, call me in the States. Here's my number.'

'Certainly,' said the shopkeeper, happily. He'd never sold so much in an afternoon. It had been a good idea to open on a Sunday, after all. 'Goodbye.'

Professor Nockman hurried out of the shop, threw his cigarello on the ground, and looked frantically right and left for the girl. He burped with excitement as he puffed his way down the street in the direction they had taken.

Molly and Petula meanwhile had returned to the hotel where Miss Adderstone and Edna were faithful-ly waiting in the minibus.

Molly went to her room, collected her rucksack and came down to pay her bill for the afternoon's rent. Then she went to the minibus and climbed in. Petula hopped in after her.

'Where to, miss?' Miss Adderstone asked, in her rubbery-mouthed voice (still not wearing her false teeth).

'The airport,' Molly said confidently. She sat back, and gave Petula a good stroke.

Professor Nockman, who'd been looking for the girl in other shops, bustled into the drive of the hotel, just as a blue minibus was pulling out. The driver had a mad look in her eye and seemed to be wearing a pair of knickers on her head. As the vehicle turned into the

113

traffic, Professor Nockman caught a second glimpse of the plain-looking talent-contest winner. She was sitting in the back of the minibus like a starlet, with a pug dog beside her and a big, burgundy-coloured book on her knee, and through the low window, he saw that she was holding what was, unmistakably, a passport.

Professor Nockman *knew* that the girl had the hypnotism book. In a useless effort to get closer to it, he dived for the back of the minibus. But he missed the vehicle completely and he tripped over his feet instead. Getting a mouthful of exhaust, he started to panic. Nockman realized that the hypnotism book, *his* book, was sliding away from him. The book was essential to his plan – his brilliantly conceived, secret plan that was going to catapult him to the top of his profession. Without it, he'd never achieve his aims. Now there was a good chance that the girl with the passport planned to take it far, far away. Desperately Nockman ran, huffing and puffing, into the hotel.

'Order me a cab an' get my bill ready,' he rudely ordered the receptionist. Then he rushed upstairs, his double chin wobbling.

'A shame you're going so soon,' the woman said on his return, as he charged towards her with clothes bulging out of his case. Professor Nockman grunted and shoved his credit card at her. He was bristling with nerves; he *must* keep track of that girl.

'So where's the cab?' he demanded fiercely as he signed for his bill.

'You'll find a rank just outside the hotel gate,' answered the receptionist, wondering whether the professor was about to have a seizure. 'Are you all right, sir?'

But Nockman didn't reply. He was already out of the door.

'To the airport,' he growled at a sleepy taxi driver who was reading the paper. It was a long shot, but he felt sure that that was where the girl was headed.

As the car moved off, Nockman willed the traffic lights not to turn red. Beads of sweat were dribbling down his forehead. Then, as the taxi made good progress out of town, he realized that he could still catch the girl and he began to cool down.

That book was his destiny. All he had to do was follow it.

# Chapter Thirteen

The airport was an hour and a half's drive from Briersville. Molly sat in the back of the minibus, stroking Petula and looking out of the window at the countryside shooting by. She drank it all in, not sure when she would be seeing it again, now she was going to America, to find Rocky. She wasn't bothered if she never came back. Nor did she care that she didn't really know where in America she was going. She felt bold, strong, rich, and eager to see the world.

Miss Adderstone drove fast and furiously to the airport and she and Edna helped Molly out of the minibus. They seemed almost sweet now as they stood huddled together for solace, Miss Adderstone in her snipped-up suit with her knickers on her head and Edna in a tight-fitting, Italian-looking mac. They dabbed their eyes with hankies. Edna's had a map of Italy sewn on hers.

'Oh, Molly, we'll bleedin' well miss you,' Edna said weepily.

'Best of luck, Molly, dear,' Miss Adderstone sniffed.

'Thank you,' Molly said cheerfully. Petula gave Miss Adderstone a dirty dog look.

'Send us a postcard.'

'Do keep in touch.'

Molly nodded. Then she decided to give each of them a farewell present. She clapped once and both went into a deep trance. 'Now, listen carefully, you two,' Molly said. 'I'm going to give you some new interests . . . so your lives get more . . . well more *interesting*. Miss Adderstone, from now on, you will have a big new passion for . . .' Molly looked about for inspiration, '. . . for, for aeroplanes and *flying*. Yes, that's it. You are going to learn to fly planes. And Edna, well you will love Italian cooking and Italy even more. You'll love Italian fashion, um . . . Italian cars, oh, and the language, of course, which you'll learn to speak. And from now on, both of you will be *nice* to *all* children.'

Molly felt satisfied that she had been generous to everyone at Hardwick House. She clapped twice and Miss Adderstone and Edna came out of their trances. Miss Adderstone started to sniff again.

'Oh, you are *so* lucky, Molly, to be going on a plane,' she said with a sob. 'I've always wanted to fly.'

Molly helped Petula inside her travelling basket. 'Goodbye then,' she said. She turned away and the sound of Miss Adderstone's and Edna's wails faded as she stepped inside the terminal building.

'Boy, oh boy,' Molly said under her breath.

'I'd like a ticket on the next plane to New York please.'

The airline clerk peered over her desk at the plain,

small girl, whose chin was level with the top of the counter. 'I'm sorry, but we can only sell tickets to passengers who are sixteen or over.'

Molly took her dark glasses off and her eyes beamed out irresistibly at the uniformed woman. 'I *am* sixteen,' Molly said, giving the woman her passport. The clerk suddenly saw a girl who was obviously *at least* sixteen. Molly held out some money.

'Madam, of course, I wasn't thinking properly, I do apologize. But I'm afraid you'll have to buy your ticket at the ticket desk over there and besides you're too late to check in for the next flight. It has nearly finished boarding. It leaves in twenty minutes.'

Molly increased her eye voltage.

'I'm *so* sorry,' the blue-suited woman said bewilderedly, 'I don't know what's come over me today. For a VIP like you, madam, of course I can arrange everything. That'll be £450. Do you have any baggage?'

'No.'

The woman took Molly's money and wrote a few details down before handing her a hand-written ticket and a boarding pass.

'Please make your way as fast as you can to gate twenty-five. Have a good trip.' The clerk smiled happily at Molly as she walked away. Then she got up and walked over to the ticket desk to make a note of the cash transaction.

Molly hurried through the departures gate and up to the X-ray machines. After a good eye flash, the security guard let her pass through without checking her dog basket, and Molly padded past duty-free shops and down carpeted corridors until she found Gate Twenty-five.

Professor Nockman arrived, sweating and panting, at the ticket desk.

'Did a young girl just buy a ticket here?' he asked aggressively. 'She would have bought it with cash.'

'Sir, we have hundreds of people buying tickets here every day,' said the ticket clerk, crisply.

'Yeah, yeah,' Professor Nockman said rudely, 'but a girl, a girl of ten or so . . . she . . .'

'Sir, we don't sell tickets to children. And, besides, we don't divulge information like that.' The telephone behind the desk rang and the woman turned to answer it. The professor leaned forwards and scanned the piece of paper in front of her, reading it upside down.

She seemed to have made a note of a cash payment for a ticket to New York for an M. Moon.

'Gimme a ticket to New York. I wanna catch the twenty-hundred flight,' demanded the professor.

The woman looked down at her list and crossly covered it with her hand. 'I'm afraid it's too late to board the eight o'clock plane, the gates have closed.'

Indeed they had. Molly had stepped on to the plane, the last passenger.

Molly showed the air hostess her 'economy' ticket and flashed her eyes. 'First class, I think,' she suggested, and was escorted to the first-class compartment at the front of the plane. She put Petula, hidden in the basket, on the empty seat beside her.

As Professor Nockman stamped and raged, Molly was doing up her belt. As a security guard put his hand on the professor's shoulder, a hostess brought Molly a drink of orange juice. Professor Nockman had to make do with a ticket on the next plane to New York, five hours later.

As the plane roared down the runway and took off into the darkening sky, Molly looked out of the window. It was her first time on a plane and she found the idea of being in a huge chunk of flying metal scary. Her hands began to get sticky. But then she noticed how calm all the air hostesses were and she felt better. She looked out of the window and watched the twinkling lights of the airport falling away as the plane climbed higher and higher. She looked to the west, in the direction of Hardwick House. It was somewhere there, miles and miles away. Molly breathed a sigh of relief. It was good to be leaving. Hardwick House had nothing to offer her now, and somehow, she was sure, she'd see Rocky again. Then everything would be hunky dory. Maybe she could hypnotize his family to adopt her too. Or they could run away together and live out of suitcases. Molly's mind boggled as she thought about America. She'd seen it so often on television programmes. Soon, she'd be living the happy life that she'd been longing for. She wouldn't have to watch the adverts to get there any more.

Molly began to investigate the small television screen attached to her armrest.

From the viewing gallery on the airport roof, Professor Nockman fumed as he saw the plane taking off. 'M. Moon,' he muttered, 'I've clocked you, M. Moon . . .' He twiddled the golden scorpion medallion that hung round his neck. 'So you've got the book an' you've learnt a few tricks. Well, ain't you a smart alec. But not so smart that you covered your tracks. You better watch it, kiddy – I'm hot on your heels. And when I hook you, woah! – you're really gonna wish you'd never laid eyes on that book at all.'

# Chapter Fourteen

The flight to New York was eight hours long but Molly was very comfortable in her massive reclining chair. She watched two films, and smelled lovely from using all the free skin creams that came in a special sponge bag. Petula behaved herself all the way, sucking on a stone that she'd picked up in the Briersville Hotel drive. She whined only once – when the chicken casserole arrived – but the air hostess thought it was Molly making the noise. Molly ordered a second helping which she put in Petula's basket.

As the plane wheeled down through low-hung clouds to the John F. Kennedy Airport outside New York, Molly pondered her next move. She only had £1,910 left of her prize money. She'd spent £5 on Petula's collar, £15 on her travel basket, £20 on the sunglasses, £50 on the afternoon in the hotel, £550 on the pendant, and £450 on the airline ticket. Over a thousand pounds. She was amazed how quickly it had gone. The first thing to do was to change her money into dollars. Then she'd have to get a train or a cab to . . . where in New York Molly wasn't sure yet. She knew that if she made some hotel her base, she'd be off to a good start. From there, safe and private, she'd be able to plan what to do next.

The plane touched down at four in the morning, Molly's time.

'Ladies and gentlemen, please put your watches back five hours,' announced the pilot. 'The time in New York is eleven o'clock at night. We hope you have enjoyed your flight and look forward to travelling with you again.'

Molly was so nervous and excited that she didn't feel at all tired. She put on her sunglasses, picked up her rucksack and Petula's basket, and twenty minutes later she was out by a taxi rank, with dollars in her pocket. $2,998, to be precise. There, whilst Petula was having a pee in the gutter, a female cab-rank attendant with a thick Brooklyn accent asked Molly, 'Where to?'

'New York.'

'Yeah, little lady, but which part of New York?'

'The Centre,' Molly said, as confidently as possible.

'You'll be wanting the island of Manhattan then.' The woman wrote *Manhattan* on a piece of paper, gave it to a driver of a rusty, old yellow cab and helped Molly and Petula inside. The door slammed and Molly slid back into the bucket-like leather seat. A tiny recorded voice from under the seat shouted, 'Hey you . . . this is the mayor of New York. Buckle up . . . I don't want to see you in hospital!'

As Molly did up her safety belt, another deeper voice inquired, 'OK, so where to in Manhattan?'

Molly looked up at the solid partition between her

and the driver. It had a metal grille at the top, with a tiny sliding door for money to be passed through. She could only see the back of the driver's bald head. He glanced at her in his rear-view mirror and said huskily, 'You're small to be travelling on your own this time of night. You know you oughta be careful, this is an unfriendly city if you go to the wrong part of it.'

'I'm older than I look,' Molly replied. 'And I'm used to being on my own. And you know what? Nowhere could be more unfriendly than the place I've just come from. Now – I want to go to . . . oh . . . no . . . oh, it's been such a long flight that I've forgotten the name of the hotel.' Molly made a convincing act of searching her pockets for a piece of paper.

'I know all the hotels in Manhattan,' boasted the driver. 'What's it like?'

'It's the grandest, oldest hotel – you know the one . . . It's got statues everywhere and gold – dead posh.'

'Oh, you mean the Bellingham?'

'Yeah . . . that's the one,' Molly said happily. 'The Bellingham.'

'OK, little lady. Well, hold on tight.'

The cab pulled into the traffic. It was the bounciest car Molly had ever been in. She and Petula bobbed up and down as the rusty old vehicle turned on to the highway and headed to the centre of New York, to the island of Manhattan.

Molly stared out in wonder. Everything was so big. Huge juggernauts thundered down the six-lane road like glaring monsters with scores of lights on their massive fronts. To the left and right suburban houses stretched away into the distance. It was a dark, moonless night, but the highway was a solid river of white headlights and red rear lights.

After rolling and bouncing along for half an hour, the driver announced, 'Here she comes.' They rounded a corner and suddenly, there, out of the window was a view of the tallest, brightest, most colossal, space-age city that Molly had ever seen. The buildings were mammoth, like buildings from another planet, and they all stood on an *island*. Petula put her front paws on the window to look out and Molly's hands started to sweat as she saw that the way on to the island of Manhattan was over an enormous, glittering suspension bridge. Her mouth dropped open as they drove towards it and as they began to cross the water, Molly saw how truly big these buildings were. Some had *hundreds* of floors and *thousands* of windows with lights still on.

'So many people are still awake!' Molly exclaimed.

'Yeah, din't ya know?' laughed the driver. 'This is the city that never sleeps.'

On the other side of the bridge, the cab turned right and drove for five minutes along the side of the river. On their right, water reflected the lights of the city, and on their left, side-streets led into the centre. These were very straight and lined with tall buildings.

'The streets in Manhattan are very simply laid out,' the cab driver explained as he honked a truck. 'They were designed on a grid system, ya know, like your math book, so it's easy to navigate. They're all given numbers. See . . . 70th Street . . . 71st Street . . . 72nd Street. Some streets are east of the park, some are west. The park's in the middle. We're heading up the east side of the island. Round about here, is what's called

"Up Town", around the East 60s 70s and 80s. Up Town's the smart part where you get all the rich people. Mind you, these days rich people live Down Town too. Yeah, yeah, Manhattan's gettin' real expensive, but still the roads are fulla holes.' The driver swerved suddenly to avoid a big pothole. At East 75th Street, he took a left turn, and finally pulled up in front of a grand old building.

'This is your stop, lady, and you owe me thirty-five dollars.'

A uniformed doorman wearing a green suit with gold braid on the shoulders and white gloves stepped up and opened Molly's door. Molly paid and thanked the cab driver, and the yellow car rattled away into the night. She and Petula walked uncertainly up a flight of marble steps, through a huge golden door and into the hotel lobby, where they stood and stared.

A heavy golden chandelier hung high above their heads, under a glistening mosaic dome. Golden-coloured marble gleamed under their feet. Chinese black lacquer chairs and coffee tables were dotted about and at the rear of the lobby a giant vase was filled with exotic flowers. Molly saw her reflection in a massive gilt-framed mirror and thought how very scruffy she looked in her old clothes. This was the most luxurious, perfumed place that she had ever been.

'Hhh, hmm,' the haughty receptionist coughed, looking down at Molly via two large nostrils. 'Can I be of assistance?'

Molly turned and stepped towards the small, smartly dressed man who was standing behind a black glass desk.

'Yes, please. I'd like a room.'

'I'm afraid you're a little young.'

Molly was tired, so it took more effort to crank her eyes up to 'zapping mode'. But after a moment, the receptionist was as impressionable as a piece of squashy dough. He looked at his books. 'I'm afraid, madam, all our ordinary rooms are full.'

'Full?' Molly said incredulously. 'But you must have loads of rooms here.'

'Yes, and all 124 of the ordinary ones are occupied.'

'Well, what about the out-of-the-ordinary rooms?'

'We have the honeymoon suite, madam, on the top floor.'

'I'll take that. How much is it?'

'It's $3,000 a night, madam.'

'Wha . . .? And do I pay before?'

'No, madam. You pay your bill when you leave.'

Molly only had $2,963 left. One night in the honeymoon suite was already beyond her, but she was too tired to set out on a hotel hunt.

'Oh. Well, I'll take it.'

'Your passport please, madam,' asked the receptionist, but Molly glared at him.

'You won't be needing that,' she said. She didn't like the idea of leaving evidence of who she was – or how old she was – in the hotel safe.

The man stepped out from behind his desk. 'Follow me.'

They took the elevator to the twenty-first floor and followed a yellow-carpeted passage to room number 125. The receptionist unlocked the door and led Molly and Petula in.

Molly felt as if she had walked into a dream.

The room was spectacular. In fact, because it was a suite it had *two* huge rooms, one with cream-coloured silk curtains and a giant four-poster bed, the other with sofas and a low table in it.

'Both rooms and the bathroom have televisions and music systems,' explained the receptionist, opening cupboards and revealing hidden TVs and hi-fi equipment. 'Here is the mini-bar and also here is a list of services we provide, from limousine hire to dog-walking to hairdressing. The jacuzzi is easy to operate and there is a pool and a fitness centre on the top floor. Room service is available round the clock so if you require anything, please don't hesitate to call. Thank you, ma'am.' The receptionist bowed and went.

Molly kicked her shoes off and jumped on to the bed. 'Yeee haaa!' she shouted, feeling suddenly very wide-awake. Petula scrambled up too. 'Isn't this great, Petula? I mean look at us. Can you *believe* it? Yesterday in grotty Hardwick House and today in the most luxurious hotel room in New York!' Petula barked happily in reply and Molly jumped off the bed and opened the mini-bar fridge. After pouring herself an orange juice with chunks of ice in it, and Petula a bowl of ice-cold mineral water, she opened the doors that led on to her balcony. Noise blasted into the room. Taxi cab horns, horns from delivery vans, the grinding of rubbish lorries, sirens from police cars, voices shouting and whistling. The whole city was buzzing with noise and life. Molly had never been anywhere as loud and busy as this. With Petula tucked under her arm, she looked out over the balcony.

It was midnight but the roads were full of traffic.

The city towered about her in a jungle of skyscrapers with insect-like cars and yellow cabs crawling about on its forest floor. Molly wondered how many people lived here. And for a second she wondered whether, maybe, somewhere out there, amongst the millions of New Yorkers, maybe there was someone related to her. Rocky must be out there somewhere – but where? She hugged Petula. 'Where are your family, Petula?' Petula licked Molly's hand. 'Yup, Petula. I guess you and me are family. We're all we've got at the moment.'

Molly gazed down at the bristling city. She supposed that New Yorkers would be as easy to hypnotize as any other people. Her eye trick had worked on the receptionist. With this room costing $3,000 a night it was vital that her hypnotic powers worked. Of course, she could move to a cheaper hotel, but Molly liked the richness of this place and she wanted to stay here. Anyway, she was too excited to worry about any of that right now.

Molly shut the balcony doors and went to have a bath. She squirted all the mini bottles of bubble bath into it to make it extra bubbly, and when the bubbles were foaming high, she sank into the sweet-smelling water. She clicked on the wall-mounted TV with a remote control. How far this was from the draughty bathroom at Hardwick House, where only recently she had been punished for having a bath more than ten centimetres deep! She laughed out loud.

There were hundreds of television channels. Molly surfed through them happily. There were news programmes, chat shows, music programmes, fitness programmes, religious programmes, and films.

And adverts *all* the time. Molly noticed that some

channels had commercials every five minutes with hardly any programme in between. Some ads were repeated over and over again. 'Buy this . . . buy this . . . You need this . . . You really do need this . . .'

As Molly watched, amazed by the regularity of the advert breaks, it struck her for the first time that advertising was like a sort of hypnotism. A hypnotism that persuaded people to buy things. A sort of brainwashing. Perhaps if people watched an advertisement that told them 'You need this' often enough, eventually they'd believe they did need whatever it was. Then Molly caught her favourite, the Qube ad, and she felt all warm inside. How much closer she was now to being one of those glamorous people on the beach. She started to sing along.

'Qube if you're cute . . . Qube if you're rude . . . Everyone loves you cos you're so Qube.'

The blue-eyed man on the TV winked. 'I'm sooooo popular – I've been Qubed.'

'Not as popular as I'm going to be,' shouted Molly, throwing a flannel at the TV and pressing the jacuzzi button on the side of the bath. A moment later she was practically blown out of the water. Molly slammed her hand on the button again and the bubbles stopped. She wasn't sure about the jacuzzi. It was like ten monsters farting in her bath all at once. But apart from the jacuzzi, she certainly felt she could get used to this kind of life. The question was, how should she go about keeping it?

After her bath, Molly got into her satin-sheeted four-poster to think. But instead, like Petula, on the end of the bed, she instantly fell asleep.

*

Nockman was four hours from landing at JFK Airport. In his mind he conjured up a picture of the girl with the book. The girl who, his taxi driver from Briersville had told him, had performed in front of hundreds of local people who had all thought her the most talented and sweet-looking child they had ever seen. Nockman realized with astonishment that the girl had hypnotized them all. He was astounded that a girl as young as her could learn Dr Logan's art. She must be exceptionally talented. But his fascination with her was soon replaced with fury. How dare the wretched kid steal his book? He'd soon wipe the smirk off her face. He looked forward to her apologies and hoped that they'd come with tears.

He ground his teeth in nervous fury. She wasn't going to escape him. He was on her trail. Even though he hadn't properly seen what she looked like, he was sure that, if he kept his ear to the ground, he'd track her down in New York. He removed his new spiral-pattern glasses from his pocket and gave them a polish. He'd read enough about hypnotism to know that when someone had the mesmerizing gift, people were powerless under their gaze. But something in the make-up of the spiral on these glasses deflected the effect of hypnotic eyes. Nockman hoped they worked. The only other thing he needed was a voice-scrambling machine, and then he'd be protected from M. Moon's voice too.

Flicking his oily moustache, Professor Nockman sat back and wondered what the M stood for. Margaret? Matilda? Mavis? He smiled. Perhaps it was a good thing that this girl had found the hypnotism book. Maybe she was better at it than he could ever hope to be. So when he found this M. Moon, all he need do was control her, which shouldn't be difficult. After all, she was only a child. And suddenly the ruthless Nockman realized that, far from being his rival, this M. Moon, whoever she was, could be a gift horse in disguise. Why, she was surely the perfect accomplice to help him achieve his ambitions. She could give him a ride to the top.

# Chapter Fifteen

When Molly opened her eyes the next morning, the hotel room made her jump. The luxury of it was a shock. The cream carpet and heavy silk curtains made her feel as if she was in a chocolate commercial. She tipped herself out of bed, opened the fridge and took out a Heaven Bar, singing the brand song as she ate it.

'*I'm in Heaven, Heaven's in me,*
*I knew I'd get to Heaven eventually.*'

Then she put on the towelling dressing gown from the back of the bathroom door. It was way too big for her, but warm and very soft, like the towels in the Cloud Nine adverts. She stepped out on to the balcony, this time to look at New York in daylight. The city buzzed away below and beyond. The buildings looked even bigger and Manhattan seemed to stretch further. A massive billboard, hundreds of feet tall, was stuck on to the wall of a skyscraper. It was a giant picture of a woman wearing blue jeans and a denim jacket.

Underneath, it said, '*Walk like a giant . . . Wear Diva Jeans.*'

The giant woman made Molly feel extremely small. An attack of butterflies gathered in her stomach. Since Briersville she'd been riding on a wave of glory, and with a spinning head she'd made her bold plans and left the country. But now, in the morning light, Molly didn't feel quite as confident as she had done the day before. She realized that she knew nothing about this city or its inhabitants. She wasn't sure how to push herself forwards. People in big cities were less friendly and less patient than country ones. She looked at the New Yorkers far below on the pavement who were walking along with purpose and determination. Very few of them were idling or stopping. Molly decided she must learn something about this place before she stepped out into it. But before she did anything, she had to have some breakfast, so she rang for room service.

Fifteen minutes later, a very old, skinny waiter pushed a table on wheels into Molly's suite. It was laid with a white tablecloth, cutlery, and delicate white china plates, cups and saucers. Two shiny pots were beside two silver domes that concealed Molly's breakfast. The waiter handed Molly a piece of paper. 'Sign please, madam,' he said in a quaky voice.

Molly looked at the slip. Her breakfast had cost forty-five dollars! She signed. The waiter hovered by the door for a moment, as if she had forgotten something. 'Oh . . . thank you . . .' said Molly. 'Goodbye.' The waiter left. He had in fact been waiting for a tip.

Molly looked at the breakfast receipt again and cringed. A second attack of butterflies, great big

Amazonian butterflies, filled her insides. She'd never had to spend money before, and now that she did, it made her panic. The main reason being that she was running out of it.

She'd nearly spent all of her prize money, and she knew that the hotel bill was going to eat up the rest and more. She knew that hypnotizing the receptionist into giving her the most expensive room at the Bellingham wasn't sensible. And she had no idea how she was going to pay for it.

On top of this, she needed money for life in general. For the little things, like chewing gum, ice creams, candyfloss and magazines. She couldn't go around New York hypnotizing everyone for everything, because sooner or later, someone would see what she was up to, and then she'd be in big trouble.

And yet, Molly didn't know how to get any cash. She hadn't thought about it. Yesterday, £3,000 had seemed like a fortune.

Molly's butterflies turned into tummy rumblings. Deciding to eat her breakfast and think about her dilemma, she lifted the silver domes. One plate had a sausage on it. This was Petula's breakfast. The other had four ketchup sandwiches. In the little silver pot was some concentrated orange juice which Molly poured into a glass. The big silver pot had hot chocolate in it.

Soon Molly and Petula were eating with relish.

But breakfast did nothing to inspire Molly as far as her money problem went. Molly bit her ketchupy lip and thought. She should approach this problem logically. Perhaps the TV might help her. So, putting her new sunglasses on, she and Petula settled down for a marathon-viewing session, paying particular attention to the adverts.

Molly learned some interesting things about how Americans lived. There was one ad about peanut butter where the peanut butter pot had a section that was full of jam, or 'jelly', as the mother on the advert called it. The lemon-haired lady was spreading peanut butter and jelly liberally on to a slice of bread.

'It's a tradition that's been handed down our family for generations,' she said, passing the sandwich to her wide-eyed daughter. 'It was good enough for me when I was a kid . . .'

'And,' said the girl, taking a bite, 'it'll be good enough for my kids too! *Everyone* loves Granny Sunshine's peanut butter and jelly!'

'Yuk,' said Molly. 'I don't. Makes me wanna puke.' And, taking another slug of orange juice, she flicked the channel. She landed in a nature programme. On the screen was a nest with three baby birds in it, all squawking for food. One chick in the middle was much bigger and noisier than the others. The commentator's voice explained: 'The baby cuckoo has hatched in the robins' nest. And already it is growing faster than the robin chicks.'

The mother robin returned to the nest with a worm. But before the smaller robin chicks had time to have a bite, the cuckoo chick snatched it.

'It's amazing,' continued the narrator, 'how the mother robin thinks the cuckoo chick is her own.' When the mother robin flew off, the cuckoo chick started to hop about. And then, with a firm movement, it pushed first one baby robin chick, and then the other, out of the nest.

Molly gasped. So, cuckoos really *did* push other birds out of the nest. Mrs Trinklebury's lullaby rang in her head, making Molly feel uneasy. Was she like those baby robins? She felt more like the cuckoo, the way she'd pushed her way to winning the Briersville loot. Mrs Trinklebury's song had never made much sense to her. Now it made even less. With a little shudder she switched channels.

By lunchtime, Molly's eyes were feeling rectangular. She'd been surfing the channels for three hours and knew much more about America, but she still didn't have a clue how she would make any money, and as for Rocky, Molly didn't know where to start looking for him. Like a helium balloon with a hole in it, her spirits were sinking lower and lower. Negative thoughts filled her mind. She must have been mad to come to America. Stir-fried crazy to have ventured to New York. Molly was beginning to feel that she had bitten off far, *far* more than she could chew.

She got up and opened the mini-bar to get a drink. Inside were all sorts: tiny bottles of whisky, gin and vodka, and cartons of fruit juice, water and Qube too. '*Be cool, drink Qube,*' sang the advert in her memory. Qube would help her. She certainly did need to cool down, she needed to be Qube cool. So she took a can and cracked it open.

Minty, fruity bubbles fizzed up her nose as she swallowed. And as she glugged, the Qube ad came on to the television screen. It was quite something to be drinking her first full can of Qube, at last, and to be watching the Qube crowd on TV at the same moment. Molly smiled.

'Hey, the world really looks better with a can of Qube in my hand,' grinned the white-toothed man.

'Yeah,' agreed Molly, drinking the rest of her can at once, and making a victory sign with her fingers at the man on the box. Suddenly the world really did look better. Molly felt certain that everything was going to be all right. For a moment, she felt just like one of the people on the screen. Then she burped and the feeling was gone. The ad switched to one about wood varnish. Molly was left with an empty can in her hand and lots of bubbles in her stomach.

Molly was startled. She'd actually *believed* that a can of Qube could help sort out her problems. Qube and its people. With Qube by her side, she'd felt sure she'd be more confident and able to charm the world. Instead of feeling cool though, she felt hot and worried and deflated. Molly felt that her favourite ad people had betrayed her, and in a blinding flash she saw that her infatuation with them and their world had been madness. Why, they were completely unreal.

As she watched the next ad, which was for plasters, featuring a boy with a grazed knee, Molly thought that maybe she could get some work as an actress. After all, those people in all the ads weren't real, they were actors, and there certainly were hundreds of ads. There must be lots of work. Maybe she could even get a part in a Qube ad. As Molly toyed with this idea, a new programme started.

A man in an orange suit sat on a pink sofa with a huge spongy microphone in his hand. Behind him a large flashing sign said 'Charlie's Chat Show'. The man had a voice so deep that it sounded as if he gargled with gravel in the mornings.

'Yes, ladies and gentlemen, as promised, we have her here with us today. Please put your hands together, and give a very warm welcome to Broadway's newest star, Davina Nuttel!'

Molly was about to flip channels, when she was surprised to see that Davina Nuttel was a small girl of about eight or nine, wearing a lot of make-up. As she strode on to the stage, the audience whistled and clapped. And as she sat down with the red-haired interviewer, Charlie Chat, he boomed, 'Well, hi, Davina! It's just grrrreat to have you on the show!'

'Hi, Charlie, it's great to be here,' came the sugar-sweet voice of Davina.

'So, Davina, let's get strrrraight to the point. I'm sure everyone wants to know what it feels like to be the star of a Broadway musical.'

'It feels just great,' said Davina, smiling beautifully. 'I love the songs, I love the dancing, I love the story. I love the other actors, I love the audiences and I love being in Manhattan.'

'You must have a grrrreat big old heart for all that love,' said Charlie, and the audience laughed.

'Well, it's all great and everyone should come and see the show.' Davina turned to the audience and beamed out a huge, persuasive grin. Her face gave Molly a jolt. She looked a bit like Hazel.

'Let's see some of it,' said Chat Show Charlie. On came a sequence of clips. First there was a picture of the entrance of a grand theatre with the title of the show, *Stars on Mars*, written above in neon lights. A slinky black car pulled up outside and Davina Nuttel, in a fur coat, got out of it. Then the picture cut to some film of the show. The stage set looked like the surface of planet Mars, full of big red rocks. Davina Nuttel was dressed in a red astronaut's suit and was tap dancing and singing. It was a space musical. More clips were shown of other parts of the show, one where four large Mars monsters tried to attack Davina Nuttel. Petula dropped the stone she was sucking and growled at the Martians.

The chat show audience clapped, and Molly felt some of the thrill she'd felt on the Briersville stage when her audience had applauded her.

'My goodness, that cerrrrtainly was something,' said Charlie.

'Thank you. You know I owe just about everything to my caring, wonderful, self-sacrificing mom and dad.'

'Aahhh,' said the audience.

'And,' said Davina, 'to my manager, Barry Bragg.'

'Ah yes,' said Charlie Chat. 'And here he is!'

On the screen appeared a man with a central parting and combed down gelled hair. He had red cheeks, and wore a chequered suit and a pair of red spectacles.

'Hi there, Davina and Charlie!' he said.

'Hi, Barry!' cried Davina Nuttel.

'Hi, Barry! So Barrrrrry, everyone here wants to know, how did you discover Davina?'

'Well, she just walked straight into my Manhattan offices in Derry Street,' said bow-tied Barry enthusiastically, 'and she bowled me over. You all know how she sings and dances, well she just came into my offices and she sang and danced about the room like the li'l bit of magic that she is. It was obvious to me that she was going to be a star, so I introduced her to the director of *Stars on Mars*, and, well, a hit and a half later, here we are.'

Davina laughed, shaking her golden locks playfully. 'My lucky stars were out the day I met you, Barry.' She turned to Charlie Chat. 'I mean, Barry knows *everyone* in show business.'

The programme continued and Molly watched bright-eyed people come and go. Molly thought that she really did fancy being an actress for a bit, but not in the adverts, they seemed very superficial compared to singing and dancing in front of a live audience. She'd enjoyed all that adulation and applause on the stage in Briersville, she'd like to experience it again. She bet actors like Davina got paid a lot. Perhaps this manager, Barry Bragg, would be a good person to meet? Acting would be a challenge, but Molly felt sure she could rise to the occasion, especially with her new skills. And what had Rocky said? That she never tried at anything? She would prove him absolutely wrong.

She got up and stretched. Petula did the same. Molly felt as if she'd found a solution. This Barry Bragg whose office was in Derry Street, wherever that was, could help to sort her out.

As she got dressed she hummed along to a number from *Stars on Mars*. It really was a catchy tune, and Molly thought what fun it must be to star in a Broadway show.

Molly put on her T-shirt and her old, holey jumper. She pulled on her worn-out, short, grey skirt, she brushed her curly hair, and she looked at her peculiar face in the mirror, wrinkling her potato nose at her reflection. She locked her hypnotism book in the room's safe, then she grabbed her thin anorak and whistled to Petula.

'Come on, Petula. Let's go and get a slice of the action!'

With her own destiny at the front of her mind, and leaving all thoughts of Rocky behind her, Molly left the hotel room.

# Chapter Sixteen

It was scary stepping out of the quiet, snazzy hotel into the busy, dirty streets of Manhattan. Hot dogs, onions, bagels, roasted peanuts, coffee, pretzels, burgers and pickles filled the air with their aromas. And everywhere there was movement – of people and of traffic. Molly had never seen such a mixture of people in one place; all colours and all kinds. There were the biggest, fattest people she'd ever seen walking past the thinnest. New Yorkers seemed to dress exactly how they felt, without caring what anyone else thought. Molly saw a guy dressed in cowboy chaps swaggering past a huge woman dressed in sparkly pink hot pants. Molly imagined Mrs Toadley in a pair of them, and smiled, and she thought how Miss Adderstone could walk down the street here in her snipped-up suit, with her knickers on her head, and everyone would just think it was a new fashion.

For a moment, Molly felt very small and unsteady,

but then a hotel porter appeared beside her in his green-and-gold uniform. 'Cab, ma'am?'

'Er, yes, please,' said Molly. The porter opened the door to another rattly yellow cab, this time driven by a Mexican-looking guy with a thick black moustache.

'Where ya wanna go, ladee?' he said.

'Derry Street,' said Molly as firmly as possible. She and Petula climbed in, and a different taped voice under her seat said, 'Miaoooow, cats have nine lives but you don't, so buckle up.' Molly didn't need to be reminded, as this driver drove like a madman. They skidded away from the hotel and turned down one of the main roads that drove south through Manhattan. '*Madison Avenue*', said a sign, and the Mexican driver slalomed down it as if he was in a computer game, laughing like a lunatic every time he nearly hit another car. Molly gripped the seat and Petula sank her claws into the leather.

Above them, on either side, enormous skyscrapers shot upwards, great walls of glass and steel. At street level, billowing clouds of steam rose up through grates in the pavements.

Molly looked at the map on the back of her driver's seat. It was a plan of Manhattan, and she saw that although most of the streets were named by number, at the bottom end of the island the streets had names as in other cities. Indeed, ten minutes and thirteen dollars later, Molly and Petula had arrived in the maze of these streets and been dropped on the one called Derry. It was a street full of brownstone buildings, more the size of buildings in Briersville, although they still had a distinctly city feeling about them. Molly and Petula picked their way along, looking at names on doorbells.

At last they came to a polished bronze sign that said, 'The Barry Bragg Agency.' Molly was relieved that finding Mr Bragg had been so simple, although it did mean that now there was no putting off meeting him. She straightened her skirt, took a deep breath and pressed the buzzer.

'Hello-o,' said a squeaky woman's voice down the entry phone. 'Can I help?'

'I've come to see Barry Bragg.'

'Come on up to the fifth floor.' The door buzzed open. Molly and Petula stepped inside into a dark, mirror-lined lobby that smelled of oranges and vanilla essence. They crossed its shiny stone floor to a small caged lift. Soon they were at the fifth floor.

'Good morning,' said the receptionist, who looked like a Barbie doll. She cast her black-lashed eyes over Molly, registering her scruffy clothes. Then she noticed Petula. 'Ah, so it's a dog act, is it?'

'No.'

The receptionist looked in Mr Bragg's diary. 'I wasn't expecting anyone this morning,' she said. 'Do you have an appointment?'

'Yes,' said Molly, thinking of how she'd made up her mind to see Barry Bragg after watching him on TV. 'Yes. I made my appointment in person, with Mr Bragg, this morning.'

'Oh, I see,' said the receptionist. It didn't cross her tiny mind that Molly might be lying. 'Mr Bragg will be out in a minute. Please take a seat.'

Molly sat down to wait. She and Petula watched fascinated as the secretary took out a make-up box the size of a toolkit and spent ten minutes painting her very pouty lips.

'Well, thank you for coming,' came Barry Bragg's treacly voice. His arm, clad in the fabric of his purple suit, opened his office door to show some visitors out. A young boy with a big bird puppet emerged with his parents. They were all smiling.

'Well, thank you for seeing us,' said the mother. 'Shall I call you?'

'He was fabulous, fabulous, fabulous,' said Barry Bragg. 'But don't call me, I'll call you . . . I need a few days.'

'Thank you, sir,' said the boy, and his duck said, 'Tankya mister!'

'Oh, Jimmy . . . He's unstoppable,' said his father proudly.

'I see, I see,' said Barry Bragg laughing loudly. 'Well, goodbye – and keep practising.'

The visitors left. Barry Bragg loosened his pink bow tie and breathed a sigh of relief. 'Gee whizz, talk about a tired act.' Then he noticed Molly. 'Come to see me?' he said, frowning. He looked questioningly at his secretary.

'She said she'd made an appointment with you,' explained the receptionist, realizing slowly that she'd been duped.

Molly nodded, steeling herself for what she was about to do.

'No . . . parents?' asked Barry.

'No,' said Molly.

'Well, how refreshing!' exclaimed Barry Bragg. 'I tell you, the worst part of this job is the parents. Pushy parents. They're the bane of my life. Gee, a kid on its own is welcome! Come in!'

This was the first time that having no parents had

been to Molly's advantage. 'Thank you, Mr Bragg,' she said as she stepped into his purple-and-gold office.

'So,' said Barry Bragg, eying Molly's scruffy outfit as he walked around her and sat down on his desk. 'What kind of act you got? Some sort of Cinderella thing? I like the raggy get-up, it's got real authenticity!' He opened a cigar box. As he lifted its lid, it started to sing, '*You've got to pick a pocket or two.*' He picked out a short, fat cigar and bit the end off it, which he spat out behind him, and picked up a lighter shaped like Charlie Chaplin. A flame came out of Chaplin's hat and after sucking and puffing cigar smoke into the room, he said, 'OK, kid, let's see what you can do.'

As the smoke cleared, he turned his blue eyes towards Molly. She was holding a pendulum, which she was swinging slowly backwards and forwards, backwards and forwards, and her soft voice was saying, 'Just look at this.'

'Oh, so it's a hypno . . .' Barry Bragg tried to finish his sentence, but couldn't remember what he was going to say. The pendulum was so beautiful to watch. Its middle was a strangely spinning spiral that drew him towards it. 'That's beautif . . .' No more words seemed able to leave his mouth but he didn't mind at all.

Molly slowly stopped the pendulum swinging and suggested calmly, 'Look into my eyes.'

That was it. Molly's green eyes zonked Barry within seconds. His eyes glazed over, and Molly set to work.

'Barry, you are now under my command, and you will do whatever I tell you, is that understood?' Barry nodded. Molly smiled. 'First thing, I want you to put out that cigar . . .'

*

146

Half an hour later, Barry was talking enthusiastically on the phone. 'I'm tellin' ya, Rixey, she's fabulous. You just gotta come see her.'

After a quick cab ride from her apartment, the producer and director of *Stars on Mars* arrived at the Derry Street office. Her name was Rixey Bloomy and she was one of New York's hottest personalities. She was thirty-six years old and was the most expensively dressed woman Molly had ever seen. She wore a black leather trouser suit, zebra skin ankle boots, and carried a matching furry handbag. Her hair was as bouncy as if she had just walked out of a shampoo commercial, her lips were plump and luscious (they had been pumped up by one of New York's top plastic surgeons), and her eyes were searingly blue. She looked suspiciously at Molly.

'Well, Barry, I know you brought me Davina,' said Rixey Bloomy, 'but, honey, this girl's no looker. Look at her spammy legs. Sweetie, I think you're losing your touch.'

'She's great, she's great,' insisted Barry. 'Even Molly will admit that she's no beauty queen, but don't you see, there's something about her. She's magic.' Barry Bragg was starting to sweat from excitement.

Rixey Bloomy looked astonished.

'Shall I show you what I can do?' suggested Molly.

Within the time it takes to sharpen a couple of pencils, both Rixey and Barry were gazing, glazy eyed at her.

'So what I want,' Molly instructed, 'is a part in a big musical, or a play, here in New York, and I want one that pays well. What have you got?'

'Nothing,' said Rixey Bloomy, her head swaying.

'All the – plays we're – doing have – adult parts in – them.'

Molly faltered. There *must* be some big acting job out there that she could take. She wanted one. More than that, she needed one. She simply had to get some money.

Then she saw Davina Nuttel's picture on the wall. Molly was reminded again of Hazel. Davina had the same spiteful glint in her eye. Memories of Hazel being mean fired through Molly's mind.

'Right then, I'll have Davina Nuttel's part in *Stars on Mars*,' she said.

There was a silence. 'That must be possible.'

'If you – say so,' said Rixey.

'Good,' said Molly. 'I'll learn her songs, I'll learn her dances . . . oh, and I want my dog in the show.'

'There – are – no – parts – for – dogs – the – show's – set – on – Mars,' said Rixey Bloomy.

'Well, *make* her a part,' said Molly. 'And design Petula some astronaut outfits.' Petula looked at Molly as if she liked this idea. 'And,' continued Molly, 'I'll need all my bills at my hotel paid for. I want to get paid *twice* as much as Davina Nuttel. Er, how much will that be?'

'Forty – thousand – dollars a – month.'

'Mmnn,' gulped Molly, 'yes, well, that is the amount you must pay me. And I want loads of new clothes, because as you can see, mine are a bit shabby, and I'd like a chauffeur-driven car that waits for me at all times, and while you're at it, make that a Rolls-Royce. And I want a never-ending supply of sweets. I'll tell you which ones I like later. And here's something *very* important. I *must* meet all the people in the show

148

separately, before we start working, and *all* the people who work behind the scenes, and I really mean *all* of them . . . is that clear?'

The two New Yorkers nodded.

'Lastly, I don't want to meet Davina Nuttel. Have you got some other show you can put her in?'

'No.'

'Oh, well, never mind . . . And why do I want all this?' asked Molly, leaning back in her chair to look proudly at her puppet creations.

'Because you are the most talented kid ever to have hit Broadway,' sighed Barry.

'Because you're pure genius,' nodded Rixey Bloomy.

Molly shivered inside. This was going to be a mammoth challenge. She hoped she was up to it.

# Chapter Seventeen

It was all so easy!

At four o'clock that afternoon, Molly was dancing around her hotel room sucking a chewy sweet, and singing along to the tape of *Stars on Mars*. The songs were easy to learn.

Scattered around were opened boxes full of tissue paper, with new clothes spilling out of them. Rixey Bloomy had chosen these and sent them round and Molly had spent the afternoon trying on jackets, dresses, trousers and shoes. The coffee table was now a candy table with two huge bowls filled with all sorts of sweets, and one full of multi-coloured marshmallows.

Petula had taken to patrolling the balcony, barking at scrawny pigeons whenever they landed.

After the last number, Molly switched off the tape recorder and lay on the bed, wearing new jeans and a very cool T-shirt with a shiny moon on it. She wished she could tell someone about all this. Namely Rocky.

Maybe he had telephoned Miss Adderstone and left his new address by now. It was five hours ahead in England – nine o'clock – so Adderstone would still be up. Molly picked up the telephone, and dialled. After six rings, the telephone was answered. 'Good evening, Hardwick Orphanage,' said the familiar voice of Gerry.

'Oh, hello Gerry,' said Molly.

'Molly! Molly, where are you? Adderstone said you'd gone on a plane! Was it good?'

'I'm in New York,' said Molly, thinking how impressive that sounded. 'And the plane was *brilliant*. But look, can I speak to Adderstone?'

'Adderstone's gone.'

'Gone shopping? Gone to have her bunions done? When will she be back?'

'She's never comin' back,' said Gerry, suddenly whispering. 'She's gone, and Edna too. Adderstone said they wanted to be nice to children from now on, so they were leavin' us to rule ourselves an' we could do *anything* we liked.'

This was the last piece of news Molly expected to hear.

'And why are you whispering, Gerry?'

''Cos Hazel's near by, down the passage. She's in charge now, see, and . . . gotta go . . . bye!'

The line went dead. Molly dialled again but this time the phone was engaged. The idea of the orphanage being run by Hazel was horrifying, but then she supposed that Mrs Trinklebury would keep an eye on everyone and she relaxed. She wondered where Miss Adderstone and Edna had gone and felt responsible. She hoped they weren't doing anything dangerous. Visions of Miss Adderstone snipping up other people's suits and Edna hitting people who didn't like Italy filled Molly's mind.

But worse than the idea of Edna and Miss Adderstone being lost was the fact that now Molly might never find Rocky, unless he called the orphanage and asked for her. Molly telephoned the orphanage once more.

Gerry picked it up again.

'Hello, it's Molly.'

'Hi, Molly,' came Gerry's tiny whisper. 'Look, the thing is, Molly, I'm not s'posed to answer the phone. Hazel gets very cross. I've gotta go soon.'

'Gerry, stop, before you do, I want to give you my number in New York. In case Rocky calls. It's important. Have you got a pen?'

'Erm, yes, I think there's one in my pocket with my mouse. No, no, Squeak, you stay there . . . sorry, Molly, Squeak nearly escaped . . . Oh yes, here's a pen and, um, some paper.'

'OK,' said Molly, and she began to give Gerry her number at the Bellingham Hotel. The line crackled. 'And if Rocky calls, give him that number, or give it to Hazel, so that if she speaks to Rocky, she can—'

'Gotta go, Molly. Hazel's not in a good mood, and I don't want her catchin' me. Bye.' The phone clicked.

'Bye,' murmured Molly, not at all confident that Gerry would relay her message to anyone.

But she didn't worry for too long. Molly looked at a box of clothes and marvelled at how quickly her dreams were coming true. She was about to become rich. Soon she would be very popular as well, and, in other people's eyes, even lovely looking too.

*

Petula gazed through a gap in the stone balcony to watch the November lights of the city start to come on. If she'd had magic X-ray eyes, she would have seen that twenty-five blocks away, in a cheap, dingy room, where he spent a lot of his dodgy time, Professor Nockman was stretched out on a bed, snoring, underneath a single light-bulb that hung from the ceiling. His building was right beside a railway track and the light-bulb bobbed about every time a train rumbled past. On the floor of the room and all over the bed were newspapers. Professor Nockman was gambling that whoever this M. Moon was, she was going to be in the papers sooner or later, for doing something extraordinary. And like a bloodhound (although not as good-looking), he was ready to pick up the scent. All day he'd scoured the papers and the streets for stories about an amazing girl, even visiting hotels, but each time he'd been asked to stop loitering in their lobbies and leave.

In his dreams, he saw the girl again, sitting in the back of the minibus with the hypnotism book in her lap and a pug dog next to her. In his sleep, Professor Nockman growled.

Back on her balcony, Petula sniffed the air. Somewhere out there, a long way off, someone was thinking about her, she knew it. And she didn't like the way they were thinking. Petula barked, then shivered and ran inside. She jumped on to Molly's bed and pushed her nose under the covers, to find one of her stones.

Molly had a nightmare. She dreamed that she was a big, ugly cuckoo in a forest with no friends. In the background, Mrs Trinklebury's song echoed through the branches, as if the very trees were singing it.

*'Forgive, little birds, that brown cuckoo*
*For pushing you out of your nests.*
*It's what mamma cuckoo taught it to do*
*She taught it that pushing is best.'*

All the other birds ignored Molly and hid from her. Some had the faces of the smaller children from the orphanage. When Molly walked towards them, they flew away. In the dream Molly felt desperately lonely. She was searching for Rocky and tried calling out his name, but all that came out of her beak was a squawk.

However, in the morning she soon forgot the heartache of her sleep. For she had work to do and money to make. Rehearsals for *Stars on Mars* were starting, and Molly had no time to pine for her friend.

# Chapter Eighteen

The Manhattan Theatre, where *Stars on Mars* was playing, closed its doors suddenly. None of the newspapers knew why. Behind the doors, Davina Nuttel had been given the sack and the theatre staff had been sworn to secrecy. Molly made very sure that everyone kept their lips sealed, and her first morning was taken up with private meetings. Molly met, and hypnotized, every single person who was working on the show; the conductor in the orchestra, the musicians, the ticket people, the ice cream sellers, the light operators, the stage hands, the make-up artists, the other actors and the boy who swept the stage. Everyone thought Molly was marvellous.

Then rehearsals began.

To Molly's surprise, she discovered that rehearsals were really fun. And she was determined to try her hardest to be good. Of course, whatever she did the rest of the cast thought she was fantastic. When she sang out of tune, no one noticed. When she got moves in the dance wrong, no one cared. Her tap dancing was useless but everyone thought it was perfect.

Petula was enjoying it too. She looked really sweet in a red astronaut's outfit and she joined in the dancing. But – not surprisingly – Petula didn't like the Martian monsters at all. They were massive things, like enormous red peppers with antennae, as big as large Christmas trees, and they walked about, because they had actors inside them. To Petula, they were trouble, especially when they attacked Molly. Petula barked at them non-stop, then bit one on the ankle. It was decided that Petula should be kept away from the Martian monsters, on and off stage.

Rehearsals started at ten every morning, with a brief break for lunch and more rehearsing all afternoon. Molly had to learn where to stand, how to dance and what to sing and say.

And then, on her third day at the theatre, came a meeting that Molly wasn't expecting.

Molly was in her dressing room, when she heard a horrible screamy voice in the corridor shout, 'WHERE IS SHEEE?'

'She's in there, Miss Davina,' a sequinned chorus girl said sympathetically. 'But, Davina, don't be too cross . . . When you meet her you'll see why . . . I mean, you'll like her.'

'LIKE HER??!!!' yelled the voice furiously. 'LIKE HER . . .? SHE'S JUST RUINED MY CAREER. She's stolen what's *mine*. What's the matter with all of you? Rixey, Barry, all of you . . . you *know I* made this show what it is.'

The chorus girl squeaked, 'Sorry, Davina, but . . .'

When Davina stormed into Molly's dressing room, Molly was ready.

'So,' said Davina, slamming the door behind her, and stamping her high-heeled boot. 'Who do you think you are? How *dare* you?' Then her mouth plunged open. 'Are *you* Molly Moon?' she said in disbelief.

Molly looked at Davina, the singing-dancing prodigy. The starlet whose performances everybody loved to watch. And Molly was fascinated. For, close up, Davina didn't look anything special. Without stage make-up, her face was pale and rather sickly looking. Her hair was blonde but limp and greasy. Her eyes were bulgy and had grey rings underneath them. But she was sparkly in the way that she dressed. She was wearing purple velvet, with high-heeled purple suede boots and a string of green gems round her neck. Molly was wearing an astronaut suit which she'd been trying on for size.

'B-but you're so ordinary,' said Davina, amazed.

'So are you,' said Molly, equally bewildered.

'They said you were really, really special,' said Davina, too dumbstruck to register Molly's remark. 'How could someone as ordinary and as lumpy-nosed as you take my part?' Davina Nuttel was overwhelmed for a moment. Then, grinding her teeth, she took a step towards Molly and in a calm, charming voice said, 'That's my costume, I think you'd better give it back.' Her eyes fixed Molly's.

Molly calmly looked back and suddenly noticed that the pupils of Davina Nuttel's eyes were huge. More than that, in fact, they were spiralling and dark, like swirling black whirlpools. Molly felt unsteady, as if the ground was starting to disappear. Quickly, she concentrated and gave Davina a strong blast of her hypnotic eyes. But Molly was shocked to find, as she increased her voltage of glare to maximum power, that Davina's eyes had a strong pull. With every ounce of focus that she possessed, Molly stood firm, until the ground felt balanced again under her feet.

This was a big surprise. Davina Nuttel had the gift. She could sing and dance too but on *top* of this, she had the gift. She had the gift without really knowing what it was. It wasn't as finely tuned as Molly's, but she obviously used this power over other people, to influence them and charm them. Molly felt as if she almost wanted to make friends with Davina. She could train her and they could become partners. They'd be unbeatable! But these ideas went out of her head when she heard what Davina was saying.

'You're so plain, so *ugly* even . . . you're not the sort of girl anyone would like to watch on stage, it's all going to go very wrong, so why don't you just give up? You're not made for stardom, you're just too boring, you've got no charisma at all, and your dog is revolting.'

Petula whined and Molly determinedly increased her eye beam again. But Davina's angry glare shot back. It was a tug of war between green and blue eyeballs. Molly's hands began to sweat. She was concentrating so hard on her look that she couldn't even begin to think how to use her voice. Molly began to worry that she wouldn't win. And as this negative thought clouded her mind, she weakened. She wondered what would happen if Davina managed to hypnotize *her*. Maybe Davina would rob Molly of all her powers and leave her empty-headed. Molly imagined herself as a tramp, on the New York streets, lost and confused, with a mind blanked by Davina. It was a future too horrid to contemplate, and so scary that it gave Molly a surge of energy. With a sizzling knock-out stare that made Molly's hair stand out from her head, the tension snapped and Molly had won.

Davina looked away. In a shaky voice she said, 'I don't know how you've done it. You may have won everyone else over, but you won't win me. You're just a spotty, ugly, country girl.' Breaking down in loud sobs, knowing that she was beaten, Davina stumbled away.

Molly was exhausted from the confrontation and shocked. She had never expected to meet someone who had the gift, and she was shocked at herself for not being prepared. She should have guessed that other people like this existed. Molly wondered how many people there were in New York, who, like Davina, unconsciously used their untutored hypnotic powers to get by. Then, Molly wondered how many there were who had those powers and knew *exactly* what they were doing. She speculated upon how many copies of the Logan book there might be. Maybe there were people out there even better at hypnotism than Molly. All these thoughts were very unsettling. She was relieved when a knock at the door distracted her and Rixey Bloomy poked her plastic-looking face into the changing room. She smiled sweetly. 'Are you ready to rehearse, dearest Molly?'

\*

That night, *The New York Tribune* had shocking headlines.

### BROADWAY BRAWL
*Davina Nuttel makes way for a new kid
on the block*

Professor Nockman bought his copy of the paper and read it eagerly on a street corner. So she was called *Molly* Moon, and she was starring in a Broadway musical. Fantastic! Nockman felt like a green light had suddenly turned on, beckoning him forward. At last, there would be no more hunting in the dark. Such a bright spotlight shone on this Molly Moon he couldn't possibly lose her again. This was brilliant! Professor Nockman couldn't wait to meet her.

It didn't take him long to discover that Miss Moon was living it up at the Bellingham Hotel. Parking his rusty, white van on the other side of the street from Molly's hotel, he sat tight, biting his long nails with excitement as he waited to spot his prey.

By the time Molly appeared, Nockman's nails were chewed to bits. All night he'd sat in his cramped van, huddled up in his sheepskin coat, trying to warm himself with a small heater plugged into the cigarette lighter socket. He slept fitfully, obsessively checking the hotel entrance.

As the working day started, a silver Rolls-Royce pulled up in front of it. Nockman shook himself awake and wiped his steamed-up windows to get a better look. A porter was opening the hotel door for someone. Nockman squinted to see and at last he saw Molly Moon.

Down the steps towards her car she came. She was dressed in a soft, white, mink coat with a fur cap to match and her feet were in cream-coloured, knee-length, low-heeled leather boots. Under her arm was a flat-faced pug. The girl looked like a starlet – altogether different to the scruffy one Nockman had seen in Briersville.

Nockman was beginning to respect this small-town girl. He was amazed and impressed by the speed at which she'd arrived. She had exceptional talents and he was sure he was the only person in New York who knew her secret.

From that morning on, Professor Nockman kept close track of Molly's movements about town. He followed her as she went shopping accompanied by body-guards, watching as more and more smart bags and boxes were loaded up into her Rolls-Royce. He waited for her as she went into amusement arcades and spent a fortune. He sat outside fabulous restaurants as Molly tasted the cuisines of the world with Rixey or Barry. And the more he watched her, the more convinced he was that he was right about the power of hypnotism. This Molly Moon obviously had everyone under her thumb.

Nockman had been looking forward to learning about hypnotism for himself for years – ever since he'd heard about the hypnotism book from a rich, old lady whom he'd met in a coffee shop. He'd found out that the ninety-year-old was related to Dr Logan, the great hypnotist, and what was more, she'd inherited his money. In her grand apartment, she'd showed Nockman an intriguing letter from the librarian at Briersville, describing the hypnotism book.

'Why, if that book ever got into the wrong hands,' the old lady had postulated, 'who knows what might happen in the world?' From that moment on, Nockman had hoped those wrong hands might be his. He became convinced that if he could get his hands on the book, he would be able to carry out the most ambitious crime of his career, which he had been planning for some time. For Nockman was no intellectual with a studious interest in hypnotism. He wasn't a real professor, but a professional crook. With a lot of experience under his belt.

Nockman had hours to while away in his van; hours to mull over how pleased he was that all his efforts had been worthwhile. In a way, Molly Moon finding the book had been a good thing. Because now, if he got his hands on her, he could very quickly jettison himself into the Super League of Crime. Nockman licked his lips greedily. He knew now that he was going to become the greatest criminal of all time.

As he dozed in his van, he imagined how much money Molly Moon must be making, and he murmured to himself approvingly. He flitted in and out of sleep, fantasizing that he too had hypnotic powers, dreaming of how powerful he could become. He had visions of himself in golfing clothes on a lawn beside a huge mansion, with a maid bringing him tea. He saw himself on a grand yacht, with a uniformed crew of ten, sailing around New York. He imagined himself sleeping on a pile of money, holding *The Book of Hypnotism*.

One day, at dawn, Nockman woke to see a huge

billboard being pasted up on the side of the skyscraper near the Bellingham Hotel. The picture on it was a giant photograph of a hundred-foot-tall Molly Moon, in an astronaut outfit, holding her dog, who was also wearing a space suit. Nockman chuckled. This girl was a *genius*! And the better she was at hypnotism, the better it was for him.

# Chapter Nineteen

After her meeting with Davina Nuttell, Molly gave strict instructions that during rehearsals no outsiders should be let in. Of course, her instructions were obediently followed.

Whenever Molly left the theatre now, or arrived at the Bellingham Hotel, there was always a flock of journalists with flashing cameras. Molly smiled enigmatically from behind dark glasses as she got in and out of her chauffeur-driven Rolls-Royce, but she never talked to them.

All over town, people were gossiping about mysterious Molly, speculating about who she was and where she'd come from. Her mysteriousness made her more and more interesting and everyone wanted to see pictures of her in the papers. One paper nicknamed her 'The Cuckoo', because she had stolen Davina Nuttel's part, and TV shows sent camera crews to try and interview her, without success.

Davina Nuttel went on television and complained about how badly she'd been treated.

Charlie Chat rang the Barry Bragg agency, again and again, to beg for an exclusive interview with this Molly Moon on his TV chat show. Barry Bragg said it might be possible if the money was right.

As Nockman's mind spiralled away in his van, his red rash broke out on his neck and face. He couldn't wait to get his hands on Molly.

But it was proving very difficult to get close to her at all.

There were always people wherever she went. It was exasperating. All he could do was watch and wait for an opportunity. Maybe after the opening night Molly would start giving interviews and he could pose as a journalist. He tried to relax, but Nockman was impatient by nature and the situation was driving him crazy. He worried that someone else would discover Molly's secret. He sat in his white van, smoking, eating cheesy biscuits and looking suspiciously at other parked cars. The van was full of rubbish and the discarded packaging, from all the junk meals he'd eaten, smelled disgusting. He smelled worse than ever. Now, on top of the chip fat and fish and tobacco was the reek of cheap aftershave, to cover up the smell of old sweat. Occasionally, he would go back to his railside room to have a wash, but not too often as he hated losing track of Molly Moon for a moment. As the days went by, he thought obsessively about her.

He had mixed feelings for Molly. He was jealous of her, because she had found the hypnotism book first, and she had learned the tricks of hypnotism, but also because she was living the life of Riley, whilst he was slumming it in this stuffy van. At the same time, he was in awe of her and her talents, and since he saw her as his property, he also savoured her rise to fame. To keep himself sane, he'd stroke the golden scorpion that hung round his neck and say a mantra over and over to himself that went,

*'The better it is for her, the better it is for me*
*The better it is for her, the better it is for me*
*The better it is for her, the better it is for me*
*The better it is for her, the better it is for me.'*

As for her dog, he hated her dog. That pug, it was so smug; a smug, ugly pug, trotting about behind her. Nockman thought jealously about Petula's luxurious bed and her fine dinners. Why, that dog was Molly Moon's partner, and her best friend. She would probably do *anything* for that dog . . . And then, as Nockman thought about Petula, he began to have a brilliant idea. His manipulative nature began to ooze with pleasure, oiling his thought and helping it grow. Why hadn't he seen the value of the dog before? Why, that dog was the key to Molly's heart! Nockman smiled and stroked his double chin. He picked at the scabby rash on his neck, flicking a piece of it on to the dashboard of the car. Then, thinking of Molly, he smudged the flaky skin across the plastic and his mind hatched a nasty plan. At last, he could see a way forward.

# Chapter Twenty

November rolled into December and temperatures in New York dropped as winter sank its teeth into the city. Molly hadn't had time to think about Rocky, since when she wasn't working hard on the show, she was busy enjoying her fame and fortune. She'd been very busy about town, always with a minder and a bodyguard, who kept journalists away from her. Molly had spent happy hours shopping, going to the cinema and seeing the sights. She'd been to an exclusive salon and had her hair cut properly, so that she no longer looked like an orphanage kid, and she'd paid ten visits to a beautician where she'd been steamed and pampered until her skin shone. Although her hands still sweated, they now looked much better after expensive manicures. Her nails were shaped into perfect, polished crescents.

Molly loved her new life. She loved the attention she was getting and the way people treated her with reverence. She couldn't see, now, how anyone could live their life in any other way. It was so much easier when everyone adored you. And the more Molly lived this life, the more she reckoned she deserved it. What was more, she began to feel that it wasn't just because she'd hypnotized people that they admired her. She suspected that, actually, she did have 'star quality'. Everyone at Hardwick House had simply been too uncultured to notice it.

After two weeks of concentrated rehearsals and hours of practising, the opening night of the new production of *Stars on Mars* arrived. The pink neon sign on the front of the theatre now read:

# STARS ON MARS
### STARRING
## MOLLY MOON
### AND
### PETULA THE PUG

Behind the scenes, Molly sat in her cluttered dressing room, with Petula on her lap, feeling very nervous. Both were dressed in silver space jumpsuits. Molly's face was thick with stage make-up, so that her face didn't shine under the strong theatre lights. Her eyes were defined with black eyeliner so that they stood out, and her cheeks were sprinkled with glitter. Petula had been groomed and both she and Molly had sparkly powder combed through their hair. Their other costumes, space wetsuits and their sequinned space dance outfits, hung on a steel rail. Vases of flowers covered every available surface; sent by everyone who loved Molly. Rixey knocked at the door and popped her face round.

'Curtains up in twenty minutes, Molly. How do you feel?'

'Fine, fine,' Molly lied.

'Well, good luck, although you don't need it, you're a star, Molly, a sparkling star, and everyone will see it tonight. New York's gonna *love* you.'

'Thanks,' Molly said, her stomach heaving. Rixey disappeared.

'Oh crikey, Petula, what have I done?' Molly moaned. Now, the idea of making her fortune by being in a Broadway musical didn't seem like fun at all. Her nerves were a thousand times worse than they had been before the talent show in Briersville. The thought of the audience tonight was truly terrifying. An audience made up of cosmopolitan New Yorkers, hard to please and ready to be dismissive. She knew the audience out there would be sceptical, critical, aggressive and very, very difficult to excite . . . but worse than that, difficult to hypnotize. Molly remembered how Davina had been such a challenge to win over. Maybe there'd be well-practised hypnotists in the audience. Like the sort of professional hypnotherapists who help people to give up smoking. Molly tried to pull herself together. What was she thinking of? Of course she'd be much better than them. She only hoped the new scene she had written into the beginning of the show, with the new props, would make things easier.

'Fifteen minutes to curtains up,' the tannoy announced.

Molly reached into her pocket for her pendulum and stared into its black spiral. 'I will do it, I will do it,' she said to herself, over and over again, and then she kissed the pendulum for luck and put it back in her jumpsuit.

Molly and Petula made their way down the corridor and up the stairs to the side of the stage. Through the curtain Molly could hear the hum of the massive audience. Her hands began to sweat and her heart began to pound. 'Good luck, good luck,' she heard people saying. She took her position in the cockpit of a silver spacecraft on the stage, ready for take-off. 'Ten minutes to go,' someone whispered to her. Molly's stomach writhed. It was difficult to concentrate.

The orchestra began to play the overture; little pieces of music from different songs in the musical. The audience went quiet to listen. Molly lowered her head, which felt useless and full of cotton wool. 'Come on, Molly, you can do it,' she said to herself in a low, quaky voice.

Then the overture finished and however hard Molly wished for time to stand still, the show started. With a dash of drums, the curtain swished upwards.

The audience sat with bated breath, and feasted their eyes on Molly Moon. The Cuckoo. At last there she sat, the new star of the show, in the cockpit of a huge spacecraft, with Petula the pug on the seat beside her.

A deep voice crackled over the loud speaker, 'Ground control to Major Wilbur, do you read me? We are ready for lift-off, over.'

Major Wilbur, with her eyes shut, replied, 'Ready.'

Then, slowly, a huge glass window began to lower itself down in front of the rocket.

This was the new part of the show which Molly had added. Because this glass window was no ordinary glass window, it was an enormous, powerful magnifying glass, that the theatre had ordered especially, at great expense, from NASA, America's space agency. And as it slowly dropped in front of Molly, it magnified her so much that she became a giant behind it. The centre of the magnifying glass was the strongest part, and when Molly leaned towards this centre, her shut eyes became eighty times as big.

This looked good, and murmurs of approval filled the theatre. The New York audience liked this spectacle and they relaxed to watch the whole stage grow dark, except for a spotlight shining on Molly's shut eyes.

'Ten,' the controller's voice boomed out over the loud speaker.

'Nine . . . eight . . .'

'Engines set,' said Major Wilbur.

'Seven . . . six . . . five,' said ground control.

'We have ignition,' said Major Wilbur.

'Four . . . three . . . two . . . one . . . And we have lift-off.'

The roar of rocket engines filled the theatre. Orange lights flashed around the cockpit like fire from the rocket's engine, and then, Molly's eyes, as huge as the hugest of TV sets, opened. Molly was composed at last and her magnified eyes swept over the audience like lasers. From the back of the circle to the back of the stalls, people were washed by Molly's strange overpowering gaze, and they were sucked into the hypnotic whirlpool of her stare.

Molly felt a surge of something like electricity in the air which made her tingle from head to toe. It was that fusion feeling, but on a massive scale.

Molly turned her gaze slowly from left to right, she stretched her gaze to the back of the theatre and then dropped it to the front. And as the fusion feeling became stronger and stronger, Molly's nerves disappeared. She felt hugely powerful, she felt sure that everyone had been 'hit', and she knew that the theatre doormen were under instruction not to let anyone in. She was safe.

'Just – look – at – me,' she said, in case there was anyone out there who hadn't looked up yet. 'Just – looooook – at – me,' she repeated slowly, her voice like a vocal magnet.

Molly had woven her hypnotic instructions into a song, which she had composed. She sang it now with no instrumental accompaniment, to a plain, haunting tune.

*You will be bowled over – by this – show*
*It'll be so good you – won't want to – go*
*My dancing and singing will – thrill you – to bits*
*My jokes will give you – giggling fits*
*This blockbuster show was – destined – to be*
*The star – of the twenty-first century – is – ME.'*

Molly clicked her fingers and the roar of the rocket launchers filled the air.

'Yes,' said Molly, her whole face now in the centre of the magnifying glass, 'we have LIFT-OFF.' The magnifying glass pulled up and away and the real show began.

For two hours, the audience was in raptures of pleasure, marvelling at Molly's dancing and singing. She could do ballet, tap dancing, jazz dancing, and break-dancing. She leaped effortlessly into the air. She glided! And when she sang, she made her audience go

172

all goose pimply and hair stand out on the back of their necks. She was entrancing.

Whereas in reality, Molly's dancing was clumsy and uncoordinated. Her tap dancing was a mess and her jazz dancing heavy-footed and out of time. But Molly was having a lovely time dancing and she got really involved with the Martians' battle scene. Her voice was flat and out of tune but no one cared. The other actors were great and helped her out whenever she forgot her lines, although it didn't matter whether she forgot her lines or not; the audience loved her whatever she did. And they thought Petula was wonderful too, even when she simply lay on the apron of the stage, chewing a stone, and looking bored.

Ice creams dripped into people's laps as they forgot to eat them.

When the show ended, the theatre erupted with applause and when Molly came forward to take her bow, the whole audience stood up to cheer and whistle and clap. Flowers were thrown at her. Anything nice that people had on them they threw: money, watches, jewellery, fancy scarves . . . It was a show of appreciation that was unlike anything that had ever been seen in New York before. The curtain opened and closed and opened and closed forty times. The audience clapped and clapped and clapped and clapped until their hands were red. And then the curtain came down for the last time.

Molly felt on top of the world, confident that everyone had seen what she had wanted them to see.

One person alone slipped through her net. One small boy in the audience had not been hypnotized, simply because he had not been watching or listening. He had been reading a comic with a torch and was too absorbed in Superman to look up at Molly's eyes. So, later when he put down his comic, he was the only one who saw Molly's true talent.

'Mom, she wasn't *that* good,' he said as he left the theatre. 'I mean we got kids at *school* better than her.'

But his mother had been smitten. '*How* can you say that, Bobby? She was *fabulous*. Beautiful. And you, Bobby, will remember this night for the rest of your life. Tonight you saw a *star* being born.'

Bobby and his mother argued about the show all the way home and finally, she came to the sad conclusion that her son needed either a hearing aid or glasses or a trip to see an analyst.

Nockman had avoided the show. He hadn't wanted to risk being inside the theatre, in case he was forced to take his anti-hypnotism glasses off. And anyway, for his plan to work he needed to be outside the stage door when the show ended.

It had begun to rain. Nockman stood in his sheepskin coat, hidden in the shadow of a wall, a few metres from the stage door. His bald pate and greasy mane of hair were splashed with the shower. Raindrops trickled down his neck and off the end of his nose.

Just after ten-thirty, hordes of people began to crowd around the stage door hoping for autographs. Twenty minutes later, the doors opened and there stood Molly Moon smiling and waving, with a burly minder on each side of her.

The shouts and cheers from her fans were perfectly distracting. Molly's mind was not on Petula.

Petula stepped out in the rain, and away from the

crowd to get a breath of fresh air. She sniffed at a lamp-post and had a welcome pee. Then an interesting sheepskin smell hit her nose. She trotted towards a shadowy wall to investigate. And as soon as she'd stepped out of the street-light, a strong, gloved hand picked her up and covered her in a cloth, while another hand clamped her mouth shut. Petula found herself under the arm of a small, fat, smelly man, who was walking briskly away down a side-street. She wriggled and struggled but she couldn't escape his grip. Poor Petula was terrified as she heard, felt and smelled Molly getting further and further away.

Nockman opened the back of his white van and bundled Petula into a cage inside. Before she'd had time to get her bearings, he'd shut the cage door and the van door too. Then he jumped into the front seat, started the engine, and was away.

# Chapter Twenty-One

After Molly had signed what felt like a thousand autographs she whistled for Petula. When Petula didn't come, she assumed that she'd slipped inside, away from the noisy, jostling crowd. But Petula wasn't inside either. Molly checked all Petula's favourite places: the cushion under the dressing table where she kept her stones; the pile of rags under the props table; the gap under the blue corduroy chair. Then she checked the toilets, the stage and even the Martians' dressing room. But Petula was nowhere. Soon the rest of the cast were helping too. They looked in cupboards, behind curtains, and in wardrobes. She wasn't in the theatre foyer or the ticket booth or in the bar. Petula was well and truly lost. Molly's heart gave an almighty lurch as she imagined the worst. The stage-door man looked in the gutters of all the adjoining streets to see if Petula had been hit by a car. After that they could only come to the conclusion that Petula had been stolen.

Molly was distraught. Who could have taken her? She shuddered as she imagined poor Petula in some strange house, lonely and frightened.

'I tell you what,' Barry Bragg tried to reassure her 'the person who took her, took her because they *liked* her and they wouldn't treat her bad if they liked her.' Inside he was already thinking about all the publicity the show would get from Petula being stolen. 'You know what we should do? We should put out an SOS interview on TV. Someone will see her. I mean, people *notice* when their neighbours get new pets. Someone will report her.'

The police arrived. Molly spoke to the sergeant privately and, using her powers, persuaded him that finding Petula was one of the most important missions of his life. The sergeant rang his superintendent and twenty policemen and women were enlisted to search for the missing pug.

In the early hours of the morning, Molly arrived at the Sunshine TV Studios where she was powdered and put in front of bright lights and cameras for an interview. Charlie Chat sat opposite her, still in his party clothes, since the producer of the show had called him in from a nightclub.

Molly found it difficult to concentrate and produce her hypnotic gaze, as she was upset and distracted by thoughts of Petula, but then she realized that she was doing this *for* Petula, and she tried her hardest to make herself utterly charming.

At Sunday breakfast time the next morning, New Yorkers eating their breakfasts of granola, pancakes and hash browns watched Molly's interview with Charlie Chat.

'It's so *sad*,' said the already infatuated Charlie to Molly, 'that a night as glorious as last night should be marred by this catastrophe. That your dog, who I understand was truly *marvellous* in the show, should just disappear.' Charlie's gravelly voice dropped to a super-sympathetic tone. 'And, Molly, you believe that Petula has been stolen, or kidnapped?'

All over the east coast of America, viewers watched the new child star and listened to her plea for help.

'If anyone out there thinks they've seen a pug dog that looks like this . . .' Molly held up a picture of Petula in her space suit. 'If you can imagine her without the space suit on . . . er . . . this is the only picture I have of her . . . it's from the show . . . She likes chewing stones . . . If anyone out there thinks they know of her whereabouts, please could they get in touch with the Manhattan Theatre. There's a reward of $20,000 for anyone who'll give me information that will lead to her. You see, I've known Petula since I was very young. Her mother abandoned her when she was a puppy, so I can't desert her now. To be deserted twice in one life is too much. Anyway, she's very special to me. She's my best friend really, although . . .' all at once Molly thought of Rocky in New York, and she wondered whether he ever watched breakfast TV '. . . although I do have a human best friend too, and if he's watching, I'd like to say hello to Rocky and I'd love to see him soon. But mainly this message is for Petula, because she's lost, and may be in danger. So please help if you can.'

People watching their screens felt incredibly sorry for Molly. She conveyed a certain hypnotic charm over the airwaves and viewers found themselves drawn to her. She wasn't wonderful-looking or anything, but there was definitely something about her. Millions of Americans went to work with Molly on their minds, alert to any dog's bark, and on the lookout for a black pug.

Throughout the day, Molly's broadcast was replayed regularly on television, and no pug in the city was safe as well-meaning, reward-seeking Petula-rescuers snatched dogs from their real owners and took them to police stations. The stations were chaotic, awash with barking pug dogs and people squabbling. Owners quarrelled with Petula-rescuers, and rescuers argued with police. The New York police investigated every dog and every report, but none of the pugs was Petula.

There was nothing for Molly to do after her interview but go back to the hotel. It was Sunday, so there was no evening show and it was very lonely in her suite without Petula. Molly thought of all the adventures they'd been through, and she looked at the show photographs of Petula in her jazzy costumes. Molly didn't know what she'd do without her. She felt utterly miserable as she thought of the soft, velvety ears that she longed to stroke. For the fiftieth time, she hated herself for losing sight of Petula, for being vain and wanting to sign autographs. And then, the phone rang.

'Hello,' Molly said hopefully.

'I've got your dog,' came a heavy voice down the line.

'What . . .? where . . .? Oh, thank you! Is she all right?' gasped Molly in relief.

'Listen to me,' said the cold voice of Nockman. 'If

you want her back, you'll do as I say. First thing is, you say nothing on the phone now. If you say anything, I'll disconnect.' He guessed Molly might try to hypnotize him with her voice and he didn't want to risk that. 'You just say OK . . . OK?' he ordered.

'OK,' Molly whispered. She was scared and shocked. This person was a lunatic. She didn't want to displease him.

The voice continued. 'If you don't do exactly as I say, I'll kill the dog, is that understood?'

Molly went cold. 'OK,' she said again. The word 'kill' began to echo like a loud alarm bell in her head and Molly's hand started to shake so much that the phone banged against her cheek as she held it.

'Right,' said the man, 'I'll meet you at the Boy Scouts' bandstand in Central Park at six-thirty. I come alone. You come alone. I *won't* be bringing the dog, but I will bring her collar so you know I'm for real. If you bring anyone with you, or if you get the cops involved, I'm tellin' you, the dog dies. OK?'

'OK.' Molly stared at the wall, hardly able to believe that this nightmare was happening. 'OK.'

'I'll make my demands. If you agree, the dog returns, OK . . .? OK?'

'OK,' Molly repeated, although she was in such a daze that she hardly knew what she was agreeing to. The line went dead. In her shock, Molly bit the receiver as she tried to absorb what she had just been told. Of all the cruel people Molly had known in her life, none was as sinister or as threatening as this unknown voice. She felt a fool. She should have been wiser and more prepared for something like this. After all, this was New York City, and under its belly lived all sorts of dangerous and revolting creatures. Molly's spine prickled as she realized that she was about to meet one of them. Then she pulled herself together. What was she worrying about? She was a hypnotist. Had she forgotten? She'd be safe – wouldn't she? Doubts gushed through her as she remembered Davina's resistance. But, she reasoned, this man was a desperado. If he had Davina's charm, he wouldn't be kidnapping dogs.

Molly looked at her bedside clock. It was already five forty-five. Central Park was nearby, but how should she get there? Quickly, she opened her balcony door, peered over the ledge, and saw to her dismay that down below there were four photographers hanging about. Molly thought fast.

She rummaged in the bottom of one of the wardrobes and found her jeans, a grey jumper and her scruffy old anorak, which, luckily, she hadn't thrown away. Putting them all on, she looked much less conspicuous. Then, with a wad of money in one pocket and her pendulum in the other, she left the hotel room and quietly made her way to the cleaners' room at the end of the corridor. She had seen the chambermaids taking armfuls of bed linen in there, and throwing it down a laundry chute. She'd have to risk it . . .

It was a fast, dark, helter-skelter ride to the basement of the hotel, and Molly landed in a pile of dirty laundry. She peeled a smelly sock off her head and looked about. With no one in sight, it was easy to make a break for the tradesman's entrance. Outside, she found a delivery man's bicycle and climbed on it, but since she was a bundle of nerves, and it was too big for her, she fell off twice and scraped her ankle on the bicycle chain before she finally managed to balance. Soon, though, she was pedalling away westwards from the back doors of the Bellingham Hotel, her curly brown hair blowing in the wind, and her expression one of anxious determination. As the tarmac passed beneath the wheels of the bicycle, Molly was persuading herself that there was no need to be afraid, that this man would simply be another of her victims. As she crossed Madison Avenue, Molly told herself that she must be strong, and then, soon, she'd see Petula again. As she cycled up Fifth Avenue, beside Central Park, she tried to feel excited. But when she got to the park entrance, her apprehension returned. With a shaky finger, she followed the paths on the park map, and saw that the Boy Scouts' bandstand was not far away. She braced herself. She knew that weirdos hung about in Central Park at night – this guy was one of them. As long as she could stare at anyone who might jump her, she was safe. So, taking a deep breath, she went in.

The park was looking beautiful. The moon had emerged from behind the clouds, throwing its light upon the giant, leafless trees. A clammy mist seeped over the ground and Molly walked ankle-deep in it. Then, she got back on her bike, and taking care to look about her often, so that no one could spring her from behind, she cycled steadily into the centre of the park. Brave as she tried to be, every snapping twig, every rustling in the bushes made her heart pound. Occasionally, a jogger or a roller skater shot by, but for the most, Molly was alone in the darkness. When she got to the bandstand, no one was in sight. She propped her bike up, climbed the bandstand stairs and stood on its icy platform. A clock broke the silence, chiming quarter past the hour, then half past six. It began to rain. Molly waited and waited, trying to compose herself. Her heart thumped so loudly that she felt it might burst through her ribs. Suddenly, a small, round figure that she faintly recognized appeared, darting from bush to bush. Then, looking up, it hurried up the path towards her.

# Chapter Twenty-Two

The man began to climb the bandstand steps. The anticipation and fear were too much for Molly and her teeth began to chatter. She clenched them shut only to find that her head was shaking. A chill December gust blew the smell of the man towards her. It was a foul smell of chip fat, sweat and old tobacco and it made Molly feel sick. As the man came up the wooden steps, Molly saw that he was wearing headphones and strange dark glasses with a spiral pattern in the middle of them. In one hand he was holding a briefcase and, in the other, a microphone. This was wired up to a machine of some sort on his belt. He was clad in a sheepskin coat and he was, Molly decided, definitely very, *very* weird. But, nervous as he made her feel, with resolute purpose and great control, Molly concentrated on bringing her eyes up to hypnotic peak. As he stepped under the bandstand's dim light-bulb, she looked up at him with her eyes on full glare.

'Wel-come . . .' she said slowly, intent on putting this nasty rat into a very, *very* deep trance. But, instead of being stopped in his tracks, the man took another step towards Molly and pointed his microphone at her.

'I'm afraid, Miss Moon, your hypnotic eyes will not work on me, since I am wearing anti-hypnotism glasses designed by Dr Mesmer himself. As for your hypnotic voice, I am not hearing it. This device is processing what you say and scrambling your tone . . . Through this you sound like an alien from outer space.'

Molly was stunned. Then she saw the golden scorpion that hung round the kidnapper's neck. Its diamond eye flashed in the moonlight, and to her astonishment she recognized the ugly face of the shouting professor from Briersville Library.

At this point, peculiarly enough, Molly's fears fell away. She actually felt relieved to see the professor, since she'd been expecting a terrifying maniac kidnapper instead. And, Molly felt strangely comforted to see someone who knew Briersville. It was almost like seeing an old friend. Molly tried to think logically and quickly. The professor couldn't be a kidnapper, so the kidnapper must be somewhere else. She must warn him. Or did he know about the kidnapper? For a second, Molly was confused. But then, her mind flashed back to Briersville Library. She saw, horribly clearly, the professor shouting aggressively at the librarian. He was demanding a book which she had lost. A book by Dr Logan. The book which Molly had stolen. Molly looked at the professor's extraordinary gear. Within the time it takes to net a slow butterfly, she realized that she was in deep trouble.

'Let's get straight to the point,' the professor began. 'I know your tricks, Molly Moon. Or should I say, "Miss Cuckoo". I know *exactly* how you operate. I know where you come from, and what you've done. That hypnotism book you found was mine. I paid for it. It was *my* property. I've known about Logan's *Book of Hypnotism* since before you were in diapers.'

From behind his squirly spectacles, Nockman stared at Molly and he found himself feeling very excited. For the truth was, deep down, Nockman was actually star-struck by Molly. Everyone else was star-struck by her because they'd been hypnotized, but Nockman actually was. In his eyes, Molly was dazzlingly talented. He'd seen her at work, and he respected her. Molly, he thought, had the makings of a great criminal herself, and it was a pleasure for him to meet her. So, since he felt they were very alike, he spoke in a more gentle tone.

'As you see, I've been *very* put out by you, Miss Moon. It has been extremely tiresome, although entertaining sometimes, to have had to chase you about. It has pushed my patience to the limit. I think you'll understand when I say that I expect something in recompense for my . . . inconvenience.'

Molly's heart thumped. This was extremely unnerving. She wished someone else would come by and she looked about for help. Nockman said immediately, '*If* you want to see your dog again, you mustn't think of getting anyone else involved. You *do* want to see your dog again, don't you?'

'Yes.' Molly nodded unhappily.

Nockman sat down on the bandstand bench and

reached into his pocket. 'Here,' he said, chucking a red leather strap into Molly's lap, 'is her collar.'

Molly bit her lip.

'Now,' he continued, 'this is all going to be very painless, I promise you. In fact, you may even enjoy what I am going to ask of you, Molly Moon. But I warn you, once again, you *must* do as I ask. Because if you don't, I assure you, you won't see your pug again, and there will be many, many more people in New York who'll learn about your little *secret*. Let me put it like this . . . I'm sure a lot of people would be very upset if they knew *how* you'd deliberately cheated your way to the top. In fact, in a court of law, you could be convicted of fraud. A crime for which you could go to prison if found guilty. Of course, someone of your age wouldn't go to jail, just a young offenders' institution instead, but I've heard that those institutions aren't very comfortable places; much worse than bad orphanages.' Nockman smiled with a sinister glint in his eye.

'B-but Petula,' Molly stuttered, 'is she OK?'

'We'll come to her.'

'What do you want?' Molly burst out. 'Money? I've got loads. Just tell me.' Molly's mind raced. How had this manipulative, sordid man found her? She hated him.

'Money?' Professor Nockman chuckled. 'In an indirect way, yes, I do want money. There is a matter,' he said, opening his briefcase, 'yes, there is a little matter which requires your co-operation.' Nockman took a large envelope out of his case, and with a gloved hand, passed it to Molly. 'This envelope contains all you need to know in order to help me. I want to borrow your skills . . . just for a day . . . It's a small favour, in return for the good fortune that my hypnotism book has brought you.'

'What do you want me to do?' Molly asked, taking the envelope as if it was about to blow up in her hand.

'I want,' sighed Nockman lazily, 'well, the first thing I want, of course, is *The Book of Hypnotism*. That goes without question. The second thing, this favour thing, is this . . . I want you to help me rob a bank.'

# Chapter Twenty-Three

'Rob a bank?' Molly gagged at the words and Nockman laughed condescendingly.

'Hadn't it crossed your mind, Miss Moon, that you might be able to use your skills to rob a bank? There you were, dancing your little feet off to earn your dough, when you could have had millions of times as much just by visiting a bank.'

'No, it never occurred to me,' said Molly, in a daze.

'Come on now,' said Nockman incredulously. 'You don't have to be shy. You're showing all the signs of being a star criminal. You should be proud of yourself.'

'But I would never rob a bank,' insisted Molly.

'Oh, yes you would. And you will. And I think that when you get back to the Bellingham and open that envelope, you're going to be very impressed.' Nockman, Molly noticed, was looking very pleased with himself.

'Inside it, you will find plans that will make your

tiny head spin. You will see, kiddo, how *big*-time crime is done.' He breathed heavily. 'I want you to rob Shorings Bank. You may have heard of it. It's in New York's jewellery district, on 46th Street. It's where every jewellery dealer and every major jewellery owner keeps their stones. The place is stuffed to the brim with rubies, sapphires, diamonds. You name a precious stone and there'll be mountains of them at Shorings. It's not a gold-bullion bank, and it doesn't hold large amounts of cash. No, what it houses is *jewels*. And why does everyone keep their stuff there? Because Shorings is the most impregnable bank in the world. Breaking into it is as difficult as travelling to the centre of the earth and back again, if you see what I mean. Every criminal's dream is to crack Shorings, and I've had that dream since I was a boy.'

'But you're a professor!' exclaimed Molly, and it sounded very prim to her, even as she said it.

'Come on, Moonie,' scoffed Nockman. 'Wake up and smell the whisky. I'm no professor . . . Well, a Professor of Crime, perhaps.' He grinned at his own joke. 'And I've been *studying* this job for a very long time. Is Shorings impregnable? Yeah. But not for a criminal genius like me. I was determined to crack it. So I worked there, as a cleaner. And I cleaned *real* good, so there was no way they were gonna fire me. I mopped floors, I cleaned latrines, but all the time I was studying the place, and seeing how it worked. But after my stint there, I still didn't know *exactly* how I was gonna rob it. Then I found out about the hypnotism book and, after that, I found out about you.'

Molly's mouth had dropped open in amazement.

'I was going to rob the bank myself,' he said. 'But since you stole the book and have held me up so much, I thought I'd let you do the job instead.'

'Thank you,' said Molly weakly.

'So I'll leave it all in your capable hands.' Nockman pulled his sheepskin coat around him. 'You should look on this as a privilege. This is your chance to be associated with the greatest bank robbery of all time. You'll see. We're gonna go down in history.'

With that, Nockman turned to go. He felt good. He'd never spoken to anyone about his ambitions, or his work. It had sounded great. 'I'll call you' he added. 'And don't go doing anything stupid like talking to the cops . . . Just remember, I've got the pug.' Then he waddled away.

The meeting was over. Molly was left clutching the heavy envelope, horrified. Molly had never shoplifted so much as a sweet in her life. The idea of stealing millions of dollars' worth of jewels from Shorings Bank made her feel sick and frightened. But if she didn't, then Petula would die. Suddenly everything felt very out of control.

Molly left the bandstand and pushed her bicycle along the path. She felt guilty about the bike now. She felt like a thief. Then she thought about what Nockman had said, about her being a fraud. She *was* a fraud. She thought about the money that she'd won at the Briersville Talent Competition, and the way she'd pushed Davina Nuttel out of *Stars on Mars*. Molly was appalled at herself. Davina might be an annoying, spoilt upstart, but at least she had worked her way to the top. Whereas Molly had *conned* her way up. How could Molly despise Nockman for wanting to rob a bank, when she had been robbing in her own way?

Then Molly imagined what would happen if she *did* rob Shorings Bank. She'd be caught, of course. Banks, unlike theatres, were on the lookout for thieves. They had all sorts of high-tech equipment – alarms, cameras. Molly would be arrested, tried in court and then sent to a juniors' prison. She could imagine how the papers would love it. Her picture would be splashed across the front pages, and the public would loathe her. Maybe the news would even reach Briersville and everyone there would know what Molly had done. Molly imagined how ashamed Mrs Trinklebury would be, crying as she made fairy cakes. Molly saw herself in a concrete cell, sitting on a bed, lonely and unvisited. Mrs Trinklebury would be too far away to come, and Petula wouldn't be allowed. What about Rocky? Would he visit her?

Molly's eyes burned. She longed for a friend to confide in. She needed Rocky. Molly thought of his face, and for the first time in weeks, her eyes filled with tears. She realized that she could have easily found him by now, if she hadn't been so caught up in herself. She felt awful for forgetting him and for chasing fame and fortune instead. Those things felt like nothing now compared with her precious friendship with Rocky. She loved him as a brother and she desperately needed his friendship now.

Tears drenched Molly's cheeks as she passed the park's wishing well. She stopped. The lines of an old song came into her head. '*You never miss your water 'till your well runs dry.*' Her well of friendship had run completely dry.

She reached into her pocket and pulled out her pendulum. Even in the dark, it shone. Molly thought how the pendulum was just like all the things she'd been chasing in New York. It was expensive, beautiful and flash, but at the end of the day, it was useless. Molly didn't need it at all. She liked her plain old soap-on-a-string pendulum better now.

She turned the heavy, golden object over in her hand, and then, with a sudden gesture, she hurled it into the well. As she did, she wished with all her heart for Petula and Rocky. With a splosh, the pendulum hit the water and sank.

Molly cycled back to the Bellingham Hotel in the rain, turning the situation over and over in her mind. If she refused to rob the bank, Nockman would expose her and she'd end up in jail. But worse than this, Nockman would dispose of Petula. Nightmare visions of Petula being left to starve in a cellar, or Petula being thrown in a river, or Petula being dropped off a skyscraper, filled Molly's mind. Molly despised Nockman and felt very violent towards him. She felt like pushing *him* off a skyscraper. She felt like bludgeoning him with a heavy spade. Her worry for Petula and her hatred of Nockman were all mixed up with her longing for Rocky and her general confusion. By the time Molly had sneaked into the tradesman's lift and was going back up to her suite, rain-soaked and bedraggled, she was in a truly miserable state.

Back in her room, she sat down sadly on the bed and opened the envelope. The first thing she pulled out was a map. It was a plan of the inside of Shorings Bank. One part showed the layout of the ground floor, another showed the layout of the bank's basement.

The basement was where all the safes and deposit rooms were. Molly groaned as she saw that Nockman had written, 'Empty all these rooms.'

One strong room was called the 'Small Customer Deposit Box Room'. Molly thought of the innocent old ladies who kept their precious family heirlooms in the bank. They'd have heart attacks when they heard their jewellery had been stolen. Stolen by Molly. She couldn't do it. She saw a note at the bottom of the page.

'The job is simple, I want all the stones, jewels and jewellery from the strong rooms. Forget any gold and cash. I have a check-list, and will be using it.'

Molly pulled out other documents from the envelope. There was a page with a list of all the people who worked in the bank, and where they worked. The last page was entitled, 'Operation Hypnobank'. It read:

'1. Hypnotize all members of bank staff, clerks, secretaries, manager, security guards
2. Hypnotize customers in bank
3. Instruct manager to close bank and to turn off all internal cameras and alarms
4. Gain entry to basement strong rooms
5. Rob
6. Load up vehicle in bank garage
7. Blank minds of all bank workers
8. Hypnotize driver and drive to warehouse (address to be given later)'

And where was Nockman to be in all of this? Miles

away, of course, where he would never be a suspect. Molly read on. She was supposed to accompany the loaded bank vehicle to a warehouse, where she would find a brown lorry. The hypnotized driver was to move all the stolen stuff from the bank truck to the brown lorry, then she was supposed to send him off with a story in his head about where he'd been. And only when this was all done would Nockman arrive to drive his lorry and his stolen treasure away. Once he had travelled somewhere else, far enough away, once he had checked that the lorry contained everything from the bank, then, and only then, would he ring Molly at the warehouse and tell her where she could find Petula.

*'When I have checked everything is there, I will telephone and give you the address of where to find your dog and you will find her safe and comfortable.'*

Molly moaned. What if Nockman didn't give Petula back? What if he held on to her and got Molly to rob *another* bank? Or what if he made off with the loot and never told Molly where Petula was? Molly wondered whether she should call the police. But Nockman's words rang in her ears. *'If you get the cops involved, I'm tellin' you, the dog dies.'*

Molly went into the bathroom to splash water on her face to try to cool herself down. She looked up at herself in the smart bathroom mirror and she stared and stared. She wanted to hypnotize herself into feeling in control of the situation.

But instead of changing, her face stayed the same. No fusion feeling crept up her legs. Her sad, tear-stained face looked back at her and, try as she might, she couldn't conjure up a confident-looking Molly. She realized how adrift she was. So helpless that she seemed to be losing her powers. This was horrible.

Molly shook herself away from the mirror and turned back into the bedroom. A light was flashing on her telephone. Someone had left a message. Her heart sank as she realized it was probably from Nockman with the address of his warehouse. Molly pressed the playback button.

'Hi, Molly!' came Barry Bragg's voice. 'Just to tell you again, you were fab, just fab in the show last night . . . Call me, it's Barry.'

*Beeeeeeep.*

'Molly, this is Superintendent Osman. Please call, we would like to talk to you about other ways we might be able to track your dog. I'm on 713 7889.'

*Beeeeeeep.*

'Molly, my name's Mrs Philpot. I got your number off Barry Bragg. He said you might be interested in some pug puppies I've got . . . Call me on 678 2356.'

*Beeeeeeep.*

'Hi, Molly! Guess who this is?' Molly sat up . . . it was Rocky's voice! 'I'm in New York, in the lobby of your hotel, but you're not in. I'm going to wait here till seven forty-five, then I'll go back to my hotel . . . The number there is 975 3366.'

Molly looked at the clock. It was seven-forty. She rushed out of her room, called a lift, and was soon whizzing down to the ground floor. As the door slid open Molly's eyes frantically scanned the people milling about in the lobby. Then she saw a head of curly black hair poking up over the back of a black lacquer chair.

'Rocky! You found me!' Molly couldn't believe it.

Rocky's fantastic brown face looked round at her in surprise. Molly had never been so pleased to see anyone in her life.

'Hey, Molly!'

The two friends rushed at each other and hugged like brother and sister. For a moment Molly forgot all her worries, she was so happy to see Rocky. It was like having a part of herself back again.

Then, they put each other down and stared at each other in disbelief. Each one had thought that maybe they'd never see the other again. Molly drank in Rocky's face. He looked as sunshiney as ever. He'd had a hair cut and was wearing a new denim jacket. Otherwise he was just the same.

They stood there with huge grins on their faces, just beaming at each other. Then Molly said, 'Quick, come upstairs away from all these people.'

As she pressed the lift button she whispered, 'You don't know how glad I am to see you. Really, Rocky, you don't know . . .'

'Same here,' said Rocky.

'Oh, Rocky, really? I've got so much to tell you. How did you find me? You couldn't have come at a better time. I've been wishing and wishing for you. I'm *so* happy you're here. How did you know I was here? Did Gerry tell you?'

'Gerry? No. I saw you on *television* this morning, when you were telling the whole world that Petula had been lost,' explained Rocky, 'and then, you actually said hello to me. It was surreal! I could hardly *believe* it was *you* here in New York. But I was really pleased because I didn't know where you were, Molly. Every time I called Hardwick House, Hazel answered the phone, and she had no idea where you were either. I don't know where Miss Adderstone was. By the way, Hazel told me you'd won the Briersville Talent Competition. You're going to have to tell me all about . . .'

'I'll tell you about that later,' said Molly, hoping that Rocky wouldn't disapprove when she told him *how* she'd won. They stepped into the lift arm in arm.

'I was just having breakfast . . . drinking a cup of tea and I *half-choked* on it when I saw you on TV. I coughed it all over the table . . . I was so, so shocked . . .'

'Sorry.' Molly began to laugh.

The lift stopped at the twenty-first floor. 'I couldn't believe it was *you*, old Molly Moon, on American breakfast TV!'


'WOW . . . this is *fabulous*,' said Rocky, as he stepped into Molly's supersonic penthouse suite. 'This is amazing. You'll have to tell me everything that's happened to you, Molly. I mean, this is *so* cool. Is this all yours?'

'Mmmnn, except, well it was mine and Petula's.'

Rocky picked up Petula's silver space suit and sighed. 'I'm sure she'll be found,' he said. 'I mean everyone's looking for her . . . you were very persuasive on that programme . . . My new parents thought you were lovely . . . They were saying things like, "Oh, isn't Molly Moon sweet . . . she's like Shirley Temple . . . she's adorable . . ."'

An awful thought suddenly hit Molly. Had Rocky been distantly hypnotized by her over the airwaves?

She couldn't bear it if her only true friend had been hypnotized into liking her, just like everyone else. 'Rocky,' she said quickly, 'before you start thinking anything about me, stop right now, because I'm going to tell you *how* I got all this, *how* I got to be in *Stars on Mars* and everything, so don't decide that you like me until I've told you. And I warn you, you may not like me when you hear what I've done, but I have to tell you the truth, because otherwise you won't know who I really am.'

'Calm down, Molly,' said Rocky, frowning and sitting down on the sofa. He helped himself to a marshmallow from the large bowl on the table.

'OK, I will,' Molly said, taking a deep breath. 'First, I've got something to show you.' Molly went to a cupboard and opened it. 'It's the thing that changed my life . . . It's what helped me get here.' Molly clicked a combination lock, and opened the safe's heavy steel door. She pulled out the white silk-parcelled hypnotism book and carried it over to Rocky. 'Inside here is the most incredible book. And I'm not joking, Rocky, it really is something special. This book is what brought me to New York. It brought me all this success . . . but it's all ended in disaster.'

As Molly poured them both a Qube, Rocky opened the package. And for the next hour, Molly told him the whole story. From when they had the argument by the cross-country track in Briersville, to hearing Rocky's voice on the answer phone just now. She showed him the envelope of instructions from Nockman and Petula's red collar. When she'd finished, Molly tried to look Rocky bravely in the eye.

'So, now you know what I've been up to. The

worst thing is, that I got so wrapped up in myself and blown away by fame and money and flashy stuff that I almost forgot about you. Then, when I lost Petula too, I realized how awful it is without friends. You'll probably want to go now, but I just had to tell you everything.'

Rocky's expression was thoughtful. He rolled a piece of golden paper from a chocolate around in his hand until it was a small ball. 'You twit,' he said. 'I'm not going to *go*. I've only just found you. Why would I want to leave my *best* friend, who has been almost *impossible* to find and who I've missed like mad?' Rocky held the golden ball up and twisted it from side to side, so that it caught the light and shone. 'I mean, she may be half-crazy and have done some things that she maybe shouldn't have, but so what? She's still the best person I know. I mean, look at this ball. If it was the *only* precious thing you owned and if you'd had it all your life, you wouldn't just go and throw it away when a little bit of rust showed on it, would you?'

Molly shook her head and looked at the golden ball.

'You can relax, Molly. I'm not going anywhere. I'm going to stay right here, by your side, OK? So you can relax and feel good.'

Molly did feel good. Better than she'd felt in ages. It was wonderful to have Rocky back. He was talking to her now but she didn't hear what he was saying. She was just listening to his warm, kind voice, realizing how much she'd missed it. It made her feel as if she had come home. But she still felt bad.

'What am I going to do about Petula, Rocky? I can't see how to get out of this trap. Nockman's blackmailing me. All because of me, Petula is somewhere lonely and scared. She'd be better off feeling sick with Adderstone's chocolate biscuits. Because now she might die, she really might . . . I mean this guy is really mean . . . and it's all my fault . . . I should have just stayed at Hardwick House and put up with life there. I may have been bad at everything and unpopular, but at least Petula was safe and I wasn't being blackmailed into robbing a bank . . . In fact, I wish I was back there . . . I wish I'd never found this stupid hypnotism book . . . I wish I could turn the clock back and all of this would just disappear.'

All at once Rocky clapped his hands and with a whoosh, the hotel room disappeared. In its place was a wood. The wood beside the cross-country track, outside Briersville. Rocky and Molly were sitting on a bench, just as they had been the afternoon of their argument. Molly and he were in games kits, with gym shoes on. It was raining and they were wet.

# Chapter Twenty-Four

Molly nearly jumped out of her skin. She looked about her in a panic. They really were sitting by the Briersville School running track, in the rain.

'Aaaah, what's happening? Where's New York gone?' she cried.

Rocky smiled. A roll of thunder growled in the sky above them.

'Your time in New York never existed,' he said calmly. 'It was all a figment of your imagination, and my imagination too.'

'But . . . how?' Molly, still in shock, managed to stammer.

'I hypnotized you,' said Rocky.

'*You* hypnotized *me*?' she said, aghast.

'Yup.'

'*You* hypnotized *me*?' Molly repeated, 'But . . . but . . . when?' Molly felt disorientated and confused. The rain started to get heavier.

Rocky sighed apologetically. 'Sorry, but just now, here in Briersville. You said, "I hate this place, in fact I can't think of a *worse* place to be in the world. My life is just *horrible.*"'

Molly felt very mixed up. 'Did I? I can't remember saying that.'

'You just said it, at the end of our argument,' said Rocky.

'What argument?' asked Molly, totally bewildered.

'Sorry,' said Rocky, 'I'll have to make this clearer. You've been cross since this morning, because Mrs Toadley was nasty to you after the word test and Miss Adderstone has been giving you punishments all week, you know like cleaning the toilets with your tooth-brush.'

'But . . .' said Molly, 'but . . . I can't believe . . . it's incredible . . .' She could find no more words as it began to sink in where she was in the world and when.

'You said,' repeated Rocky, 'that you couldn't think of a *worse* place to be, and that your life in Briersville was a *horrible* situation. So I hypnotized you and showed you a worse place to be, which was an imaginary situation in an imaginary New York.'

'So Petula's OK?' asked Molly, shaking from shock.

'Yes,' replied Rocky. 'She's probably curled up on Miss Adderstone's lap, right now.'

'So Nockman doesn't exist?'

'Nope.'

'And Adderstone's still at Hardwick House?'

'Yup.'

'And she doesn't click her false teeth like castanets?'

'Nope.'

'And you haven't been adopted?'

'Nope.'

'And I'm plain old, unpopular, Molly Moon?'

'You got it.'

'Wow,' said Molly. The worry of Petula and the worry of having to rob a bank lifted off her shoulders. Her stomach relaxed and she felt a hundred times better. 'Wow,' Molly said, still dizzy from shock and still half-disbelieving that she was really back in her old world. 'Wow, Rocky! But where did you learn how to hypnotize? Wow! That story was amazing. Did you just make it up?'

'Yup,' said Rocky.

'But, Rocky, you could probably *really* hypnotize your way to the top. I mean you're *really* good. That felt *completely* real. I actually felt like I was in New York, for weeks and weeks.' Raindrops splashed on Molly's gym shoes. 'I can't believe that I really thought *I* was a hypnotist, and all along it was *you*.'

'Mmmnn,' nodded Rocky.

'But that was *amazing*,' Molly said, remembering everything. 'I *really* felt like I was in that show.' Molly shivered. 'And Nockman was so real. Uuurgh, he was horrible, and it felt really bad when he had Petula. Rocky, your imagination is *wild*. I can't believe you made that all up. And how long have you been able to do that? When did you learn? Does the book really exist? Why didn't you tell me?' Molly looked suspiciously at Rocky. 'Why haven't you hypnotized me before? Or have you?'

'We'd better get back,' said Rocky. 'I wonder what's for supper.'

'Probably Edna's fish in cheese-and-nut sauce,' said Molly, thinking of the food at the Bellingham which, in her imagination, had been so delicious. 'Mind you, Rocky, there were lots of parts of that story that you told me that were really nice.' Molly licked her lips. 'The food in the hotel was amazing, and that bedroom was so posh. Room service . . . I liked room service, and I liked the view from the hotel room and, even though I shouldn't have stolen Davina's part, I liked being in *Stars on Mars*, and I liked New York, oh, and I really liked having money.' Molly laughed. 'It would be lovely if it was all true, with just Nockman cut out of the story. I mean, he spoiled everything. Although I suppose I *was* starting to feel a bit guilty for being such a fake. But otherwise, it was . . . pretty good.' Molly chuckled. Then there was a flash of lightning and Rocky clapped his hands again.

# Chapter Twenty-Five

*A* flash of lightning lit up the New York skyline. Molly found herself back in the Bellingham Hotel room with Rocky.

'What . . .? Why . . .? Rocky! What's happening? Oh, Rocky, what are you doing? Why are we back *here*?' Molly felt spooked. She didn't know what was real any more and she didn't like the feeling at all.

'Rocky,' she said slowly, 'I don't understand . . . Is this real, or are the woods in Briersville real? I mean, we were just in Briersville, or was that my imagination?'

'New York is real. Briersville was in your imagination.'

'Definitely?' asked Molly.

'Yes. New York is real and everything that you've been doing here is real,' said Rocky.

'Are you sure?' asked Molly, still unsteady.

'Yes, I'm sure,' said Rocky. 'I just hypnotized you

206

then, using my voice and this ball of golden paper.' Rocky held up the sweet wrapper. 'I made you think we were still on the cross-country run. I wanted to make you think that all this,' he pointed out of the window at the New York skyline, 'never happened. Sorry about that.'

'But it felt *wet* . . . that rain. Everything felt so real,' said Molly.

'Well, that's the power of hypnotism,' said Rocky.

'But why . . . why did you do that?'

'I'm sorry,' said Rocky again. 'But, well, you were saying you wished you'd never found that hypnotism book . . . so I wanted to show you how *lucky* you were to have found it, and I wanted to show you that *I* could hypnotize too.'

'So you're a hypnotist too! I can't believe it,' said Molly, still reeling from the trip Rocky had taken her on, and completely amazed by his talent. 'And that's what it feels like to be hypnotized . . . Quite nice! So how did you learn?'

Rocky smiled. 'Guess.'

'I don't know, your new parents are hypnotists?' guessed Molly.

'No.'

'I give up.'

'OK.' Rocky reached into his denim jacket pocket and carefully pulled out two tissue-paper packets. 'Do you recognize this?' he asked, passing the more lumpy one to Molly. Molly unfolded the tissue, and found inside a small, shabby piece of hard, burgundy-coloured leather. She turned the leather over in her hand to discover on the other side, a large, golden, capital letter:

# H

'The missing H!' she said, amazed and, picking up the hypnotism book, she carefully placed the H in the space on the spine. It fitted exactly, and the strange word, YPNOTISM, became HYPNOTISM again.

Then Rocky passed her the other parcel. In this one was some neatly folded, old, yellowing paper. Molly opened the paper up. 'I can't believe it! So you were the one who ripped those chapters out!'

'I couldn't resist them,' Rocky said. 'Chapter Seven, Hypnotism Using the Voice Alone, and Chapter Eight, Long Distance-Hypnosis. They're my specialities.'

'And I thought *I* was the naughty one,' said Molly.

'Mmmnn. You see, I had the book first,' explained Rocky. 'I found it in the Not-To-Be-Lent-Out section in the library, so I read it there.

'It took me *ages* to read. Every time I had a spare hour, I'd sneak to the library. I think you thought I didn't like you any more, because I kept disappearing. The truth was, I was trying to learn how to be a hypnotist, because I had a plan. I wanted to get you and me away from Hardwick House by hypnotizing some of the Americans who came. I wanted to hypnotize them into seeing how great you are. I wanted them to *tell* you how much they liked you because everyone else was always so mean to you. I wanted them to boost your confidence. That's why I never told you about the book. Anyway, while I was reading, that bit of the cover fell off so I kept it. And I decided to . . . um . . . borrow those pages. But you know what? I think I ought to put them back now.'

Rocky took the pages and flattened them out and, opening the hypnotism book, he put them back into their rightful places. 'Home sweet home,' he said. Then, he gave the whole book to Molly.

'We'll glue the H back on,' she said, wrapping it up with the book. Putting the bundle back in the safe, she imagined Rocky practising Dr Logan's lessons, just as she had. 'Did you hypnotize an animal?' she asked, very intrigued.

'Yes, a mouse in the library.'

'You're kidding!'

'I've never seen a mouse roll over like the one I talked to,' chuckled Rocky.

Molly laughed. 'And what about people? Who did you hypnotize?'

'Well, people weren't easy,' remembered Rocky. 'I could *half* hypnotize people but it never really worked. Do you remember when Edna did your washing-up punishment for you?'

'Yes.'

'Well, I managed to hypnotize her to do that, but my powers weren't very strong and that was all I could get her to do. And, do you remember our argument, on the cross-country run when I made that blowfish face?'

'Yeah,' Molly said, smiling.

'And you told me I looked really stupid?'

'Yes,' said Molly, laughing as she remembered.

'Well,' explained Rocky, 'I was trying to hypnotize you into calming down because you were in a really bad mood.'

Molly grinned at the memory. 'So when did you get good at it?' she asked.

'Well, something clicked the day the Alabasters

came to Hardwick House, at least enough for them to fall under my spell. I was flabbergasted, I couldn't believe it when they actually wanted to take me home. They just turned up again on the Saturday morning, and wanted me to come away there and then, and Miss Adderstone, of course, was really pleased to get rid of me, and I couldn't get to spend enough time with them to persuade them to take you.'

'But, Rocky, maybe they really *genuinely* liked you,' Molly interrupted.

'Well, maybe,' admitted Rocky. 'Maybe. Anyway the thing was, Molly, that you were upstairs ill and I wanted to say goodbye to you and explain that I'd come back and get you too, and then all the little kids as well, eventually. Wow! I had such a plan . . . But Miss Adderstone wouldn't let me see you. She said you were highly contagious, and that you were asleep, and I knew I wouldn't be able to hypnotize Miss Adderstone, and the Alabasters said that since we were travelling I ought not to catch your illness and it was awful because I didn't want to make a scene just in case it put them off me, but I knew you'd be really upset and I wrote you a note, but I expect Adderstone never gave it to you and oh, Molly, I'm sorry.' Rocky stopped, out of breath, and took a gulp of Qube.

'That's all right,' said Molly, 'I knew something like that must have happened.'

'Now though, I'm more practised at hypnotism,' said Rocky, smiling craftily. 'Voice-only hypnosis is my strongest point. And *most* of the time, it works.'

'Mmmnnn,' said Molly, very impressed and putting on the voice of a learned expert. 'I never managed to master voice-only hypnosis, myself. *Since I couldn't find the lessons*. My speciality is eyes-only hypnosis, with a bit of voice on top. When you saw me on the telly, did you guess I'd found the book?'

'You bet I guessed,' said Rocky.

Molly sat back down and smiled. It was great to have Rocky back and someone to confide in. 'Real friends are the best thing,' she said. 'Better than popularity, or fame or money. Rocky, I'm *so* glad you found me. But – what are we going to do about Petula? And what are we going to do about Nockman and the robbery?'

'Well,' Rocky nodded slowly. 'Things are a bit different now, because Nockman doesn't know about me.'

'I hope not,' said Molly quietly.

'When do you think he'll ask you to rob the bank?'

'Who knows?' said Molly. 'He's so greedy . . . tomorrow?'

'That soon?' said Rocky. 'In that case, we've only just got time to sort ourselves out. I think I know what we can do. I've got an idea. It's a long shot I have to admit, but it might just work.'

# Chapter Twenty-Six

A flash of lightning lit up Petula's cell. She hated thunderstorms and on her own she was even more terrified of them. She shivered in the corner of the damp basement room where Nockman had imprisoned her.

After the kidnap, Petula had been driven away from the theatre, and had spent the night in Nockman's white van with Nockman stretched out flat in the back. Through the bars of her cage, Petula had studied the man's walrussy face and his scorpion necklace and as he snored, she'd wondered why this strange-smelling person had stolen her. She'd managed to claw at an old half-eaten baloney sandwich, pulling it into her cage. Then with a full stomach, she'd fallen asleep. The next day, the man had driven to the empty, chilly industrial building they were in now. He'd parked the van inside the building alongside a big lorry and then, with gloved hands, he'd carried Petula's cage down to this basement room. He'd undone the latch of the cage, roughly taken off her collar, left her there and gone away. Luckily, a dripping pipe in the room meant that Petula had something to drink, but she had nothing to eat.

Petula circled round and round on an old, broken sofa that smelled of mould, trying to find a comfortable position. She wished that she had a stone to suck. She wished the lightning would stop.

The same sheet of lightning lit up the pavement as Nockman scurried though the rain. He was hurrying through dark downtown streets, some distance away from Central Park where he'd just met Molly Moon in the bandstand. His feet were sodden from stepping in puddles and his hat was soaking, but inside he felt elated. He'd blackmailed Molly Moon beautifully, *perfectly*. There was no way she could refuse his demands. Within a few days he'd be richer than any criminal in the history of crime. How he loved that pug!

Every so often, Nockman stopped in a doorway to catch his breath and to listen, to check that Molly hadn't brought the cops with her. Each time, all he could hear was the heavy fall of rain. So on he went, dashing down alleys and side-streets, making his way back to his warehouse. Fifteen minutes later he arrived, his hand shaking as he fumbled with the keys. Inside, he slumped on a chair, his heart still pounding from the anxiety of the run. After a few minutes, he got up and poured himself a big whisky and, five whiskies later, he was asleep.

Nockman slept restlessly in the chair and woke up at six the next morning, with a dry mouth and a terrible headache from the whisky. As he reached for a bottle of water and looked about the dark warehouse, he realized that no one had come after him, and this made him feel a lot better. At eight, he was in a phone box, dialling Molly's number. To be safe, he was wearing his earphone contraption and was holding the microphone to the telephone.

Molly sat up in bed to answer the phone.

'Good morning, Molly,' said Nockman. 'And congratulations for not doing anything stupid. Your dog is still fine.'

Molly nodded frantically to Rocky, who was on the sofa, to indicate that it was Nockman on the phone. Rocky sat up quickly.

'I assume you agree to do the job?' he said.

'Yes,' said Molly, her voice sounding like an alien through the voice-scrambling machine.

'Good. Have you got a pen?'

'Yes.'

'Then I have the address of the warehouse, where you are to bring the *bank* truck, once it is *full*. You'll find the place open.'

Molly wrote down the address of the warehouse. It was on the west side of Manhattan, on 52nd Street, by the docks, where there were lots of derelict buildings.

'So I bring the bank truck to the warehouse, driven by a hypnotized security guard,' said Molly, 'and then . . . ?'

'Dear me, Molly,' said Nockman impatiently, 'it's all in the instructions I gave you. I do hope you are up to this job.'

'Yes, yes,' Molly said. 'Sorry, it's just I'm a bit nervous.'

'You better not be so nervous that you fluff it, Molly. Because I won't look so kindly on your dog if you mess this up.'

'No, I'm so sorry,' apologized Molly. 'I remember everything. The security guard loads the jewels from the bank truck into *your* lorry. I send the security guard back to the bank, mind blanked, and *then* you come to fetch the lorry, and after you've driven to a different place, far enough away, you will ring me, and let me know how to get Petula.'

'That is correct. And, Molly, I won't be calling until I am absolutely satisfied that you have delivered all the goods. Every last emerald.'

'And when do you want me to do this?' Molly asked.

'Today. This morning.'

'This morning!'

'Yes,' said Nockman. He'd decided that it was best to push Molly before she changed her mind. If he gave her time, she might track him down or work out some way to foil him. Besides, he was very impatient and wanted to feel those rubies pouring between his fingers.

'These are your final instructions. I want the people in the bank to be in a trance *until two-thirty*,' he said. 'I will pick my lorry up from the warehouse on 52nd Street before they even report that their bank has been robbed. I will collect the goods at a quarter to two.'

'Quarter to two today?! But . . . OK,' Molly agreed.

Nockman put down the phone and took off his anti-hypnotism device. Then he left the phone box and went back to his chilly warehouse. He tossed his coat into the back of the van, patted his brown lorry, which was soon going to be stuffed with precious loot, and went down the stairs to get Petula.

Petula's room smelled horrid. Poor Petula had peed on the floor, which was against all her training. When Nockman entered she tried to put up a fight, but he was wearing gloves again, so her bite didn't hurt him. Besides, she was feeling weak. Nockman grabbed her by the scruff of the neck and pushed her into the cage. Petula felt dejected and very, very hungry.

With the cage in the van, Nockman then drove across Manhattan island, and over a bridge to Brooklyn, to a small leafy industrial estate, where he owned another, larger warehouse. Over the years, Nockman's crooked business had brought him a certain amount of wealth and so he owned two storage facilities. They were useful for business. This second warehouse was where Nockman kept all his stolen property. It was crammed to the ceiling with boxes and bags full of stolen things, ranging from glass goblets to cutlery to lawn mowers to garden gnomes; anything that Nockman had stolen and planned to sell on.

He drove inside the warehouse, parked the van, got out, and happily kicked one of the smiling garden gnomes. Operation Hypnobank was going to plan. Nockman had nearly frisbeed himself into the Super League of Crime. He was nearly there! No more small-time crime for him now. He'd be rolling in money soon. The next step was to put this stupid dog somewhere and be ready to go back to Manhattan to collect his booty. Nockman was tense with excitement. He had a quick drink of whisky to steady his nerves.

\*

A room-service table stood in Molly's room with the leftovers of two half-eaten breakfasts. Molly looked at Rocky and pulled at her hair.

'Today! I can't believe he wants us to do it today. It's eight-fifteen now, and he wants the jewels and stuff in his first warehouse, repacked into his lorry by *quarter to two*. That gives us . . .'

'Five and a half hours,' Rocky calculated, 'to rob the bank, to pack up the loot in the bank truck, to drive it to his warehouse, and then to transfer it to his lorry.'

'But we haven't memorized the plans.'

'We'll take them with us.'

'I mean, is it possible?'

'We'll just have to try.'

'More than try,' said Molly. 'We've got to do it one hundred per cent right.'

'True,' said Rocky.

They both sat quietly for a moment summing up the monstrousness of the task. Then Molly said, 'What are we waiting for? Let's get it over with.'

It was time to move.

# Chapter Twenty-Seven

At eight-forty, Molly and Rocky, dressed in jeans and anoraks, were outside Shorings Bank. It was a huge, austere fortress, with walls steep and solid like the side of a small cliff. On two balconies were window boxes full of holly and red berries. Hidden in the holly were cameras that filmed the bank's entrance. It didn't open until nine o'clock.

Molly and Rocky sat on a bench on the other side of the street, hidden from sight by a bush. Hiding Nockman's plans behind comics, they were testing themselves on the layout of the bank, trying to visualize where everything was, and where all the people who worked there would be. Through the bushes they watched New Yorkers hurrying to work. Two hundred metres away, they could see the bank security guards patrolling the bank's entrance on the look out for would-be robbers. Molly and Rocky threw pebbles into the gutter as the last few minutes ticked by.

'I just hope they're all easy to hypnotize,' said Molly. 'And you can do it, can't you, Rocky? I mean I'm not being rude, it's just you said that *most* of the time it works for you. I mean, how often doesn't it work? The thing is, if you do it wrong and they get alerted to the fact that we're trying to hypnotize them, then we're in big trouble . . .'

'I hypnotized you, didn't I?' said Rocky.

'That's true,' admitted Molly. 'But are you sure you can still do it when you're nervous?'

'Yup. Well, I think so.'

'Are you feeling nervous now?'

'Yup.'

'Same here.'

Molly wasn't entirely confident of Rocky, but she knew he would try his hardest, and she needed an accomplice, so she tried not to think about things that could go wrong. 'Rocky, you won't do one of your wandering-off tricks when we're inside, will you? Don't disappear on me just as we're supposed to be leaving or anything.'

'Keep calm, Molly,' he said. 'You're just getting the last-minute jitters. We can do this. As long as you remember everything we worked out last night?'

'OK,' said Molly, trying to relax.

A clock on the side of the bank chimed nine, making them both jump. And then, the heavy cast-iron doors of the bank opened.

'Do you reckon all the people who work there are in now?' she asked nervously.

Rocky shrugged. 'I suppose so.' He stuffed the bank plans into Molly's rucksack alongside the hypnotism book which was all wrapped up for Nockman.

The two friends bobbed off the wall and walked slowly to the bank. The closer they got, the bigger the bank got, and the more their stomachs churned.

'I've got butterflies,' Rocky said.

'You're lucky,' said Molly, wiping her hands on her jeans. 'I've got jellyfish.'

Gingerly, they stepped up the stone steps. As they walked through the immense entrance, Molly noticed the huge metal bolts that kept the doors locked at night, and two hairy gorilla-like security guards, who seemed to look straight through her.

Inside the bank it was cool and quiet. Copper fans and green lamps hung down from the high ceiling, and the floor was polished black marble. Molly glanced up at the high, barred windows and saw cameras, like menacing black flies, crouched on the walls. Dotted about were smart-looking, leather-topped desks with weighing scales on them, where bank clerks sat. Here and there were tables where customers could lay out rubies and gems on white cloths for bankers to inspect through magnifying lenses. Along the back wall were glass-fronted booths shielding more bank workers from the public and strung out across the room were heavy, red ropes held up by brass posts. A few customers were already queuing up. Telephones were ringing and being answered. The place was buzzing with activity.

'Oh dear,' whispered Molly, losing her nerve. 'Look at the cameras. This is going to be tricky.'

'Not if you stick to our plan,' said Rocky encouragingly. 'You'll see, we'll be fine . . . and . . . and good luck, Molly.'

Molly swallowed hard and nodded. 'Likewise,'

she said. And Rocky went to sit on a chair by the wall.

Molly walked towards a desk in the corner of the hall. She sat down opposite a young, freckle-faced clerk. 'Good morning,' she said, 'I'd like to deposit some rubies.'

'Certainly, madam,' said the clerk, innocently looking up. The poor young man was an easy target. He fell into Molly's web like a blind caterpillar.

Soon Molly had nearly finished her instructions.

'From now on you will do exactly as I say, or as my friend says. Until *ten* o'clock you will behave normally to other customers. Then *at ten* you will come to the front of the bank and await instructions.'

The clerk nodded. 'And when would you like to bring these jewels in?' he asked, behaving normally.

'That's very good,' said Molly. 'Now, please take me to see the bank manager.'

The clerk led Molly through a security door. Acting as innocently as possible, she looked straight ahead, ignoring anyone who might be watching her and following the freckly man along a grand corridor until they came to a door with a golden plaque on it that read, *'Mrs V. Brisco. Manager.'*

The clerk knocked and they entered. This startled the manager's secretary, who stopped her typing and looked very irritated by her unannounced visitors, but after a few seconds of Molly's glare, she too was captive, and she spoke to Mrs Brisco through an intercom. 'Sorry to bother you, Mrs Brisco, there's someone here to see you called . . .'

'Miss . . . er . . .' Molly's eyes darted desperately about the room, for inspiration. 'Miss Yucca,' she said, seeing a spiky potted plant on the window-sill, and wincing inside as she heard the stupid name coming out of her mouth.

'Miss Yucca,' repeated the secretary. 'I think you ought to see her.'

'Send her in,' came the manager's sober reply.

The bank manager was a small, thin woman of fifty or so, with shaky hands and a weak face. She greeted Molly with an impatient frown, examining her through horn-rimmed spectacles, wondering what on earth a child could want with her.

'I'm afraid we don't give tours of Shorings to school-children. But you may pick up some Shorings bank literature from our inquiries desk for your school project. I'm sure that will be adequate for your needs. Goodbye.'

'No,' said Molly, 'I would like your *personal* assistance on my project please.'

As a bank manager, Mrs Brisco had learnt to be very untrusting of people. So she was tricky to hypnotize. Molly found her surprisingly resistant. She was like a dog, pulling on a lead, refusing to come, but Mrs Brisco's coming was inevitable, since she was on Molly's lead. She twitched and she twisted, and tried to defend herself, but she couldn't resist Molly's tugging eyes. In half a minute Molly had her well and truly disorientated.

Soon, Mrs Brisco had agreed to do everything Molly asked.

With no time to lose, she had all the bank workers brought one by one, into her office, where Molly worked her magic on them. She gave each one the same instructions; to keep working as normal until ten o'clock, then to assemble in the lobby of the bank and wait for more orders. Molly wanted to keep the bank working normally for as long as possible. It was already after nine-thirty.

Meanwhile, Rocky was at the front of the bank, keeping an eye on any new arrivals. He saw customers come and go, and he watched as the clerks behind the glass partition left their desks and came back again with a glazed look in their eyes.

From the office, once Molly had covered all the security guards, including the two gorillas from the main door, and all the other workers in the bank, she concentrated on the cameras, which were spying from every corner. Some, she found out, were secretly hidden on the sides of waste-paper bins. Already, Rocky and Molly would have been recorded by twenty or more. It was very important to wipe this evidence clean away, and then work could begin. Mrs Brisco took her to the video suite and every camera was switched off.

'Now,' said Molly, breathing a sigh of relief. 'I want you to rewind the tapes and rub off all this morning's film.'

'Im-possible,' said the manager. 'It goes – electronically – straight to our – records office.'

'What?!' exclaimed Molly, incredulously. She couldn't believe what she was hearing. Rocky and her on film, at the records office! This was terrible. Molly would be recognized! Even the thickest of detectives would be suspicious, seeing her walking around the back rooms of the bank. Nockman's notes hadn't said *anything* about a records office. Molly was filled with fury and thrown into panic at the same time. 'Wait here,' she commanded. With her stomach lurching from nerves, she hurried out to Rocky.

'Rocky,' she growled, 'we've got a problem. We're on film and it can't be rubbed off because the film is automatically transmitted to the records office . . . We can't go ahead, we'll be caught straight away, but, Rocky, if we don't, what will happen to Petula?'

Rocky looked worried. 'Take me to the video room,' he said. 'I'm not promising anything, but, I may just be able to sort this out.'

After extracting the telephone number of the records office manager from Mrs Brisco, Rocky settled down with a telephone and tried to focus. He'd only hypnotized over the phone a few times before, so he was extremely anxious about whether he would be able to do it now. It was very difficult to relax with Molly sighing and biting her lip beside him. Then he took a deep breath and went for it.

Concentrating as if his life depended on it, he dialled the number. A gormless-sounding operator answered the phone, and since the person was very unsuspecting, it was much easier than Rocky expected to hypnotize him long-distance. Soon the operator had rubbed off all that morning's film. Feeling much more confident, Rocky then telephoned the bank's security company and had the guard there switch off the Shorings Bank alarm.

'Phhheewww,' Molly murmured. 'That was brilliant, Rocky!'

'Lucky it worked,' said Rocky, breathing more easily. 'For a moment I thought it wouldn't. It just shows though,' he pointed out, 'that Nockman's plans are out of date. I hope there aren't any more nasty surprises waiting for us.'

Molly nodded, feeling sick. Then on they went.

Both the front-door security guards were summoned to Mrs Brisco's office. As they stood beside each other in their hypnotic states, with their tongues dangling from their mouths, Molly thought how like stone-age men they looked.

'Which one do we chose as our driver?' she asked Rocky. 'Which is the most intelligent-looking one?'

'I wouldn't say either has a brain bigger than a sugar lump,' said Rocky, 'but I think the one on the left looks the cleverest.'

'How can you tell?'

'Because he's not trying to eat his collar.'

The security guard they chose was the most muscly and also the hairiest. Rocky took the hungry one back to the lobby of the bank, and Molly was led by the other guard to the bank garage. This was at the back of the building, down a narrow passage, at the end of which was a black fire door with a metal handle. Behind this door was a steel balcony and a flight of steps that led down on to the concrete floor of a garage the size of a tennis court. There stood their truck. A grey truck, the size of a small elephant. Molly imagined that she would just be able to stand up in the back of it.

'Is that the only truck you have?' she asked, worrying that it would be too small to take Nockman's load.

'Urghyeah,' grunted the guard.

'Do you think it will carry the contents of the bank's strongrooms?'

'Urghyeah.'

'What makes you so sure?' asked Molly, hoping that the guard's sugar lump brain was functioning.

''Cos de stones ain't heavy, they're real expensive but they ain't that heavy.'

'OK,' said Molly looking at the truck's dark, slit, side windows and bullet-proof doors. She hoped the man was right.

Molly went back to the lobby and subtly hypnotized the thirteen customers who were there. Soon they stood in a line like toy soldiers, standing to attention. And as the clock struck ten, the doors of the bank were closed. A notice was put up outside.

*'Closed for four and a half hours, due to staff training. We apologize for any inconvenience.'*

Some very annoyed customers who wanted to come in were left on the steps, complaining. Then, hypnotized bank workers started to fill the lobby and soon, they too all stood in a line like dummies.

'This is like a dream,' Rocky whispered.

For a moment he and Molly stood still. It was eerie to be standing there, with the working day on hold.

In the background a ringing phone made Molly jump, but it was quickly answered by a receptionist, who, as instructed, said, 'I'm afraid he isn't available at the moment. He will call you back, goodbye.'

'OK,' said Rocky, 'let's hit the basement.'

Mrs Brisco led them down a grey passage to a lift. There, she tapped a ten-digit code number into a small silver box. The doors opened with a swish, and Molly and Rocky followed her into the elevator. As it moved down its shaft, Molly started to feel very claustrophobic. She and Rocky were well and truly stuck in now. They'd hypnotized roughly thirty-five people, who would all be straight on the phone to the police if they came out of their trances. And these people were all *upstairs* whilst Rocky and her were about to conduct their business *below*. If anyone were to wake up, she and Rocky would be trapped. Molly banned the thought from her mind, and tried to concentrate on the matter in hand. Her knees were feeling all prickly and she kept shivering from nerves, and on top of this, her fear kept making her want to go to the loo, even though she didn't *really* want to go at all. Rocky's brown face, she noticed, was looking distinctly pale. Molly was reminded of all the times he had helped her out of trouble at Hardwick House. She felt guilty now for getting him involved. 'I'm sorry about this,' she whispered, as the lift doors opened.

'Forget it,' he said with a nervous smile.

Now they were standing in the basement. Ahead of her Molly recognized the entrances to the private counting rooms, from Nockman's bank plans. As Mrs Brisco led them down the tight, low-ceilinged passage to the strong rooms where the jewel vaults were, Molly lagged behind. She'd wondered what one of these counting rooms would look like and she also wanted to check that no guards were inside them, unhypnotized. So, peeling away from Rocky and Mrs Brisco, she went inside one. It was extremely lucky that she did.

A stony-faced man wearing a heavy striped suit looked up. He had a safety deposit box tray on the table in front of him, and was pawing over a very large diamond. 'What da hell is a kid doin' down here?' he demanded, his eyes narrowing, and his nose runkling into an aggressive scowl. Quickly, Molly zapped him, and she removed the diamond from his grip. The diamond was heavy and hard and enormous. It caught Molly's reflection as she rolled it around in her hand.

'Jeepers, this must be worth a fortune,' she marvelled.

'You betcha,' the gangstery man growled. 'Stole it – today.'

'Where from?' Molly asked, shocked and fascinated by the underworld man.

'From – another – crook.'

Molly shuddered, put the diamond in her anorak pocket and caught up with Rocky, who was three doors away, with Mrs Brisco by the strong rooms.

Rocky looked as if he'd just been told that Petula had been made into mincemeat.

'What's the matter?'

'The locks,' whispered Rocky hoarsely. 'That *idiot* Nockman doesn't know a thing about this place. It's all been *updated* since he was here. There's absolutely no way we are ever going to get into these strongrooms and get these safety deposit boxes open.'

'Why not?'

'Because, Mrs Brisco here has told me that she can't open them on her own. Both she *and* the customers who rent them have to be present to open their boxes. There are five strongrooms each with eighty deposit boxes. That's *four hundred* boxes, and four hundred customers who need to be here.'

'But why?' asked Molly.

'Because,' explained Mrs Brisco, 'we have – a – new

device – which only – opens the – boxes once it has – information from me – and from an authorized customer.'

'What kind of information?'

'Iris-read information.'

Molly's legs felt all wobbly suddenly. What was Mrs Brisco on about?

'Show me the device,' she said.

Mrs Brisco led her to a black box on the wall. On it was a panel with buttons labelled from nought to nine, and an electronic display board where numbers came up in green. At the moment, this display read zero, zero, zero. To the right of the zeros was a yellow light, the size of a billiard ball.

'Explain how it works,' said Molly.

'Firstly – I punch – in the number – of the safety deposit box that needs – to be opened. Then – the device matches my iris – with my iris pattern – in its memory. Next, it reads the – customer's iris and matches that – with the one in its memory. If all the information on irises is – correct, the computer – in the machine – knows that I am present – and so – is the customer. The device can then authorize the deposit box – to open. It is so that – the safety boxes cannot be opened – by anyone who wished to steal – their – contents.'

Molly's lip curled. This was completely unforeseen. She looked at Rocky who was looking as if he might be sick.

'And what exactly is an iris? A fingerprint of some kind?'

'In – a – way it is – like a fingerprint – in that no two human irises – are the same. That is why – the device – works.'

229

'Yes, I know *why* it works,' said Molly, knowing that they were beaten, 'I just want to know *what* an iris *is*.'

Mrs Brisco's answer was flat as if she was reading from a boring text book. 'The iris – is the coloured part – of the eye. The part which gives a person – their eye colour. The iris has the muscles that – contract and dilate – the black pupil – in the centre of – the eye. Everyone has – a different-looking iris. Yours is lovely – it is a beautiful shade of green.'

A glimmer of hope shot through Molly. She nodded at Rocky. 'It's worth a go.'

A minute later, Rocky had punched the number one into the iris-reading device, to open safety deposit box number one, and Mrs Brisco was bending over, peering into the machine, having her iris read.

Then it was Molly's turn. She leaned forwards and glued her eye up to the yellow hole. She looked inside, into the iris reading equipment, and the machine, in turn, looked into Molly's eye.

There was Molly's eye, like a great, speckled, green tyre, flecked with emerald rays. The machine began to read the branches of tiny veins and muscles, making a pattern in its computer memory. It made pipping noises as it assimilated the information.

Then, all of a sudden, the eye in front of it changed. The machine began again. Pipping away as it read the iris. When the eye changed once more, quicker than before, the machine started yet again. The eye shifted, the machine shifted. Then the pupil in the eye grew larger, the machine adapted to the growth. The pupil shrunk, the machine shrunk its data. The tyre-like iris started to turn. The machine was confused. It hadn't

230

been programmed to read turning eyes. And now the green flecks in the eye were flickering. The machine's temperature went up as it searched its silicon memory to find instructions on what to do. The eye began to pulse, the computer pipped faster, the eye started to twist and pulse at the same time, the computer started to panic. Its temperature was soaring, its chip was bending, its reading device was . . . was . . . all of a sudden the computer couldn't remember what or where the reading device was. Suddenly all it could compute was how perfect the eye in front of it looked. Its silicon chip felt as warm and comfortable as the day it had been made. The computer liked this eye. Liked its iris. It was better than all the other irises it had *ever* read, put together. The computer relaxed and gave instructions to itself to open up completely.

PING CLUNCH, PING CLUNCH, PING CLUNCH, PING CLUNCH, PING CLUNCH, PULLYOONK, PULLYOONK, PULLYOONK, PULLYOONK.

Four hundred safety deposit box doors opened at once. And simultaneously, five steel-barred gates on the deposit rooms unlocked themselves.

Molly took her eye away from the machine. And admired her work.

'That's what I call style,' she said.

'That's what I call extremely lucky,' said Rocky.

He accompanied Mrs Brisco up the stairs – the alternative exit from the basement, and went back to the lobby of the bank. There, he ordered the thirty-five hypnotized people to make a human chain from the safety deposit boxes all the way to the bank truck in the garage. Mrs Brisco provided Molly and Rocky with football-sized jute sacks, and lots of big, brown envelopes. Immediately the two of them set to work.

The strongrooms were stuffed with a daunting amount of treasure. Each of the rooms had eight columns of ten boxes. So there were eighty boxes in every strongroom. Four hundred boxes in all.

Each box had a small metal tray in it, which could be pulled out, and every one of them, Molly and Rocky soon discovered, was different. There were trays with large single rubies carefully laid out on velvet. There were others with tiny fingernail-sized packets stuffed into them like sardines. There were trays full of pearl necklaces and others covered in diamond rings. Some held leather, silk or suede pouches. Each pouch was filled with gems. There were trays of expensive antique jewellery and specially cut jewels. Molly and Rocky emptied each tray, putting their contents into a separate brown envelope, doing one column of boxes at a time. Ten full, brown envelopes filled every football-sized sack.

Finally the last of the sacks was passed on to the human conveyor belt and transported to the garage. There they were loaded by the gorilla.

It was exhausting work. Millions and millions and millions of dollars worth of jewels left the vaults. But eventually every last crystal in the bank had been lifted and packed, and a pile of plump bags sat expectantly in the back of the truck.

Molly and Rocky assembled the sweaty hypnotized subjects and duly blanked all their minds.

'All of you will wake up when you hear the clock outside strike two-thirty,' Molly said. 'You will all tell the police that an armed gang of robbers with stockings on their heads robbed the bank and, well, each of you will have your own story to tell, like how frightened you were, and what they said to you, that sort of thing, um . . . and until two-thirty, you can all sit on the floor and er . . . sing songs. The last thing is this. You will have *no memories at all of my friend here and me.*'

The people in the lobby all obediently sat down and began to sing songs. Molly thought how sweet they looked, like kindergarten children sitting on the floor. Then she and Rocky jumped into the front of the security lorry with the hypnotized driver, the garage door opened, the lorry left, and the door shut behind it.

It was a nerve-racking drive, from Shorings Bank to West 52nd Street, because the gorilla was not in complete control of the lorry. But soon, near the docks, they had located the run-down building that was Nockman's warehouse. Molly tried to read its graffitied exterior whilst Rocky hopped out to open its shabby doors.

Then the transplanting began. The jute bags had to be repacked into Nockman's brown lorry. When the job was done, the hairy guard sat down, red in the face from all the effort, and Molly gave him a drink.

'Thank you very, very much,' said Rocky, feeling sorry for him. 'Now, you must drive the empty lorry back to the bank, but you won't wake up or get there until *three* o'clock. You won't remember this address. You will tell everyone who asks that you were made to unload the stolen stuff into all sorts of different cars, Mustangs, Cadillacs and station wagons. And you'll say that afterwards, you were tied up and blindfolded, that when you finally broke loose, you found yourself on . . . on . . . 99th Street, and you drove back to the bank from there.'

The gorilla grunted, and then slurped his water, spilling half of it down his chest as he drank. Soon, he was gone.

At twenty to two, Molly sat nervously on a chair, waiting for Nockman to arrive.

# Chapter Twenty-Eight

At quarter to two precisely, the door of the warehouse creaked open. Nockman, in his sheepskin coat, and wearing his anti-hypnotism device, entered. He shut the door behind him. His body shook slightly, made cold by the walk from the subway, and his hand trembled from nerves. He wasn't one hundred per cent sure of Molly. However, he had to make it look to *her* as if he was in complete control. He took a deep, raspy breath.

There she sat on a chair. He couldn't see her too well with his squirly spectacles on, but it was definitely her. His footsteps sounded squeaky with his earphone contraption on, and his own voice sounded like Micky Mouse as he spoke. 'So the vehicle's full, is it?'

'Yes. It's got everything from the vaults. Every last pearl.'

Nockman was amazed. This girl was better than he'd thought. But he didn't let his astonishment show. 'And the job went according to plan?'

'Completely. They all think they were robbed by a bunch of armed bandits. And your lorry has everything in it. You'll see.' Molly studied the fake professor as if he was an insect under a magnifying glass. He really was a low-down dirty louse, and he looked at Molly like a louse might look at a human it was about to suck blood from; without compassion.

'Good,' he was saying. 'You're learning. Next time you can rob a bank on your own without my help. Now, what about the book? That was part of the deal too.'

Molly reached behind her and picked up the silk-wrapped parcel, and offered it to Nockman. He grabbed it and roughly pulled the silk off it to check it was the real thing.

'Mine,' he said greedily, like a spoilt child. Now he was itching to get away.

He climbed hastily inside his lorry. The vehicle shook as the engine started up and exhaust spluttered into the warehouse.

'I'll call you when I've gone through my check-list,' he said hurriedly. 'Now, open the door.'

'How is Petula, is she all right?' Molly asked, standing on tiptoe and speaking to him through the front window.

'Fine, fine,' lied Nockman. 'She's been eating well, steaks and bacon and chocolate biscuits.'

'Chocolate biscuits?'

'Yeah, and the sooner you open this warehouse, the sooner I'll ring you, and the sooner you'll be seeing her.'

Molly saw Nockman out, and watched as he drove his brown lorry away along West 52nd Street.

*

As soon as Nockman got off the road by the docks, he tore off his squirly spectacles and the earphones from the voice-scrambling device. The lorry's gears ground noisily as he fumbled with the shift stick. Then, with his heart racing, he drove. Although he knew he would easily be off the island of Manhattan before the robbery was even reported, he felt dreadfully nervous. Beads of sweat were dripping from his forehead into his eyes, making his vision blurred. He cursed every traffic light and swore at anyone who wanted to cross the road. Soon though, he was driving into the tree-lined industrial estate in Brooklyn, to his gnome-filled warehouse, safe from prying eyes.

Here, Nockman looked forward to catching his breath, steadying his nerves and inspecting the precious loot that was in the back of his lorry.

Having driven safely inside the building and locking the doors behind him, he slumped against the concrete wall.

'Boy, oh boy, I need a big drink,' he said out loud.

He collected his bag with the hypnotism book, anti-hypnotism kit and his passport from the driving compartment, and unloaded it on a low table where a large bottle of whisky and a dirty glass stood. Sitting down in a plastic armchair, surrounded by garden gnomes, he poured himself a drink and took a slug. He drank the whole glassful and poured himself another. He lit a cigarello and, breathing out a cloud of smoke, sat back with his feet up on the table. Then he began to laugh.

Inside the lorry, hidden behind a stack of cartons, Rocky heard him laughing. He wondered whether Nockman was alone.

From inside her room, Petula could sense that Nockman's mood had changed. She barked.

'Awh, shut up, you stupid animal,' Nockman shouted. A loud shuttery noise resonated through the building as he opened the back of the lorry. Rocky shrank behind his boxes.

'Happy Chrismasbirthdayanniversary to me!' Nockman shouted, grabbing two sacks and hauling them out. He carried them over to his plastic armchair and carefully tipped one out on to the table. Ten heavy brown envelopes thudded on to the Formica top. Nockman smiled greedily, puffing at his cigarello. From under his chair, he pulled out a light blue file with several sheets of typed paper in it, and sitting down, he began to rip open an envelope. From inside the paper, a cluster of rubies, hard and blood-coloured, peeped up at him.

Rocky crept to the end of the lorry and peered around the edge. There sat the sluggy Nockman, drooling over a packet of gems and beside him on the table was *The Book of Hypnotism* and his anti-hypnotism kit. Nockman smiled as he poked at his treasures.

Rocky couldn't do the eye trick, like Molly. He could only hypnotize people by talking to them. All he had to do was wait and hypnotize Nockman when he finally fell asleep.

Nockman smiled again as he counted. He dropped his cigarello on the floor and stubbed it out with his foot. Then he put on his earphones and his squirly glasses, and laughed to himself.

He walked over to the lorry.

Rocky scuttled back to his hiding place.

238

Casually, Nockman pressed a button and elevated himself up on the lorry's electric lift. Rocky shivered from nerves. Nockman unhooked a rope from the inside wall of the lorry. He heaved the boxes from in front of Rocky and he seized him by the wrists. 'Nice try,' he said menacingly, pulling him roughly off the lorry. 'You stupid fool. I saw your reflection in the side of my whisky glass.'

Nockman was flabby, but still he was much stronger than Rocky. So, struggle as Rocky did, he was incapable of resisting as Nockman tied his wrists behind his back and gagged him. Nockman dragged him across the warehouse floor and roughly cast him into the back room with Petula. Rocky fell backwards on to the hard floor.

'Make yourself comfortable, titch,' Nockman spat, shutting the door and locking it. Petula jumped on to Rocky's lap and licked his face. Nockman approached the lorry suspiciously. If there were any more rats on board, he'd catch them.

And then he heard a faint noise above his head. Someone was climbing in through the roof.

# Chapter Twenty-Nine

Molly knew Petula hated chocolate biscuits. And from the way Nockman had boasted about how he'd been feeding Petula, Molly just knew he hadn't been. She trusted him about as far as an ant can jump. She knew she had to follow him.

So when Nockman had driven the brown lorry to the end of 52nd Street and was turning the corner, Molly stepped out of the warehouse door and ran as fast as she had ever run in her life on to the main street to hail a taxi.

Nockman's lorry was almost out of sight when she climbed into a yellow cab, but luckily the driver was nifty and soon they were tailing him.

Molly felt like a spy. If the situation had been less critical, she would have enjoyed this. Instead, her hands were so sweaty they were practically dripping, and by the time her cab arrived at the Brooklyn industrial estate her mood was very grave.

She watched carefully as, in the distance, Nockman

stopped by a warehouse. Once her cab had gone, Molly stepped behind a tree and spied on Nockman as he drove inside.

'Got you,' she said under her breath.

The muffled thud from upstairs had sent Nockman into a panic. He had a sudden vision of a squad of crime-busting police closing in for an ambush. He didn't know the intruder was only Molly, who had managed to scramble up a tree, clamber through a half-open skylight on the roof and drop quietly into an upper room. Frantically, he threw the bags of gems, his check-list file, the hypnotism book and the anti-hypnotism device into the back of the truck and slammed it shut. Shoving his passport into his pocket, he heaved himself into the cab and hit the ignition.

Molly heard an engine start and realized in a panic that Nockman was leaving. She rushed down the stairs, but already the vehicle was changing gear. Nockman put his foot on the accelerator. By the time Molly reached the pavement outside, it was too late. With a screech, and spewing exhaust, the truck sped away.

Molly dashed out on to the street and chased, but the diesel fumes made her cough and the lorry was too fast. She was left standing in the empty road surrounded by old, deserted warehouses and trees.

She'd really done it now. Rocky must still be in the truck, and Nockman would find him. And what about Petula? Nockman would *never* ring Molly now. Molly moaned. She felt sick to the core.

As she worried about Petula and Rocky, she realized that the only safe way out of this now was for her to tell the police everything. She'd have to, otherwise Rocky could be in real danger. As for Petula, there was still a faint hope that she was in this building. Molly sprinted back. Once inside, she found a door and heard scraping noises and muffled cries coming from behind it. Molly burst into Petula's – and Rocky's – prison.

Petula leaped at Molly and Molly hugged her as she pulled a gag off Rocky's mouth. Rocky started talking as soon as he could. 'Molly, I'm really sorry, but he saw me and he put all his gear on again and he grabbed me and . . .' Rocky was shaking and breathing asthmatically.

'Rock, I'm so sorry, this was all *my* fault,' said Molly, undoing the ropes around Rocky's wrists, and hugging Petula at the same time. 'I'm *so* glad you two are OK I thought I'd lost you both – I really did.' She reached in her pocket for a small tin of emergency dog food that she'd been carrying for a few days now and, peeling back its lid, tipped the chunks of meat out on the floor. Petula gobbled it up frantically. Then Molly poured some mineral water into her cupped hand. 'I can't believe it. I don't think he fed Petula or gave her a drink at *all*,' she said, disgustedly. 'Poor Petula!'

When Petula had finished drinking, Molly picked her up and held her very close. It was wonderful to feel her warm in her arms once more. 'I'm sorry, Petula,' she said. 'I won't ever let that happen again.' And Petula nuzzled into Molly's anorak to feel as safe as she possibly could.

Then both the children stroked her and thought about Nockman.

'So, he's driving as far away as he can now,' said Rocky.

'Yeah,' said Molly, 'and feeling nervous I bet . . .'

She and Rocky grew silent for a moment and looked out of the door, imagining Nockman on the highway. Then, curiously, they both began to smile.

'Mmmn,' said Rocky. 'No doubt, he'll have to stop at a petrol station, to fill up on fuel. He'll buy himself a Heaven bar.'

'And maybe a can of Qube,' suggested Molly.

'Then, he'll get back in the lorry and drive on.'

'And on and on and on,' echoed Molly.

'And then?' asked Rocky.

'Then he'll get tired.'

'And then?'

'Then he'll start to feel he's dropping off, and he won't like that.'

'No, because he won't want to stop driving, will he? Because he wants to get right out of New York State . . . So then?'

'So then, to keep himself awake, I suppose he'll turn on the radio,' imagined Molly.

'Let's hope he does.'

Nockman drove away from the gnome warehouse, fast. Adrenaline pumped through his veins as the lorry hurtled through the suburbs of Brooklyn. Every police car he saw made his rash itch, even though, he told himself, he knew that his lorry had no reason to look suspicious. The police would think that all the lorries *already off* the island of Manhattan were as good as gold, not full of gold. But still Nockman was a bundle of nerves. He drove as fast as he could away from New York, sticking to the smaller roads, looking in his rear-view mirror constantly, chain-smoking and sweating like a hot cheese. After two hours of torment, Nockman began to feel confident that he wasn't being tagged. He loosened his shirt and turned on to the interstate highway.

He drove on and on for hours, until he had driven so far that his fuel tank dial was pointing to empty. He pulled up at a gas station, filled up and bought himself three Heaven bars and four cans of Qube. Then he tramped back to his lorry and off he set again.

By nine o'clock Nockman was starting to feel tired. This worried him. He didn't want to fall asleep at the wheel and crash. He imagined the lorry cracked open on the highway like a very expensive Easter egg, all the gems and jewellery spewed over the road. But he didn't want to stop to rest. He must keep driving. He'd pull up somewhere soon and drink a pint of coffee, that would keep him awake. In the meantime, he decided to turn on the news.

'Drive time,' sang a jingle on the radio.

'Yeah,' said a chirpy presenter. 'We'll be keeping all you drivers across the east coast of America wide, wide awake, now you needn't worry about that, so relax while you drive . . . We're the station that gives you motion! And boy, oh boy, have we got entertainment for you. We've got hours and hours of grrrrrreat music. In a second we'll bring you the news but first a short break . . .'

Nockman felt a lot better. This was just the sort of station he needed, and he was very excited about hearing the news because his robbery would be reported. As the radio played adverts, he changed up a gear.

'I'm in Heaven,
Heaven's in me,
I knew I'd get to Heaven eventually.'

Then a voice sang out, 'Hey you, you want to have a taste of heaven? Pick up a Heaven bar!'

Nockman took another bite of his Heaven bar and felt very happy. He listened to a Qube advert.

'Qube if you're cute . . . Qube if you're rude . . . Everyone loves you 'cos you're so Qube.'

'I'm sooooo popular – I've been Qubed!'

'Oooh you're so cute, can I sip your Qube?'

'Hey, the world really looks better with a can of Qube in my hand.'

'Qube . . . It'll quench more than your thirst!'

Nockman opened his can of Qube, took a sip and smiled. He was going to be so, so popular now. He'd never been popular in his life and the idea of it made him tingle with pleasure.

The presenter came back. 'So, now, the *news*. The main story of the day is that Shorings Bank, in Manhattan, was robbed today . . .' Nockman turned the volume up. 'The operation was conducted earlier today by a gang of armed robbers. They made off with precious stones and jewellery to the value of over one hundred million dollars.'

Nockman guffawed. It was more than that!

'Experts are trying to ascertain how the robbers managed to secure the building and turn off all the alarms, since Shorings Bank has one of the world's finest and most sophisticated alarm systems. It is believed that the gang are still somewhere on the island of Manhattan. The robbery was reported immediately after the thieves left, and police were able to set up road blocks at all the bridges leaving Manhattan within five minutes. Police have also been checking boats docked around the island. All water traffic has been stopped. A bank worker who was forced to go with the gang has given accounts of how he was made to unload the stolen goods from a bank truck into different cars which were driven away. It is believed that the criminals have hidden the stolen property all over the city of Manhattan. The police have asked people to be on the lookout, and also to be careful, as the gang are likely to be dangerous. The police would be very interested in any information that might lead them to the thieves.'

This was the best news that Nockman had ever heard. He loved this news reader for bringing it to him.

'Thank you for listening,' said the news reader.

'Thank *you*,' said Nockman.

'Great news, isn't it?' said the news reader.

'Yeah,' said Nockman. He really liked this news reader, and especially his voice. It was perfectly pitched and very soothing.

'You must be feeling *fantastic*,' said the news reader.

'I am!' laughed Nockman.

'You're feeling fantastic, the best you've felt in years.'

'I am! I am!' agreed Nockman.

'All that effort was worth it. You deserve this, don't you!'

Nockman nodded. How right the voice was.

'And now you need your well-deserved rest. Take a nice deep breath and breathe out, slowly.'

Nockman breathed deeply in and out and felt much, much better.

'Breathe slowly in and out and, as I count down, you will feel more and more relaxed. Keep driving as I count ten – nine – eight – seven – six – five – four – three – two – one and now, Mr Nockman, you are complete – ly under my power. Understood?'

'Understood,' said Nockman stupidly. He felt wonderful. He'd fallen into Rocky and Molly's trap, and he felt fabulous.

'Now,' said Rocky. 'I want you to turn this lorry round and drive back to New York, back to the place you left this afternoon. OK?'

'Fine,' smirked Nockman. 'Fine, just fine.'

As Nockman drove, the tape in the radio/cassette player reeled to its end. The rest of it was blank. Molly and Rocky had only had time on the Sunday night before to record a short fake radio show. So Nockman drove grinning in silence.

Molly and Rocky had relied on two things to achieve their ends:

The first thing was a fact – that many adults underestimate the intelligence of children.

The second thing was a design point – if radio/cassette players have tapes in them, when the machine is turned on, the tape automatically plays first.

# Chapter Thirty

olly, Rocky and Petula sat patiently in the gnome warehouse. As the light outside faded, Molly went out to a phone box. From there, she rang Rixey Bloomy and told her that she was too upset about Petula being stolen to go through with that evening's performance of *Stars on Mars*.

'I'm sorry, Rixey, it's just I might collapse on the stage.'

'Oh, Molly, the public will understand,' sympathized Rixey. 'And don't you worry, your understudy, Laura, will play your part tonight.'

Molly felt a bit guilty since she knew that the people coming tonight would be bound to be disappointed. But then she thought of Laura the understudy, a girl who was longing to show everyone how she could dance and sing, and Molly felt better. Rocky didn't need to call anyone since he'd programmed the Alabasters into thinking that he'd gone on a boy scouts' trip to New York. So, instead, he ordered pizzas. Then, full of pizza and hope, they waited for Nockman.

Petula, meanwhile, was venting her anger on Nockman by attacking the coloured garden gnomes that stood like a small army in the shadows. They reminded Petula of the Martians in *Stars on Mars*, even though they were smaller. And one or two of the gnomes bore a nasty resemblance to Nockman himself.

Molly and Rocky ventured upstairs where there was a window looking out on to the dark street.

'Do you think he listened to the tape?' asked Rocky.

'If he didn't, I'm in big trouble. He'll definitely blow the whistle on me,' said Molly, wincing.

'If he did listen, I hope the tape worked,' said Rocky. 'I hope my voice was up to it.'

'We'll just have to wait and see.'

While they were waiting, Molly and Rocky had a snoop around Nockman's warehouse. They discovered two more rooms on the first floor; a tiny kitchen and a loo. The kitchen had a sink, with Bubblealot washing-up liquid and gloves on its draining board, a dirty cooker and a fridge that smelled of sour milk. And everywhere were boxes for Molly and Rocky to open. Boxes of perfume, jewellery, ornaments, antiques and expensive watches. 'Wow,' said Molly, 'these must be worth a fortune!'

'I don't think so,' said Rocky, pointing to a stamp on one of the boxes which read, 'Made in China'. 'These are fakes, but I expect Nockman sells them as if they're the real thing.'

In another room they found boxes full of leather handbags. 'Fakes too,' said Rocky. 'They're copies of posh designer handbags. If you look closely, you'll see they're glued not stitched . . . They'd fall apart in seconds. I've heard about crooks selling these.'

'Bet he sells them for a mint,' said Molly.

'Yeah, you bet he does.'

Downstairs were boxes of precious old porcelain, again, every piece a modern fake. Other boxes were full of anything Nockman could lay his hands on: hair-dryers, cat baskets, hammers, mops, TV sets and hi-fi equipment. There was even a box full of cuckoo clocks.

'I bet all of this is stolen,' said Rocky.

'"Fallen off the back of a lorry" as they say,' Molly agreed.

Shortly after midnight, headlights lit up the road by the warehouse.

'It's him,' Molly and Rocky said in unison. They bolted downstairs to open the huge metal door. Nockman drove in and parked, his lorry's tyres crushing a box of teapots. Molly and Rocky opened the driver's door and found him staring straight ahead with a idiotic expression on his face, clutching the wheel.

Driving in a semi-daze had been quite an experience for Nockman. At one point, he had driven off the highway and around a piece of spaghetti junction sixty-two times before hitting the main road again.

'You can get out now,' Rocky said. Obediently Nockman stepped down on to the warehouse floor. Petula growled at him and Nockman blew his cheeks out until they were full of air. When his eyes began rolling in their sockets, Petula backed off. This was not the tough man she had known. This one looked like he might suddenly explode. Petula decided to leave him and to attack a garden gnome instead.

Molly rescued the hypnotism book. 'Pheeew,' she whistled.

Then, she and Rocky walked around Nockman. 'With the right outfit,' Molly said, 'he'd be perfect by a pond.'

'Mmmmm,' said Rocky. 'You,' he ordered Nockman, 'will be under this person's power too. She is called . . .' Rocky looked about, 'hairdryer.'

'I've had worse nicknames,' Molly said.

'And I,' continued Rocky, 'am called Cat Basket.' Nockman nodded seriously and Molly and Rocky started to giggle.

'Who am I?' asked Rocky.

'Cat Basket,' said Nockman as if he was saying 'God'.

'And this person is?'

'Hairdryer. I will do – whatever Miss Hairdryer – and Mr Cat Basket – say.' Petula's barking disguised Rocky and Molly's stifled laughter.

'Sshh, Petula,' said Molly. Turning to Rocky she whispered, 'What next?'

Rocky pulled at the hairs in his eyebrow. They had talked about what they might do should Nockman return well and truly hypnotized, but they hadn't come to any decisions.

'Let's do what I said,' he suggested. 'Let's just leave the lorry here, dump Nockman in Manhattan with his mind blanked and call the police anonymously. Once they've got this address, they can sort everything out.'

'No way,' whispered Molly hoarsely. 'I told you . . .

251

when the police come here they'll probably trace the warehouse back to Nockman and then when they investigate him, maybe they'll find out he's been hypnotized and maybe they'll undo all the hypnosis we've done and they'll eventually track us down.'

'Couldn't we just park the lorry somewhere?' asked Rocky.

'No, because they'll probably trace the lorry back to Nockman too. It's too risky. No, what we should do, is put the jewels somewhere *else*, like in bin bags. We could put them in bin bags *outside the bank*.'

Rocky looked doubtful.

'Why not?' insisted Molly. 'The bank doesn't need security guards now there's nothing left to steal, so it would be safe. No one would expect the robbers to come back to the bank. We could ring the police and tell them where to come.'

'We can't put it in bin bags,' whispered Rocky. 'What if the rubbish collectors think its rubbish? And we can't dump it all at once, there's tons of it. It would take ages to get it all out of the lorry. Someone would see us.'

Petula, sensing the tension in the discussions, was barking ferociously at a pink-faced gnome as if it was all his fault.

'Yes, you're right, bin bags are bad. How about those handbags then, from upstairs?'

'They're too small,' whispered Rocky. 'And anyway, people would steal them. I mean, handbags almost always have money in them, don't they?'

'Hmm, we need big bags that won't be stolen *or* picked up.'

Petula was leaping at another red-hatted gnome,

trying to bite his nose. Finally, she knocked him over. The gnome cracked noisily as his hat hit a concrete step and his head smashed open. Petula looked up proudly as if she'd just killed a gorgon.

'The gnomes!' Molly gasped. 'I don't believe it, they're hollow! Look, they've got screw-on bases so that you can fill them with sand and they don't fall over.'

'Perfect,' said Rocky, picking up the gnome's pipe. 'Thanks, Petula.'

'Raoof raoof,' barked Petula, feeling pleased with herself.

Over the next two and a half hours, Molly, Rocky and Nockman, all with Bubblealot rubber gloves on to avoid leaving fingerprints, set to work transferring the envelopes of stolen stones and jewels into the gnomes. They gave each gnome a mixed stuffing. Delicate, lighter jewellery in the heads and upper parts of the gnomes so that they wouldn't be crushed and the heavier packets of jewels in their bottom parts to weigh them down. Most of the gnomes had enough space for a couple of the little football-size bags from the bank. Once their bases were screwed on, the garden statues looked as innocent as before.

Eventually, Nockman, sweaty and smelling like a dirty sock, pushed the last of them into place in the lorry.

Molly and Rocky, holding Petula, admired the line-up of smiling pixies, all ready for action, and watched as Nockman descended on the lorry's electric platform.

'Shall we leave him here?' asked Rocky.

253

'No, he's too dangerous,' whispered Molly. 'He knows too much. He might have a bank-robbing map or something that would jog his memory.'

'But, but that means he has to come with us,' moaned Rocky.

'Sorry,' said Molly, 'but he could be useful to us. Look how he helped us load up. Anyway, Rock, for starters, you or I can't drive.'

'I could if I had to,' said Rocky, smiling.

'No way, Rocky. You must be off your rocker. Come on, we've got to get going. It'll be dawn in a couple of hours.'

'I know,' said Rocky, yawning.

'We'd better deliver these things before everyone in Manhattan wakes up.'

Molly and Rocky checked the warehouse for any incriminating evidence. Then, with Rocky and Nockman in the cab of the lorry, and Molly and Petula in the back, they drove away from the warehouse, through Brooklyn, towards Manhattan.

Nockman's driving was very, very loose, a bit swervy, but just about all right. As they crossed the Manhattan Bridge, Rocky noticed that all the vehicles coming out of Manhattan were being stopped and checked by police. There was a long traffic jam. But the road into Manhattan was empty and so they headed straight over the bridge.

Once in Manhattan, 'Operation Plant a Gnome' began. They had decided to drop the gnomes in different places over the city. That way, they didn't have to stop the lorry for too long and so reduced the risk of being seen. Every time they came to a quiet grassy area, where there were no prying eyes, Rocky, sitting in the front, told Nockman where to stop and banged on the partition behind him, signalling to Molly to plant a gnome. Molly then opened the back of the lorry from the inside, rolled a gnome out on to the electric platform and lowered it down to ground level. Petula acted as watchdog as Molly rolled and heaved each gnome into position. Rocky noted exactly where each gnome was.

They left gnomes under trees, beside bushes and on tiny triangles of grass. They decorated playgrounds with gnomes, and put gnomes by fountains, by sidewalk benches, and beside city flower beds. One looked very brave laughing beneath a ferocious fake dinosaur on the grass outside the Museum of Natural History. Another looked pleased that his pond had frozen over, as he sat on a grassy ledge overlooking the Rockefeller skating rink. They put two gnomes by the gates of the Manhattan Zoo, and two at the Strawberry Fields entrance of Central Park.

Each gnome took five minutes to plant.

Each hair-raising five minutes was a window for them to be seen, and there were a few tense moments when Molly thought they might have been. By the park at Riverside Drive, Molly halted the electric door halfway open, since she saw a police car approaching. As it coasted by, like a hungry shark, she crossed her fingers that it wouldn't stop. At Gramercy Park, Petula ran off into the darkness to investigate a stray dog and Molly had to call quietly for her until she returned. By Union Square, two Japanese men came out of the shadows and tripped over a gnome. Molly worried that they'd seen her, but when she saw that they could hardly walk straight through being blind drunk, she knew they wouldn't be seeing straight either.

One by one, they got rid of the twenty-five brightly coloured gnomes. Manhattan was littered with them. The last two were placed teasingly outside Shorings Bank.

'They look great!' said Molly admiringly, climbing into the front of the lorry with Petula, Rocky and Nockman.

Then they drove back to the warehouse by the docks on West 52nd Street to ditch the lorry. Rocky took his tape out of the radio/cassette player.

They left the dockside and walked quickly back to the main streets. At a phone box, they telephoned the police and held the receiver to Nockman's mouth. 'The – Shorings – jewels – are – safe. Look – for – gnomes – on – the – streets – of – Manhattan,' he said. And then they hung up. They flagged an early morning cab and, by six o'clock, before the December sun came up, they were back at the Bellingham Hotel.

# Chapter Thirty-One

The hotel receptionist was tired from his night shift. Molly easily used her powers to persuade him to give Nockman a room, just for that day, and to bring him a clean outfit, whatever outfit the hotel had that would fit him, and a shaving kit. The receptionist nodded and led them to a room on the sixteenth floor.

'Lastly,' Molly instructed him, 'you won't remember seeing this man after you have delivered his outfit. Understood?'

'Un-der-stood – madam.'

'You may go.'

Then, to Nockman, Molly said, 'Sleep in here until two o'clock today, then have a bath, wash your hair, shave off your moustache and your goatee beard and make yourself smell nice. At two-thirty, when you are dressed in your new outfit, come to room 125.'

Molly and Rocky then went upstairs and, peeling off their top layers, flopped on to the bed fully clothed.

Petula made herself a bed on Molly's old anorak and fell asleep too.

Molly slept until her alarm went off. For a minute or two she lay on the bed looking at Rocky's doodle-covered hands and listening to him snoring and the rain, which was starting to pelt down outside. Their early-morning adventure already seemed like a dream. Molly smiled and rang room service to order some food.

Rocky woke to the smell of eggs and toast, and then he and Molly sat down for a TV brunch.

The news channels were full of reports about the gnomes. The TV reporters were going bananas. This was a fabulous news story. On Channel Thirty-eight, a reporter, under an umbrella, was talking excitedly into a furry microphone outside Shorings Bank.

'Amazingly, the Shorings' jewels have *all* been returned. The bank has verified that every last pearl has been accounted for. *Every* diamond, ruby and gem! In fact, goods to the value of a hundred *million* dollars! And the method of delivery adds a bizarre twist to what was already a teasing story. Twenty-five garden gnomes stuffed full of the stolen property were discovered dotted about Manhattan in the early hours of this morning, after an anonymous phone call. The male caller had a Chicago accent but, apart from that, nothing else is known about him. Police have released these pictures of the gnomes as they found them.'

The screen filled with photographs of the gnomes, looking startled in the darkness, lit with police torches like criminals caught in the act. They looked very funny.

The reporter continued. 'The reason for the return of the jewels is baffling detectives. Some think that the robbery was some sort of dare, others believe the robbers themselves were robbed. The police are asking the public for any information that could help them solve the mystery. Now, back to the studio.'

'More! More!' Rocky shouted at the TV. 'We want more pictures of the gnomes, and more of the police looking baffled.' He fired the remote control at the TV, skimming through the channels, trying to find more news. 'Owh,' he complained, 'lunchtime news is over. I've never been on the news before. That was brilliant!'

'We were brilliant,' agreed Molly. 'We robbed that bank like professionals and returned the loot like undercover agents.'

'Except, though, we did have a few hiccups doing it . . .' chuckled Rocky. 'Molly, you didn't look quite so pleased with yourself in the bank when you thought you'd been caught on film. Your face was *so* worried.'

Molly remembered and grinned. 'OK, but not half as freaked out as you looked when you thought we wouldn't get past those eye scanners . . .'

'Yeah, yeah, yeah, but what about you, Molly, in Gramercy Park this morning when Petula went running off. I thought your bottom lip was going to fall off . . .'

Molly and Rocky laughed as they relived the scariest moments, scene by scene.

'And the crazy thing is, no one will ever know who did it or how it was done. In fact, you know what?'

Rocky pointed out proudly. 'This crime will go down in history.'

It would go down in history. Molly remembered how Nockman had hoped for that himself. Then, other things he'd said ruffled her. Molly switched the TV off and started twiddling her napkin with her fingers.

'You know, Rocky, I'm no better than Nockman really. I'm a criminal too.'

Rocky looked surprised.

'Yes I am, Rocky. If you think about it. I mean, look at this place. I conned my way here, I conned people to pay for it, I conned Davina Nuttel out of her part. I conned the audience at Briersville, so I *stole* the prize money really, and I cheated all those other kids out of a chance to win the talent show.'

'Oh, shut up,' said Rocky light-heartedly. 'You are a genius hypnotist. That's what you're good at. That's what your talent is. I mean none of those other people in Briersville could have got to New York with their talent. You're brilliant. Everyone's happy. New Yorkers loved your show, they had the best night of their lives. And Rixey and Barry love you. Just look at all the publicity you've got them for *Stars on Mars*. Now everyone in New York knows about it and loads of them will buy tickets. You're not a *real* thief, you just get what you want using a different method to everyone else. The only thing you ever actually really stole was Davina's part, and she wasn't an angel herself, was she? You and me are the only ones who know the truth, so really, Molly, what does it matter?'

'Yeah, I know, but being truthful is better, isn't it, Rocky?'

'OK, it is but, Molly, I'm not having you going on some kind of guilt-trip now. Loosen up.'

Molly did feel guilty, but more than that. Like a runaway horse that had galloped and galloped, she'd found herself in a place where she didn't really want to be. Being with Rocky had made her slow down and look about.

'Rocky, it's not just that. There's something else that is making me feel . . . well, bad, really. I know this hotel room is amazing and everything, but the thing is, Rock, I'm starting to not like being Molly Moon the Star. Maybe I would do if I really *was* the person who everyone thinks I am, but the thing is, I'm not. And it may seem funny to you but I'm getting tired of this thing where people like me just because they've been hypnotized to like me. People aren't liking the *real* me. They're liking something unreal. They're liking a sort of adverty, fake Molly Moon. So it makes the *real* me feel like rubbish, and my life here is just a waste of time, because it's not the *real* Molly Moon's life, nobody is getting to know the *real*-life Molly Moon.' She looked at Petula, sound asleep. 'I mean, even *Petula* doesn't properly like me. I hypnotized her to like me.'

'Molly! But that was ages ago. Your hypnosis on Petula must have worn off by now.'

'Worn off? What are you talking about?'

'Molly, it doesn't last for ever, you know. Didn't you realize? The *lessons* that animals or people learn from hypnosis *can* last for ever, like Petula not eating chocolate biscuits, and liking you. She got into new habits that made her feel good so she carried on being like that. But the hypnotism doesn't last for ever. Petula's not hypnotized any more. Now she likes you because she does.'

'What, so you mean that the hypnotism I did on Barry Bragg and Rixey Bloomy will wear off?' Molly's mouth fell open.

'Sure. Eventually. They won't ever know that they were actually hypnotized and they'll always remember you as brilliant. But, if you didn't see them for six months, they wouldn't think you were as brilliant as they thought you were before. You'd have to hypnotize them all over again.'

'And the audience I hypnotized?'

'The same. They'll remember you being good, but if they saw you on stage again, you'd have to hypnotize them afresh, otherwise they'd see your little singing and dancing routine for what it was.'

'But how do you know all of this?' asked Molly.

'From the book of course,' said Rocky. Molly looked perplexed. 'Oh, whoops,' he said, covering his mouth with his hand, 'it was written at the end of chapter eight.'

'So that piece of *vital* information was in your pocket. Jeepers!'

'Sorry.'

'Don't worry,' said Molly thoughtfully. 'So, hypnotism wears off. Well, you know what? The sparkle of my life here has worn off too. I wanted to leave New York with you and Petula anyway. Now you've told me all this, I *really* want to go. Having to charm and hypnotize everyone all the time, forever . . . uuurgh! The idea is like a nightmare!'

'Where do you want to go?' asked Rocky.

Molly looked up at the ceiling. 'I've been worrying,'

she admitted, 'about everyone at Hardwick House. Not Hazel or Gordon or Roger, but about Gemma and Gerry, and Ruby and Jinx.'

'Mmmnn, so have I,' agreed Rocky. 'Imagine what it must be like there with Hazel in charge. It's probably worse than when Miss Adderstone was there, even with Mrs Trinklebury coming in.'

'And it's all my fault,' said Molly. 'I bet Hazel has them doing all the work. I want to go back. But you, Rocky . . . You won't want to come back, not now you've got your new parents.'

'Ah. Well, Molly, I've got something to tell you about the Alabasters. They weren't very nice.'

'Not very nice?'

'No. In fact they were horrible.'

Rocky proceeded to tell Molly about the dreadful Alabasters who had seemed wonderful the day they visited Hardwick House, but who had soon shown their true colours once back in the States. They'd been very, very strict and Rocky found their house like a jail.

'They wanted to dress me in stiff, old-fashioned suits and make me sit inside doing puzzles or making origami.'

'What's origami?'

'You know, that Japanese art of folding paper. I wouldn't have minded doing it a bit, it was just that they gave me a book to learn it from, and the instructions were impossible to follow, and they wanted me to do it all day long.'

'All day?'

'Well, a lot. They said it would discipline my mind. I hypnotized them, of course, to drop the origami.'

'What else?'

'Well, they didn't like me going out in case I muddied my clothes. Or in case I caught a bug from another kid. Not that I saw any other kids. Their neighbourhood was full of old people. Once, when I went on a wander they called the police! I tried to hypnotize them to loosen up but it didn't always work. I wasn't as good at it as you, Molly. If they'd had their way, I wouldn't have been allowed to sing or whistle or go for a walk or watch telly. They liked me reading but the only books were ancient annuals that Mrs Alabaster had when she was a girl. Oh, and the food they ate was gross – they were both on special diets and so I had to eat their rabbit food with them.'

'Rabbit food?'

'Well, it looked like rabbit food. Sometimes, it looked like cat food with goldfish food sprinkled on top. Everything they did was weird. It was hard work living with them. I got what I wanted in the end, but they were not the people I'd hoped they might be and I hated my life there. Worst of all, I missed you. I mean, you're my family, Molly. I've known you for ever.'

Molly felt all warm inside. 'Thanks, Rocky.' There were a few moments' silence as the two smiled at each other, appreciating what they had. Then Molly asked, 'But how will you get away?'

'I'll call them and put some ideas into their heads. I'll hypnotize them that it never worked out because they didn't like me. I'll make them think that they sent me back and that it was all for the best, you know, that sort of thing.'

'It's going to be difficult disentangling myself from New York,' said Molly, with dread in her voice.

'You can fix everything,' said Rocky, thoughtfully. 'I know what you should do. And I think I may know how you can make up for all your guilt about the conning you've been doing. You just need to make a few phone calls.'

Ten minutes later, Molly was on the phone. 'Yes, Barry, so Petula got returned in the night.'

'Just like the Shorings Bank gnomes!' said Barry.

'Yes, like the gnomes. But you see, Barry, the whole kidnap thing has freaked me out. And I've decided I want Davina to have the part back. I want to take a *long* break.'

'But . . .'

'I have to go,' said Molly firmly.

'I see,' said Barry. 'Well, Rixey and I and the cast will – miss you.'

'Thank you. I'll miss you too. Now, Barry, listen carefully. You must organize the hotel bill to be paid and I want some wages. Er, how much do you think is really fair?'

'Well – con-sidering the – amount you've cost – to keep – and the cost – of that massive – magnifying glass – balanced against the – great publicity – you got the show – well – I think – thirty thousand dollars,' calculated Barry, thinking about his ten per cent cut.

'OK,' said Molly, very pleased by his sums, 'great. Please will you get that delivered to the Bellingham, by four o'clock today. Oh, and I'll have it in cash.'

'A-greed.'

'And, Barry, tell Rixey that I can't do the show again tonight. Let Laura, the understudy do it . . . oh, and talking of Laura, will you look after her, Barry? Make sure she gets a really good lead part in something . . . take her under your wing sort of thing . . .'

'A-greed.'

'Then, with me, no one is to know I'm actually leaving until tomorrow.'

'A-greed.'

'Tell Rixey you had a long, long, conversation with me and that I said goodbye. Say, I'll call her.'

'A-greed.'

'So, goodbye, and, well, thank you for everything.'

'A-greed,' said Barry and he put the phone down.

'See, that wasn't so bad, was it?' said Rocky.

'No,' said Molly, although inside she was feeling slightly sad. She'd grown fond of barmy old Barry Bragg, and she would miss him.

# Chapter Thirty-Two

Soon after they'd had their brunch, Nockman knocked at Molly's door. He looked smart in the green doorman's outfit with its matching green felt cap that that the receptionist had given him. He shuffled obediently into the room and Molly and Rocky studied him. His hair was still a straggly black mane and his face, although clean and shaven now, was bloated and unhealthy looking and he had a scabby red rash under his chin.

'A haircut, I think,' said Rocky. And soon he and Molly had put a towel round Nockman's shoulders.

Without his tail of hair, Nockman looked much better. Still bald as an egg at the front with a fringe of hair around the back, like a monk.

Rocky gave him a banana. 'For a few days you will eat nothing but fruit. It will do you good. And you will give up smoking.' Nockman tore open the banana and greedily stuffed it into his mouth. Bits of banana fell out all over the floor.

'What about his manners. They're *revolting*,' Molly pointed out.

'OK,' agreed Rocky. 'From now on, Nockman, you will eat like . . .'

'Like a queen,' suggested Molly.

'Er, could I have a napkin and a finger bowl please?' Nockman asked.

'And his accent must change,' said Molly. 'A Chicago accent might get us caught. From now on, you will talk in a . . . a German accent.'

'OK, I vill do zat,' Nockman agreed.

After Nockman had finished his banana Rocky asked him to stand up. Rocky and Molly walked around him again and observed his slouched back, his squashed neck and his double chin.

'Couldn't we make him look a bit friendlier?' asked Rocky. Experimenting, he demanded, 'Look like a puppy.'

Nockman immediately stuck out his purple tongue and raised his hands like paws. His eyes were wide and keen.

'That's nearly it, just put your tongue back in.' Rocky whispered to Molly, 'He's so weird. I feel sorry for him.'

'*Sorry* for him? He's a *rat*,' Molly replied.

Nockman began to do a rat impersonation, crouching on the floor, sniffing. 'I didn't say *be* a rat,' said Molly.

'Sorry, Miss Hairdryer,' Nockman apologized.

'But he's got no friends,' whispered Rocky.

'Bet he has. Lots of other rats. Let's ask him. Let's find out about him. Do you have any friends?' asked Molly.

'No, no. No friends ever,' stated Nockman robotically in his adopted German accent. 'Except, I did have a fluffy pet budgie – once. Eeet used to sing so – beautiful, and fly – around ze garden.' Real tears welled up in Nockman's eyes. Molly was taken aback. The last thing she wanted was to feel was pity for Nockman.

But Rocky was intrigued and sympathetic. 'What happened to it?' he asked.

'It – vas – killed in – Mr Snuff's – rat trap. I found it – dead.'

'How horrible, and sad,' said Rocky. 'Molly, you have to agree, that is sad . . . Poor budgie, poor you. But who was Mr Snuff?'

'He vas our landlord. Vee shared a garden vith him.'

'And why, why didn't you have any other friends?' asked Rocky.

'Because – I – vas veird.'

'Weird? How?'

'Just veird. Unpopular.'

'I didn't realize. This is awful,' said Rocky. 'I do feel sorry for him.'

'I don't,' declared Molly. 'He was really nasty to Petula and very mean to me. Just stop it, Rocky. What's come over you? The guy's a jerk.'

'I don't think he's mean right at the bottom,' said Rocky.

'You don't? Let's ask him. Right, Mister. Please will you list all the nasty things that you've done since, since your budgie died.'

Nockman nodded his head and began to talk in a childish voice. ' I set a rat – trap and put it under ze table where – Mr Snuff sat – and it snapped shut – on his foot – just like it had – on – my b-b-budgie.'

Rocky looked at Molly with a well-that-was-fair-enough look.

Nockman continued, 'I tipped ze budgie food into Mr Snuff's cereal box and he ate it.' This too sounded fair.

'OK, OK,' said Molly. 'Don't tell any more nasty things you did to Mr Snuff, because he obviously deserved it. Tell us *other* nasty things.'

A flood of confessions now tumbled out of Nockman's mouth. 'I stole Stuart Blithe's watch – and blamed it on another boy – and he got a beating from ze headmaster. I scribbled all over – ze homework of Shirley Denning – and I drew all over her best pictures. I made Robin Fletcher eat fifteen – dead flies, and zen when he was sick – I made him eat ze sick. I pushed Debra Cronly's head through ze banister in the stairs – and ze fire brigade had to come and cut her free. I stole – children's sweets – and said if zay told, I'd flush zair 'eads down ze toilets . . .'

Molly interrupted. 'That's deep-down mean, isn't it, Rocky?'

Rocky shrugged. 'I suppose so.'

'What else?' asked Molly. 'And skip a few years.'

Nockman's voice now sounded older. 'I burned Danny Tike's model aeroplane zat he'd spent three weeks making. I stretched string – in between two posts near – ze nursing home and tripped up – old Mrs Stokes so zat she – broke her nose. Eeet vas very funny. Zen I tripped up – ze blind man. Zat vas easy – and I stole 'is vallet.'

'Stole his wallet?!' Molly was really shocked. 'And later?'

'Later.' Nockman's memory fast forwarded, past numerous foul deeds. 'Later, I learned – to steal elsevare. Zis vas very – useful. Kids' toys, anything I could steal. And I learned how – to sell zem – to a second-hand store. Zis vas – ze start – of my career.'

'And how old were you then?'

'Eleven.'

'What else?'

'I stole a girl's bicycle and locked – her in a storeroom. No one knew she was zare for – a day and a – night. I got small kids to steal from zare parents. If zay told – I beat zem up. I forced one kid to rob – an old man's house – for me. He fit frew ze – small vindow. Zat vas good – verk.'

'Zat, I mean *that*, was not good work,' Molly corrected him.

'No, no, not good,' said Nockman, his mind suddenly changing.

'What about the recent years?'

'Vell,' explained Nockman, in a flat voice, 'I did very vell vunce, – ven I managed – to per-suade – an old lady – to give me her life-savings for a stray-dog home. She gave me – a hundred and fifty – thousand bucks. I bought my varehouses – and set my business up.'

Rocky made a face as if he'd just swallowed a pickled egg.

'Your business?'

'Yes. I deal in – stolen goods.'

'Not any more you don't,' said Molly.

'No,' agreed Nockman. 'No.'

'So,' continued Molly, 'what do you consider was the highlight of your career?'

'Ah . . .' said Nockman, his hypnotized eyes going all dreamy suddenly. 'Ah – vell ze best – sing I ever deescovered – vas a hypnoteesum book. Ze old lady – she told me all about eet. Wis ze book – I master-minded ze greatest – bank robbery – of ze world. I robbed – Shorings Bank eetself – een New York.'

'Crumbs,' said Molly, under her breath to Rocky, 'he isn't half deluded.' Then to Nockman she said, 'I've just got to stop you a moment there. Let's get things straight. *You* didn't rob the bank. Some extremely talented chil . . . I mean, *accomplices* did. Anyway, that's beside the point, as from now on you will completely forget the hypnotism book and the trips you made searching for it. You will forget any ideas you had about robbing Shorings Bank. You will forget that it was robbed. OK?'

'OK. I forget – now.'

'Right. Any other big bad things you've done?'

'Yes,' admitted Nockman. 'I sold a car with a broken – chassis – to a man. He crashed.'

'Was he killed?' Rocky asked, his mouth agape.

'No, but ze lady he hit vas.'

'Uuurgh, stop,' said Rocky angrily. 'This is horrible. I can't believe you. Why do you do all these things if you know they're nasty?'

'I like being nasty,' came Nockman's simple reply.

'But, why? Why?' asked Rocky, completely per-plexed. 'Why did you *like* being nasty? Why couldn't you have liked being *nice*?

'Never – knew vat – nice was.'

'But weren't people nice to you?' asked Rocky.

'No – ov course not. Eferybody hated me. My father – he heet me eef he saw me – een ze house. Even my muzzer laughed when my budgie – died. She vished I – vas dead too. She vas nasty. I learned ze nasties – vrom her – not ze nices. I don't know nice.'

Rocky looked horror-struck. Then his appalled expression turned to one of realization. 'Molly, it's like Mrs Trinklebury's lullaby . . . It's what mamma cuckoo *taught* it to do. She taught it that pushing is best.'

Molly slowly nodded, as she too saw both Mrs Trinklebury's rhyme and Nockman in a new light. How could she blame Nockman for being unkind, if he'd never been treated kindly himself? If his cuckoo childhood had only taught him spite? 'You're right, Rock. I almost hate to feel sorry for him, but you're right. I suppose it's not surprising that he's mean, if no one taught him otherwise . . . I suppose being kind is a bit like . . . like reading . . . if no one had ever taught me to read, I'd find it very difficult to know how . . . I mean the pages of letters would just look like a jumble. Being kind must look like a jumble to him.' Then she added, 'And you and me thought our lives had been bad.'

'Yeah,' sighed Rocky. 'At least we had Mrs Trinklebury, and each other. Perhaps we can teach Mr Nockman to be a better person.'

'Mmmmnn,' hummed Molly. 'I wonder . . .' Then she asked Nockman, 'Do you feel bad about the things that you've done?'

'No, vhy should I?' answered Nockman.

'There's a problem here,' said Molly to Rocky. 'It will be difficult to teach him to be better, if he doesn't see why he should change. He won't want to be taught. And I'm not sure that just hypnotizing him to be good will fix him. He won't *really* change until he feels sorry for what he's done before. He might *want* to change if he realized how much he'd hurt people.'

'But how do we do that?' asked Rocky. 'We'd have to make him feel what those people felt.'

'Well, I reckon,' said Molly, feeling like a surgeon about to conduct an operation, 'I reckon we tap into the one thing that upset him, the only thing that we know he was upset about.

'His budgie?'

'Yup, his budgie.' Molly turned to Nockman.

'I tell you what, um, what's your first name?'

'Simon. I'm Simon,' said Nockman, reaching inside his green jacket for his passport and offering it to Molly. She took it and studied his photograph, in which he looked more like a goldfish than a person. Or maybe a piranha.

'Well, Mr Simon Nockman,' she said, 'first I want you to do a dead-dog impersonation, on your back with your arms and legs in the air, yes that's right, and now bark.'

'Voof, vooof, voooof,' barked Nockman from the floor, his legs and arms waving.

'Good,' continued Molly. 'Now, while you're like that, I want you to imagine what it was like for Petula, that pug dog that you stole, to be treated badly by you.'

'Voof, arf, voooof.'

Molly could see he wasn't feeling much, so she added, 'And if you can't feel anything just think about your poor dead budgie.'

'Aaaaaooouuuuoooo,' howled Nockman pitifully.

'There. You see,' said Molly, 'he's thinking about poor Petula and mixing it up with his sad feelings about his budgie. He's learning.'

Nockman howled again. 'Aiaaaouuuuuouoooo.'

'Now,' shouted Molly over his wailing, 'whenever any one says "hello" to you, you will get on your back and bark like this and feel like this and imagine how Petula must have felt kidnapped by you.' And turning to Rocky, she said, 'Every time someone says hello should be often enough to really make the lesson sink in, don't you think? And doing it this way will mean we don't have to keep prompting him.'

Then to stop the noise, Molly told Nockman to get up and hop about like an excited orangutan.

'Oooogh, oooogh uuuugh,' he grunted.

'Now,' said Rocky, getting the idea, 'for all your other bad behaviour, whenever anyone says "good evening" to you, you will remember the nasty thing you've done, that *that* person reminds you of, and you will tell them what you did, remembering your budgie again. OK?'

'Oooooh, ooogh, uurgh, aah, OK,' nodded Nockman, absorbing Rocky's complicated instructions.

'That should get him thinking, shouldn't it?' said Rocky.

'Most definitely,' agreed Molly. 'And,' she ordered, 'you can stop being an orangutan. Good. Right, you work for us, Mr Nockman. You will do everything we ask. We will treat you well and you will be very happy working for us. Now, you may wake up.' Molly clapped her hands.

Then Rocky went to the fridge and poured everyone a glass of Qube.

Preparations to leave began.

Molly had some extra suitcases sent up from the lobby showcase, since she had so many new things, and Nockman began to pack her clothes. Rocky went to the second suite room to make a series of important telephone calls. And Molly saw to the hypnotism book.

She took it from the safe, carefully stowing it away in her rucksack. Then she picked her way through the hotel room debris, through fan mail and New York souvenirs, through toys and gadgets, accessories and clothes, and she thought about what to take with her. When she saw Petula lying on her old anorak, she decided to leave it behind. She unhooked her new denim jacket from the wardrobe door and, with an umbrella, went out on to the balcony, to take a last high-up look at glistening Manhattan.

Rain poured down outside, but the afternoon sunlight was also hitting the buildings, so that everywhere, brick and steel and glass were shining. Molly still felt small there, because the city was so tall and dense and full of people who she'd never meet. But now, instead of finding the city scary, as she had done the first morning she'd looked out at it, she now loved the place. She loved the skyscrapers, the noisy streets, the crazy drivers, the shops, the galleries, the theatres, the movie houses, the slick people, the city's parks and all its dirt. And she knew that, one day, she'd be back.

Petula, after a restful sleep on the anorak, was woken by the sound of Nockman emptying Molly's wardrobe. For some reason the man in the room wasn't as frightening as the one who'd kidnapped her, so she ignored him. She picked up a nice stone from the floor and began to suck it. And sleepily watching Molly on the balcony, Petula felt relieved to be back.

Finally, the hotel receptionist brought up a fat envelope that had been delivered for Molly and it was time to go.

Molly's Rolls-Royce was driven to the tradesman's entrance. With some help from a hotel porter, Nockman loaded it up with luggage. Soon Molly, Rocky and Petula were sitting comfortably in the car's leather seats, behind its tinted-glass windows. Nockman was in the driving seat as chauffeur, butler, porter, general servant.

The Rolls-Royce engine revved and with a stately lurch they left the Bellingham Hotel.

# Chapter Thirty-Three

Before they left New York, Molly and Rocky wanted to make one last stop. The Rolls-Royce wove its way down busy avenues until Nockman parked it outside a tall building with a triangular-shaped entrance and the name Sunshine Studios above the doors.

A scruffy man in a dark blue suit hurried down the white marble steps to meet them. He took off his dark glasses and smiled, revealing a golden incisor in his top deck of teeth. 'Welcome, welcome,' he said excitedly, 'and thank you for your phone call. We are so pleased to have you. I'm the director you spoke to, Alan Beaker.' He thrust his hand out for Molly and Rocky to shake. 'Please, follow me.'

Molly, Rocky and Petula followed the director inside, along white passages and then into an enormous studio, full of booms and cranes and cameras and people standing about staring at Molly. The new starlet, Molly Moon.

A grey-haired woman, dressed in a very smart suit, stepped out of the throng. 'This,' said Alan Beaker, introducing her, 'is the chairwoman of Qube Incorporated, Dorothy Goldsmidt.'

Dorothy Goldsmidt raised her hand to shake Molly's. A huge emerald ring flashed on her finger. 'How do you do,' she said smoothly and grandly. 'It's *such* a pleasure.'

'Nice to meet you too,' said Molly. 'I think you spoke to my friend Rocky on the phone.' Rocky stepped forwards.

'How do you do,' he said.

'It's a huge pleasure – to meet you, too,' said Dorothy Goldsmidt, only slightly haltingly, 'and we are ready – ready for everything.'

Twenty minutes later, Rocky, Molly and Petula had been brushed up and were all on the studio stage.'

'Lights,' shouted Alan Beaker. 'Camera roll, and . . . *action.*'

And Molly and Rocky began. It was a simple rap jingle Rocky had made up, but with Molly's eyes on full glare, and Rocky's voice at its most hypnotic, and Petula looking as sweet as possible, the advert they performed was very, very powerful. It went like this:

*'If you want to be cool and feel good,*
*Do something that we think you should,*
*Do a check up, a check up, a check up,*
*On the kids in your neighbourhood.*
*Some kids may be having a bad time,*
*So check out those kids, make 'em feel fine,*
*Do a check up, a check up, a check up,*
*On the kids in your neighbourhood.*

Yo, listen up . . .
*For some kids this life isn't one ounce of fun,*
*This world should be good for everyone.*
*Happy childhood . . . Understood?*
*Check out the kids in your neighbourhood.'*

The advert finished with Molly and Rocky pointing straight at the cameras. 'Cut!' shouted Alan Beaker. 'That was fabulous! You two are professionals all the way.'

'Well,' said Molly, smiling at Rocky, 'we have been doing ads for years.'

'Yes,' said Dorothy Goldsmidt, 'that was wonderful, and we will air it, like you said, every hour, every day. It will be Qube Incorporated's pleasure to pay for the TV time. Thank you *so* much.'

'Oh, no,' said Molly, 'thank *you*. And so goodbye now. We have to go.'

'Goodbye,' called everyone in the studios, starstuck.

Back in the Rolls-Royce, Rocky said to Molly, 'See, brainwashing *can* be used for good. Feel less guilty now?'

Molly nodded. 'I know that advert won't change the world, but it will do something good, won't it?'

'Definitely,' agreed Rocky. 'Even if only one person is kinder because of it, it was worth it. But you know what? I think thousands of people will see it. You never know how many kind things will be done because of it. Plant a seed and hope it grows.'

# Chapter Thirty-Four

The Rolls-Royce left the island of Manhattan through the Queens Mid-town Tunnel, and rolled on down the highway to the John F. Kennedy airport.

Once there, Nockman parked alongside the International Departures Entrance, and a porter came to help. He and Nockman loaded Molly's twelve suit-cases on to an airport cart, whilst Petula hopped into her travelling basket and Rocky went inside to pick up their tickets. The porter drove the cart inside and everyone followed him to the check-in desk.

'Thank you,' Molly said to him as he heaved the last case on to a conveyor belt. 'And if it's not too much bother, could you keep the car?' She put the Rolls-Royce keys in the tired man's hand.

'Keep? You mean garage it?'

'It's a present,' said Molly. The man's mouth dropped open. 'You're kiddin'?'

'These are its papers.' Molly took a crumpled

envelope out of her jeans pocket. 'If I just put your name here, it's all yours. What's your name?'

'Louis Rochetta. You're joking though, ain't cha? Hey, am I on some sort of game show? The man looked about for a hidden camera.

'Nope,' said Molly, trying to get her biro to work. 'There you go, Mr Rochetta. Take it easy now.'

Mr Rochetta was too stunned to say anything, but, 'Th . . . th . . .'

'That's a pleasure,' said Molly, smiling. 'Goodbye.' She'd always wanted to give someone a jackpot surprise like that. Then she turned to talk to Rocky who'd sorted out the tickets. Fifteen minutes later, Molly was hypnotizing the airport staff once more, to get Petula unnoticed past the passport officers and past all the X-ray machines.

Rocky and Molly went shopping in the duty-free lounge. They had to visit a bathroom shop, a sweet shop, an electronics shop and a toy shop. After a mammoth spree, their plane was ready to board so, staggering with all the weight of their purchases and carrying Petula's basket, they made their way to Gate Twenty where they had arranged to meet Nockman.

Nockman, like a good servant, was making his way to the gate as instructed. He felt quite peculiar. He knew who he was, and exactly what his life had been like so far. However, he didn't know how he'd come to be a servant to Mr Cat Basket and Miss Hairdryer. Nor did he know exactly why he liked them so much. He still hated other people. At Gate Twenty, where everyone was queuing to get on the plane, he presented his

282

passport and ticket to the air hostess. 'Good evening,' she said politely.

Nockman was halfway through an insincere smile, when his mind suddenly filled with memories of a teenage girl he'd once known who looked like the air hostess. Nockman recalled how rude he'd been to her. And, without meaning to, he started to babble. 'You are fat and ugly just like 'er,' he found himself saying. 'Yes eendeed, eet ees true. You look like a constipated frog. And sis ees vat I alvays tell 'er too. And I alvays bloow ze blubber face noise.' At this point, Nockman found his mouth suddenly filling with air, and before he could stop it, a very loud, bubbly raspberry blew its way out of his mouth. And if that wasn't enough, Nockman then uncontrollably began to remember his old budgie, Fluff, who Mr Snuff had killed, and he began to howl. 'Aaaaaeeeeouuuuooo!'

The air hostess looked appalled. She crossed her arms and narrowed her eyes. 'Sir, we have a policy against rude passengers. If you are rude to staff or other passengers, you will be barred from flying.'

Nockman was amazed at himself. He couldn't understand how that had happened. He wasn't drunk. Maybe he was ill. And all those nasty memories gave him the creeps.

'I'm zo zorry. Please accept my apologies. Eet vas a joke.'

'Strange sense of humour,' said the air hostess. But, uncrossing her arms, she let him through.

Nockman stumbled down the tunnel towards the aeroplane door, tripping on his shoelace and wondering again what had just come over him. As he lumbered along, he considered how strange that encounter had been, and how out of control he had felt. He'd felt like he was a machine but that someone else had the remote controls. Nockman shuddered again as he thought of his poor budgie, and he wrinkled his nose as he recollected the teenage girl he'd taunted so meanly. He couldn't understand why all these memories had just spewed up in his head. He didn't like it. Then he thought of his new employers and he hurried on.

'Er, 'ello, Miss Hairdryer and Mr Cat Basket, I'm back.'

'Oh, hello,' said Molly and Rocky, looking up from their first-class seats at the green-suited Nockman. Nockman looked at them both and seemed to pale, as if he'd seen a ghost.

'Are you all right?' Rocky asked.

All of a sudden, Nockman felt peculiar again. This time he found himself diving down on the plane's gangway floor, rolling over on to his back and waving his legs and arms in the air. And, like before, his mouth opened of its own accord. He found himself barking and howling piteously.

'Voooof, voooof, aaarf, aaaarf,' he barked as his hat fell off. Then, 'OOOoooooOOOooOOooooowwvooof,' he howled, as again, he thought of his poor dead budgie.

Other people on the plane looked very concerned and an air hostess came up to see what the problem was.

'You can stop now,' said Molly, authoritatively. Then she beamed her eyes at the air hostess. 'It's all right. He just needs his medicine. Don't worry about it, please.' And the air hostess walked away.

Nockman got up, all out of breath. That had been a fit. He *must* be sick. Again, out of the blue, he'd been crying about his pet budgie and how horrid Mr Snuff had been.

And now, as he sat down, another feeling made his eyes water. He felt pity for a dog he had once been unkind to; a dog not dissimilar to Mistress Hairdryer's.

Nockman saw that he was no better than Mr Snuff. As he did his belt up he wondered how he could have been so blind. As a boy he hadn't been blind. He'd known how much his budgie had suffered, and he'd cried for her. For nights he'd cried. And yet, as an adult, he'd been cruel to a dog. He'd left the animal alone, cold and hungry, in a dark, dirty room. The S for Simon, he thought, should stand for Snuff. Snuff Nockman. Nockman hung his head and an emotion that hadn't troubled him for years now throttled him. Shame.

Nockman looked out of the aeroplane window and thought. He'd been unkind to people too. He'd never let other people's feelings bother him. He'd persuaded himself that they didn't matter. But now . . . It was very strange, and he didn't know how, but today, he knew he couldn't ignore people's feelings any more. Nockman was waking up to the fact that, just like his budgie, people had feelings too.

More memories of horrid things he had done began to fill his mind. One by one, the ghosts of his bad deeds introduced themselves to him. And the more they came, the more sick with himself Nockman felt.

As the plane took off, he felt heavy in a way that was entirely new to him. His spirit was lagging behind him, low and sad and drenched with guilt.

# Chapter Thirty-Five

When it was time for supper on the plane, Nockman found himself only wanting to eat fruit. Then he went to sleep. Rocky and Molly, on the other hand, stayed wide-awake, making the most of the first-class menu.

'I wonder what the rest of the plane are having,' said Molly brightly, biting into a ketchup sandwich.

'Meat in congealed fat, followed by lumpy trifles with fruit that tastes of cardboard?' suggested Rocky, biting into a crispy pancake that oozed lemony syrup. 'That's what the Alabasters and me had on the way out.'

'The Alabasters and I, you mean,' said Molly.

'You weren't with them, what do you mean?'

'Awh, forget it,' said Molly. 'Just trying to improve your English.'

'You know what?' Rocky added, looking up from his in-flight magazine. 'It says here that you can get a neck massage in first class.'

'Who by?'

'I dunno. The captain?'

This made them both giggle and Rocky got quite a lot of his syrupy pancake on the magazine.

'Mmmnnn, first class is gggrrrreat. Luxury!' Molly added, taking a slurp of concentrated orange squash. 'But, you know what, Rock? It's going to be difficult coming back down to earth when we land.'

'Why? Hasn't the plane got wheels?'

They started laughing again.

'Pathetic joke . . .' said Molly, her eyes watering as she recovered.

'No, what I mean is . . .' she glanced at Rocky. 'And don't make me laugh, Rocky, because I'm about to say something serious.'

'Are you?' Rocky pulled a very serious face.

'What I mean is, it'll be difficult to not use our hypnotism any more when we're back. I mean, think of all the times you've used it over the last few weeks. It's so *useful*. I know we agreed we should make our ways honestly from now on, but what if, let's say, you saw an old man crying on the street because his wife had died, and because he was lonely . . . Wouldn't you want to hypnotize him to not feel quite so sad? Hypnotize him to join the old peoples' party club, or something? Or let's say you saw a kid crying because she'd got a bad school report, and on the same day her gerbil had been eaten by a cat and her friend had gone to hospital with a terrible disease and . . .'

'Molly,' interrupted Rocky, 'stop it. We agreed.'

'Yes, but I just think it's going to be difficult to resist the temptation.'

'True. It will be. But we have to resist, because if we

start using it for good deeds, soon we'll be doing useful deeds, and before we know it, we'll be using it again every time we don't get our way. And then, we'll be living unreal lives again.'

Molly looked disappointed. She knew Rocky was right. They'd talked this all through already. 'But,' Molly tried, 'if we don't hypnotize anyone, maybe we'll forget how to do it.'

'Nope,' said Rocky, raising an eyebrow, 'it's like sucking your thumb. Once you've learned how, you never forget.'

'OK, you're right,' said Molly glumly, turning her head to look out of the window.

Outside, the night sky was full of stars and beneath – 35,000 feet beneath – the Atlantic Ocean's tides moved with the moon. Molly stared out, finding it difficult to believe that she would never hypnotize anyone again. It struck her that it would be hours before they landed, however. It wouldn't be breaking the rule if she used her powers on the plane.

Rocky was watching a music video. Molly got up and stretched. Then she went for a little walk.

Molly had quite a few conversations over the next two hours.

She met a man by the toilets who was shaking, because he hated flying. Molly persuaded him that from now on he would love it. She talked to an exhausted mother who was up holding a child who wouldn't sleep. After ten minutes they were back in their seats, both completely conked out. She spoke to a weepy air hostess who'd just broken up with her boyfriend, and Molly mended her broken heart. Then she helped three kids who hated school, she turned a grumpy old codger into a mild old man, and she fixed a small boy so that he would love eating green vegetables, especially spinach.

Molly sat down in her seat feeling very satisfied, and a little bit like a fairy godmother.

The plane touched down at six o'clock in the morning. This was like one o'clock New York time, so Rocky and Molly felt very disorientated. But they'd slept a little and were excited to be back.

'Remember what we agreed,' said Rocky, coming down the aeroplane steps.

'Here goes,' said Molly, stepping on to the airport tarmac.

Once in the terminal, Nockman collected their mass of luggage and shopping from the baggage carousel. Then Molly and Rocky decided that it would be cool to travel back to Hardwick House in style. So they chartered a helicopter.

The journey in the helicopter took twenty minutes. As its blades whirred above, Molly looked out, seeing the coastline in the distance and then, from afar, the town of Briersville. As the pilot flew closer, she pointed out the hill where Hardwick House was. Approaching the dilapidated, unkempt building, Molly was reminded of how she used to shut her eyes and picture flying away from Hardwick House, into space.

Very soon, they were hovering directly above the grounds of the building and the pilot began to bring the helicopter down. He landed just outside the orphanage, on a small area of flat ground, the wind from his propellers whipping up the bushes and thistles and grass.

He turned the engine off. 'Here you are.'

Molly looked out expectantly, to see who would emerge from the building first, but no one came out.

'I suppose no one's up yet,' said Rocky. 'I mean, it is early. At least it shows Hazel's not strict about getting up.'

'The place looks as crumbly as ever,' said Molly, letting Petula out for a pee.

Whilst Petula sniffed enthusiastically about the frosty drive, Nockman unloaded the helicopter. Once that was done, the pilot wished them all good luck, and with everyone standing back, started up again. With a thumbs-up signal, he was off. In a minute the machine was only a blot in the sky.

Molly and Rocky turned to look at Hardwick House. A small face dodged from one of the windows.

'Someone's up.'

'Something's up,' said Molly. 'It's all a bit too quiet round here.' She rang on the front door bell, but then she noticed that the splintered door was already open.

# Chapter Thirty-Six

The first thing that hit Rocky and Molly when they walked through the door was the smell. The hall smelled awful. It smelled something rotten. Of decayed food and rubbish and dirt. The chequered floor, instead of being black and white, was so dirty that it looked all black.

'Yuk!' said Molly, putting her cashmere scarf up to her nose. 'Revolting!'

'It smells like someone's died,' said Rocky. 'And it's cold, like a morgue.'

'Oh, don't say that,' winced Molly. 'Please don't. You're spooking me out. But I wonder why it smells so much, and where is everybody?'

'I think the smell is coming from the kitchen,' said Rocky, shutting the door that led to the basement passage. 'Everyone must be upstairs. Nockman, please bring in the luggage, and leave the front door open so we can air the place.'

'Yes, Mr Cat Basket,' said Nockman obligingly. And

Molly, Rocky and Petula ventured up the stone staircase.

On the first landing all the bedroom doors were shut and there was a pungent, unwashed, vinegary smell about the place. Molly pushed open the door to the room where Gordon and Rocky used to sleep.

The room was quiet, with the curtains shut, but holes in the curtains let in enough light to see that no one was there. And the place was a tip. Sheets, blankets and lumpy mattresses were scattered on the floor, leaving the criss-cross wire-framed beds bare and cold. Orange peel, apple cores, old milk cartons, cans, empty baked-bean tins and dirty plates were dropped everywhere. And when Rocky opened the flimsy curtains, a cloud of moths fluttered out of the material.

Molly and Rocky shut that bedroom door to open the next.

That one was empty too, and in a similar chaotic state. The third and fourth bedrooms were empty, but tidier, with the mattresses on the beds. In every room, the air was so cold that Rocky and Molly could see their breath.

'But we saw someone,' said Molly. 'Maybe they're in here.' She pushed open the fifth bedroom door to find that it was jammed with a piece of furniture. However, it wasn't jammed well, and with another bigger push it gave way.

In this room the curtains were open. And there, sitting in the harsh December light, were Gerry, Gemma and the two five-year-olds, Ruby and Jinx.

They were huddled together under blankets, their hair mangy and their faces grimy, their eyes wide open and scared.

'What are you doing in here with the doors all barricaded up?' was the first thing Molly asked. Then when none of the children answered, not even Gerry or Gemma, she walked over and crouched down in front of them. The children shrunk towards each other, like magnetized bits of iron filings. Their behaviour was shocking.

'Gemma,' said Molly quietly, 'don't you recognize me?'

'N-no,' said Gemma, looking quizzically up at Molly's face.

'I'm *Molly*.'

'But,' said Gemma weakly, 'Molly's flown away, and anyway, Molly din't look like you. She din't have nice clothes an' stuff, like you've got, an' her shoes weren't clean lookin' like yours, an' her 'air weren't tidy, an' her face were different.' The little girl wiped her runny nose with the edge of a blanket, and shivered.

'Yeah, Molly had a blotchy face,' said Gerry.

'I *am* Molly. It's just I'm a bit fatter and better kept. You know, like your mouse, Gerry, after you'd looked after him. You know.'

Molly glanced about her. Piles of dirty clothes were strewn messily about. White feathers, from a pillow that had burst, covered the mattresses and the floor, so that the room was more like a nest than a bedroom. A toothpaste tube that had been trodden on had squeezed its contents on to the wooden floor, in a sticky, minty mess and a can of Qube lay beside it, crunched, empty and sad-looking.

'My mouse *died*,' said Gerry hanging his head.

'Oh no, Gerry, did it? That's awful. Isn't it, Rock?' Rocky looked very concerned.

'Yes,' he said. 'That *is* very bad news, Gerry. I'm very sad to hear that Squeak died. Do you remember me, Gerry? I'm Rocky.'

Gerry nodded.

'And this is Petula. She's changed too. See, she's not fat any more, and you know, she actually likes running about now.'

Gerry stared numbly at Petula who licked his hand.

Molly looked anxiously down the row of children. 'You all seem *sick*,' she said. She could hardly believe the change in them, and how quickly it had happened. Whilst she'd been fattening up, they'd all been half-starving. They looked seriously ill. A few more weeks, and Molly might have returned to find them all dead. She recoiled from the thought and felt entirely to blame. As she looked at their little faces, which were as familiar to her as brothers' and sisters' faces might have been, she felt completely responsible for their misery.

She leaned over and gave Gemma a hug. 'I'm so sorry,' she said, from the bottom of her heart. The little girl clung on to her, and Molly felt how frail and cold she was. Rocky gave Gerry a hug, and then Ruby and Jinx too. Jinx and Ruby began to cry. Utterly shocked with herself, Molly wondered how she could have been so uncaring; leaving this lot at Hardwick House, with mad Miss Adderstone. Then later, why hadn't she come back when she'd known that horrible Hazel was in charge? Molly saw that she'd been self-centred and, she remembered, desperate, too. But how could she have left for America in the first place, thinking that there was nothing left in Briersville for her? Molly supposed it was because she hadn't realized, until now, how much she loved these children.

'Is there any food in the house?' Molly asked Gemma, determined to make things better as soon as possible.

'Yes, yes, we still get deliveries, like 'tatoes an' eggs an' groceries an' stuff, but I'm not very good at cookin', an' we run out of saucepans, but the kitchen's full o' rats so we're scared to go down, but we do make a trip sometimes, with sticks.'

'So what have you been eating?' asked Molly aghast.

'Cold baked beans . . .'

'But the tin opener is difficult to use . . .'

'An' we eat bread an' fruit an' cheese sometimes, if we can get to it before those 'orrid rats do.'

'But why's it all gone wrong? Doesn't Mrs Trinklebury come in and bring you fairy cakes and help you to clean and cook?'

'No,' said Gerry, piping up, 'Miss Adderstone gave Mrs Trinklebury the sack, and she never come back. Adderstone said we'd be happier on our own. But we're not . . . an' my mouse died.' Gerry looked down at the floor.

'I know, Gerry, that is very, very sad,' said Molly, touching his head.

'But listen,' said Rocky, trying to be positive, 'you must be really hungry. So how about if we make you omelette and chips and hot chocolate for breakfast?'

All four children stared at Rocky in amazement. 'Yes, please,' they said.

'OK then. Put on your dressing gowns and slippers and let's take you downstairs and we'll light a fire and you can all get warm.'

The small children looked so worn out and grateful that Molly felt compelled to say, 'And listen, you lot, you mustn't worry any more. Everything's going to be lovely from now on, I promise. We've come back to look after you, and we've got someone else to help too, and everything will be tidied up and there'll be nice things to eat and we'll be warm and . . . well just you wait.'

With that, Molly led the waif-like children, in their straggly dressing gowns, downstairs. In twenty minutes a fire was blazing in the hall hearth and they were sitting round it warming their grubby feet. Molly wondered where the older children were, but decided to ask Gemma later. First of all, she had to sort out breakfast, so she called Nockman and Rocky and they made their way down to the stinking kitchen.

They found the kitchen in a diabolical state. Bin bags lay on their sides with rotten food and maggots in them. The sinks were piled high with dirty saucepans, plates and cutlery. In fact, every piece of kitchen equipment was dirty, either in the sink, on the side, or dropped on the floor. Chairs were pulled up to the cooker, where the small children had tried to cook.

Petula sniffed about and smelt rodents. When Molly opened a cupboard three mice, who were eating some crumbs, darted down holes.

'You know, Molly,' observed Rocky, 'there can't be rats here, because I heard that where there are mice, you don't get rats. Which is good, because rats carry nasty diseases, whereas mice are just a bit dirty. If Nockman cleans the surfaces with some sort of disinfectant, it should be safe to cook.'

'Just shows how scared they were. I mean, Gerry loves mice, but his imagination saw the mice as rats.'

Nockman, thanks to the days when he'd worked at Shorings Bank, was very good at cleaning. First he took the kitchen rubbish outside, then he filled one of the sinks full of bubbly water and another full of hot, clear water, for rinsing. He washed up frying pans, bowls, plates and cutlery, and then he started to peel potatoes. Rocky cracked twenty eggs into a bowl, and began to whisk them, whilst Molly found two trolleys, which she wiped down. Then she went to the back door to see if the milkman had been.

Near the doorstep were two crates of extremely rotten fish, several more smelly bins, and milk bottles with their silver tops pecked by small birds. Molly grabbed the milk basket with its five new bottles and hurried back inside.

'Nockman, when you've finished breakfast, and had some yourself too, please can you spring clean the kitchen?' she asked.

'Yes, Miss Hairdryer,' said the willing Nockman.

A terrific smell of omelette and chips and logs burning on the fire soon filled the house. Molly and Rocky watched with satisfaction as the small children, now sitting on the floor around the fire, ate up. With every mouthful, more colour came back to their cheeks.

Gerry was the first to get his curiosity back. 'So,' he said. 'What was the place you went called again?'

'It was called New York,' said Molly. 'Do you remember, I called you?'

'Yup. So what was it like in New York?'

'Amazing,' said Rocky.

'And what did you do there?'

'Well, we did different things,' said Rocky. 'I lived with a family and I found that I liked you lot as my family better.' Gerry looked pleased at this. The other children nodded and smiled.

'And I,' said Molly, 'I lived on my own, and had everything I wanted.'

'What, everything?' asked Gemma.

'Yes. I had posh, posh everything, like everything you've seen in the adverts and more. I had clothes and cars and TVs and films and shops and as *many* sweets as I wanted. And I was in a play and I was on telly and people rang me up all the time and I did some scary things and I was famous!'

'You were famous?' the children echoed.

'Yes, I was as famous as . . . as a person from an advert.'

'So why didn't you stay?' piped up Gemma, looking very perplexed.

'Because,' explained Molly, 'I also had something I *didn't* want.'

'What was that?'

'Lice?' guessed Gerry.

'No, not lice. I had loneliness.'

'Loneliness?'

'Yup. Loneliness. And you know what?'

'What?'

'Loneliness makes all those snazzy, posh, posh, adverty things look like rubbish.'

'Rubbish?'

'Yes, like bins of rotten old rubbish.'

'But why?' asked Gerry.

'Because, when you're lonely without friends or family, what you want more than anything is *not* to be lonely. All those posh things don't make you feel better. You don't care about the posh things then, you just want to be with people you like.'

'So,' said Rocky, 'when Molly bumped into me, she was very pleased to see me. And we decided we were both lonely for you lot, and we were worried too, and so we came home.'

The children seemed very impressed and chuffed that they'd pulled Rocky and Molly home. None of them felt resentment. They were too sweet and forgiving for that. They all stared in wonder at Rocky and Molly and slurped their drinks.

'An' was Petula lonely too?' asked Jinx, stroking Petula's soft head.

'Yes,' said Molly.

''Cos we were lonely, too, weren't we, Gemma?'

'Yes,' admitted Gemma, 'an' it weren't very nice.'

Tiny Ruby was sitting by the fireplace, next to Nockman, with a big moustache of hot chocolate above her lip. She slipped her hand into Nockman's. 'Thank you, Mister,' she said, blinking up at him. 'That was the *best*.'

Nockman had been feeling different since his fit on the plane and now, looking down at the little girl, he felt something he hadn't felt for years. He felt all warm inside. Warm because the little girl had found the way into his heart and because he was glad he had helped her. He could hardly believe the feeling. 'Zat vas my pleasure,' he said quietly.

'Now,' said Molly to Gerry and Gemma, 'tell us everything. Where have Hazel and the others gone?'

'Gone? They're not gone,' said Gemma. 'They're still here.' And she took a deep breath to tell them everything that had been going on at Hardwick House.

# Chapter Thirty-Seven

$\mathcal{G}$emma began. 'After you flew away Miss Adderstone and Edna left too, but before they went, they sacked Mrs Trinklebury, an' they told 'er *never* to come back. They said they wanted to be *nice* to children from now on an' that us children didn't want grown-ups bossing us about. So they said it would be happier for us if they *all* went.'

Molly remembered the instruction she had given Adderstone and Edna at the airport. How could they have been so stupid as to think that leaving kids all on their own, without anyone to help, could make them happier?

'But Mrs Trinklebury *was* nice,' insisted Jinx.

'Yes, but she did what Adderstone bossed her to and left all the same,' continued Gemma. 'Then, Miss Adderstone packed her cases an' so did Edna an' they had an argument 'cos Miss Adderstone snipped some of Edna's clothes up . . .'

'She cut up Edna's coat,' said Ruby.

'An' both their hats,' added Jinx.

'Yeah, they looked silly when they went away, with their clothes all snipped,' said Gerry. 'Edna gave us some sweets, 'cept they were funny ones with 'orrid stuff in them.'

'They was kinda Italian grown-ups' sweets,' explained Gemma. 'They were both nice to us afore they went, though. Miss Adderstone gave me a bag of moffballs.'

'An' she gave me 'er bottle of mouffwash,' said Jinx.

'But you were naughty weren't you, Jinx?' Gemma reminded him.

'Yeah, I drank it.'

Rocky ruffled Jinx's hair.

'Anyway,' Gemma continued, 'Miss Adderstone said food and groceries would keep bein' delivered an' paid automatic by the bank and she said we *must* keep going to school or else nasty Mrs Toadley would come 'ere. So we had to *pretend* Miss Adderstone and Edna were still 'ere so no one outside knew they'd gone.'

'And where did they go?' asked Molly.

'Dunno.'

'Then what happened?'

'Well, then, Hazel took over,' said Gemma.

'And she was *worse* than Adderstone,' whispered Gerry.

'She was horrible an' bossy,' continued Gemma, 'an' she made us work so 'ard. We had to cook an' clean. She said we 'ad to look *really* tidy for school or else Mrs Toadley would guess we was 'ere on our own . . .'

'An' Hazel left her room and moved to Miss Adderstone's old rooms an' she frew lotsa paper out of the window,' said Gerry. 'She said Roger and Gordon must go in Edna's room. But then . . .'

'Then, they all started arguin',' said Gemma. 'An' Roger wanted to be in charge because he said Hazel was lettin' the place run wild. An' Gordon wanted Edna's rooms all to his self. So Roger an' him had a fight an' Roger had to go up to the sanatorium room . . .'

Gemma and Gerry were talking very quickly and animatedly, and Ruby and Jinx were watching them with wide eyes. Molly and Rocky realized how disturbing the last few weeks must have been.

'An' then they *all* shouted at us all an' bossed us about,' said Ruby, 'but they *never* helped.'

'And then they all argued so much that they stopped talking to each other.'

'An' us. They stopped talking to us,' said Jinx.

'Most of the time,' Gemma remembered. 'Sometimes they'd get *really* cross with us if we answered the phone. Or the door. And Hazel was very strict. She said we mustn't tell anyone that Adderstone left. She said if we told, Gordon would hit us. But now it's OK 'cos it's the Christmas holidays and school's finished.'

'So we don't 'ave to be clean any more,' said Gerry.

'But we don't get school lunches now, so we're 'ungry,' murmured Ruby.

'An' we can't go to the village, or the town.'

'Never,' said Jinx, 'Or they said the *Bogeyman* would get us.'

'Well you mustn't worry about that,' said Molly. 'The Bogeyman's just rubbish.'

Molly looked about her. Her surroundings looked

more like a rubbish tip than a room in a house. Hockey sticks and burst footballs were kicked into corners along with cardboard boxes and plastic bags. A few saucepans with mouldy insides still lay about and the walls had been splattered with black ink.

'So where are the others now?'

'Probably asleep,' said Gemma, sipping her drink. 'At ten, Roger gets up. He goes foragin' in the Briersville bins. But Gordon an' Cynthia an' Craig don't go out. They stay in Edna's rooms, watching TV. An' Hazel stays in her room, 'cept she does come downstairs for her special deliveries. She takes the boxes back to her rooms.'

'Well,' concluded Molly, turning to Rocky, 'I think it's time we went to wake Hazel and the others up. Don't you?'

The door to Adderstone's old apartment was shut. A huge, black beetle crawled out from under it. Petula sniffed nervously at the air, detecting a faint smell of the old spinster. Molly looked at Miss Adderstone's portrait that hung on the landing wall. Someone had given her a moustache and a beard. Molly knocked at the door, pushed, and the door swung open. Molly and Rocky entered.

The place smelled stuffy and rank. Miss Adderstone's old, brown parlour was even darker than normal, with the heavy wine-coloured curtains shut.

Molly switched on a light. Boxes, discarded cans and files from Miss Adderstone's cabinet were dropped everywhere. Empty crisp packets and piles of sweet wrappers littered the floor like dry autumn leaves.

From the darkness on the wall, the cuckoo clock sprung open and cuckooed nine times.

'Who is it?' came Hazel's groggy voice from the bedroom. Rocky and Molly crunched over the debris on the floor and opened the door.

In the semi-darkness they saw Hazel, sitting up in bed. Molly stepped through more rubbish and pulled the curtain cord.

Light flooded into the room, hitting Hazel in the face. She shielded her eyes and, squinting, whined, 'Get out, Gemma. No one's s'posed to come in here.'

'It's not Gemma. It's Molly and Rocky,' said Molly.

As Hazel's eyes became accustomed to the light, she let her hands drop from her face. And she revealed a very different-looking Hazel to the one Molly had last seen. This Hazel had a much fatter, paler, spottier face. Her eyes were bloodshot with dark rings around them. Her lips were crusty with cold sores at their edges. Her hair was longer because it hadn't been cut, and stuck to her head because it was so greasy. She also had the look of a mad person, which now, coupled with the shock of seeing Molly and Rocky, made her look very alarmed. She clutched a pillow. 'D-D-Drono. I'm dreaming,' she panted hoarsely, and she lightly hit herself on the head with the pillow.

'No you're not. We're back,' said Molly. 'And this may seem like a nightmare to you, but we're staying.'

The old Hazel would have jumped out of bed and challenged Molly, but this Hazel simply whimpered, 'Whatever.'

Hazel reached for a cardboard box beside her bed, and took a Heaven bar from it. She unwrapped the chocolate and frantically crammed it into her mouth.

'Gotta have a sugar hit,' she said, biting a chunk off, concentrating on the chocolate. All of a sudden, she seemed to have forgotten that Rocky and Molly were in the room.

'Hazel,' said Molly, 'you look terrible.'

'Yeah, I know,' said Hazel, biting a second chunk.

'You look *ill*,' said Rocky. 'Have you been eating only sweets?'

'Yeah, there's nothing better to eat,' said Hazel, her eyes darting desperately about the room, at the boxes and boxes of sweets. Then she suddenly looked petrified. 'You're not going to take my sweets away, are you?'

'No,' said Molly, 'but we've got some better food for you. Would you like some omelette and chips?'

After Rocky had fetched some proper food, and Hazel had devoured it, Rocky and Molly talked to her.

She told them how everything had gone wrong.

She told them she'd enjoyed being in charge at first, but then, after her rows with Gordon and Roger, she'd become more reclusive. She'd started to spend more time alone, eating only chocolate and sweets. She'd even smoked a packet of cigarettes that she'd found in Miss Adderstone's cabinet. She confessed that she'd felt tired and ill and alone, and that finally, she'd started to look at herself.

'I felt bad-tempered all the time, and I tried to feel better but I couldn't. I wanted to have good feelings for other people, but they wouldn't come. I just hated everyone and I hated myself for being so . . . so full of hate. And I'm a liar.'

Hazel reached for a green file on the side table, and threw it to Molly.

'You should know who I really am. I always lied to everyone. Read it. Go on, read it.' She sank back on the pillows behind her, with tears in her eyes. 'There's no point in hiding any more.'

Inside the green folder was Hazel's record. Molly and Rocky started to read.

| | |
|---|---|
| Name | Hazel Hackersly |
| Date of Birth | ? |
| Place of Birth | ? |
| How came to Hardwick House | Seriously unstable home life. Child, age six, arrived undernourished and bruised because of maltreatment. |
| Parents | Mother alcoholic. Father violent and prone to fits. Both unfit to care for child. |
| Possessions | None |
| Description of child | "Hazel reminds me of myself as a child. She is quick to learn and eager to please." |

'See,' moaned Hazel, 'I never was the glamorous kid you all thought. You thought I had the best parents ever, but my parents never loved me, they only hit me.' Hazel's eyes brimmed over with tears. 'At least Adderstone never beat me, so I liked her. But you. I was jealous of you because you had Mrs Trinklebury. She was like a mum to you two. But not to me. I came too late. I had a mother who screamed at me.'

'But,' said Molly, frightened by what Hazel was

307

saying, 'but Mrs Trinklebury would have loved you too, eventually. You just never let her.'

'But I'm horrible,' sobbed Hazel. 'I know no one likes me. I don't blame you. I don't like myself. I'm bad. And you know, it's not a nightmare you coming back. I don't care about being in charge any more. I don't want to run this place. I'm sick. I just want to get better. I want to *be* better.' Hazel's face crumpled up into a desperate mass of furrows and creases and her mouth opened. No noise came out of it. A silent cry was there though, and tears streamed down her cheeks.

Molly put her hand on Hazel's shoulder. 'It's OK, Hazel. Please don't cry. We understand. Thanks for showing us your file. You should have seen mine, it made out I was a real nobody. We'll help you get better now. From now on, things are going to be different around here.'

'Good,' Hazel managed to gasp, between sobs. 'And . . . thank you for coming back.'

Molly and Rocky helped Hazel out of bed and ran her a bath. Then they left the room to investigate Gordon Boils.

They found Gordon sitting in an armchair in Edna's rooms, wrapped in a duvet, with his feet in a huge double slipper. Next to him, on a sofa, under eiderdowns, were the two other big children, Cynthia and Craig. Their eyes were glued to the telly which had been removed from the common room downstairs. When Rocky and Molly appeared, they all looked up briefly as if they had seen a couple of flies, and then turned back to the TV.

Gordon's face, which he held in his hands, was anaemic, thinner and less aggressive. Molly read his tattoos. 'KING GORD', his fists read. There was nothing majestic about him now. Cynthia and Craig looked equally ghost-like and sad.

Molly switched the telly off. 'Hello, you lot.'

After Rocky had brought them all breakfast, Gordon at last talked. His voice was weaker and as he spoke his eyes shifted about uneasily.

He told them how they'd all been in a terrible black mood since the school term had ended. Their only consolation had been the telly, and so they'd watched it non-stop.

'It's horrible here. We all feel sick,' Gordon groaned. 'I feel like I'm sick right down to the core. Really, I think there's something wrong with me. Rocky, I think I need a doctor.'

Cynthia and Craig said nothing.

'Listen,' said Molly. 'We'll help you lot get better, but on one condition; you have all got to change your ways.'

'How do you mean?' asked Gordon feebly.

'You've got to stop being mean.'

'Oh, that,' said the downtrodden Gordon, whose eyes were soft and wet like a bull calf's now. 'Of course we can. I haven't bullied anyone for wee . . . days.'

'But how can *you* help us, Bogey Eyes?' asked Cynthia.

'I just will,' said Molly. 'Wait and see. Oh, and by the way, I'm Molly to you. Molly Moon.'

Molly spoke firmly, but inside she was pleased that Cynthia had called her Bogey Eyes. It showed that any adoration that Cynthia might have felt after Molly's hypnotism at the Briersville Talent Competition had worn off.

As they left Gordon, Cynthia and Craig to have baths and get dressed, Molly wondered whether the three would be quite as compliant when they were better again.

'We'll have to see,' agreed Rocky.

The last person to visit was Roger Fibbin, up in the sanatorium room. They found him sitting on the edge of the bed doing up his shoelace.

Roger jumped with shock when he saw Molly and Rocky.

His face was bonier than ever, his sharp nose was pink and dripping and his hands were purple from cold. His clothes were just as tidy as they had been before, but when Molly got closer she noticed that his shirt had a brown dirt mark round the inside of the collar and his grey trousers were stiff with grime. His fingernails were tipped with muck.

'What . . . what are you doing here?' he demanded, his left eye twitching. 'I'm off. Got to . . . got to go and check the bins.' He looked at a broken watch on his wrist. 'I'm late and if I don't check them soon, they'll be emptied.'

After Molly and Rocky had calmed Roger down with some nourishing food, they discovered that he too was a broken person. He'd developed a foraging habit whereby he found food to eat in the bins of Briersville town. He'd caught a few nasty stomach bugs, he said, but he found it the easiest way of getting a varied diet.

'That,' he said, half-weeping, pointing at the empty breakfast plate, 'was the best food I've had in . . . in . . . weeks.'

'Don't worry, Roger. There will be lots of good things to eat from now on,' Rocky assured him. And at these kind, promising words, Roger flung his arms around Rocky's neck and broke down in tears.

Wandering back up to the sanatorium room, Molly caught a glimpse of herself in the mirror. The very mirror she had looked into and seen herself as a punk.

She thought how different she looked now. Her hair was shinier, her face wasn't blotchy, her complexion was healthy. And as for her potato nose and her closely set green eyes, instead of seeing these features as ugly, Molly now liked them, because they were hers.

She had definitely changed since that November night when she'd stood on the hill hating her life and herself.

Molly reflected upon how everyone at Hardwick House had changed since that time. And, the changes had all happened because of *The Book of Hypnotism*.

Hazel, Roger, Gordon, Cynthia and Craig had been humbled. Without the structure of school and rules, and by not having anything to fight against any more, they'd fought with each other and broken their alliances. With their gang smashed, they'd all had to stand alone. And then they'd had to face themselves. And they didn't like what they'd found. Hazel had broken down so completely that she'd told the truth about herself. Molly knew she couldn't ever rule like before again. And she trusted that Hazel had meant it when she'd said she wanted to be a better person.

Molly wasn't so sure that Gordon, Cynthia and Craig would change their ways. She couldn't imagine Gordon helping an old lady across the road, or Cynthia or Craig being kind. Molly thought that when their strength returned, so would their aggression. It would be hard work living with them. As for Roger, Molly was worried that the strain of the last few weeks had tipped him over the edge into a sort of madness. She hoped he would recover.

Then there was Nockman. He was definitely improving, becoming more considerate by the hour. Although he was still a bit of an experiment, Molly hoped he would be changed for ever, like Petula had been. She was running about now, as fit as a puppy.

And Miss Adderstone and Edna? Molly didn't know what they were up to or where they were. She knew that the instructions she had given them would wear off soon, but hoped that both would have discovered that they actually did love planes and flying and Italian cooking. And if these hobbies were new passions, they wouldn't come back to Hardwick House. Neither of them were children-loving types anyway. Molly had done them a huge favour by guiding them away from kids.

Then Molly went downstairs, to hide the hypnotism book where it had always been safe before. Under a mattress.

# Chapter Thirty-Eight

Mrs Trinklebury was delighted when she got Molly's telephone call. She arrived at Hardwick House, jolly and rosy-cheeked, like a roly-poly pudding, wrapped in a woolly coat. She held shopping bags that were packed with delicious things to cook for supper, and her old knitting bag which was stuffed full with home-made fairy cakes. Once inside the house, she handed these out.

'Oooh, my w-word,' she said, looking about her. 'This place has gone to seed, hasn't it? D-deary me. It smells like an uncleaned kennel.'

After Molly and Rocky had explained the situation to Mrs Trinklebury, it didn't take much pleading to persuade her to come and live with them.

'You've got to come, Mrs Trinklebury. We need you to help look after us,' explained Molly.

'Otherwise they'll send some other Miss Adderstone,' warned Rocky.

'Please come, Mrs Trinklebury, cos we really need a mum,' said Ruby.

'Someone to make us fairies,' declared Jinx.

Mrs Trinklebury sighed and folded her arms. 'You know, it's been lonely at home since my A-Albert died. And I've been even lonelier since Miss Adderstone sacked me. I'd love to c-c-come.'

Molly and Rocky gave her a hug. 'You're a star, Mrs T.'

They then took Mrs Trinklebury downstairs to meet Nockman.

Nockman had an apron on and his arms were elbow high in Bubblealot bubbles. He'd already disposed of the smelly bins and cleared the kitchen cupboards. The kitchen now smelled of lemony cleaning cream.

'Mr Nockman, this is Mrs Trinklebury. She's coming to live here, and she's going to be in charge.'

'And you will get on with her,' Rocky whispered quietly.

'Ah, hello,' said Nockman, taking off his rubber gloves and shaking hands politely.

'Nice to meet you,' said Mrs Trinklebury. 'You're doing a l-l-lovely job of clearing up.'

'Thank you,' said Nockman, smiling, chuffed that his hard work was appreciated.

'W-well,' said Mrs Trinklebury, embarrassed and not knowing what to say next, 'as I s-said. Molly, I'd l-l-love to come back. I'll be bringing P-Poppet, if that's all right.' Then, she explained to Nockman, 'She's my pet budgerigar and she sings beautifully. I'm sure you'll like her.'

'You have a budgie?' said Nockman, gazing at Mrs Trinklebury as if she was a goddess.

'Oh, y-yes,' said Mrs Trinklebury, embarrassed again by Mr Nockman's attention. She pulled on a spare pair of rubber gloves. 'If we're going to slap this place into shape, Molly,' she said, 'I'd better get started.'

By suppertime, wonderful smells of a roast dinner with potatoes and peas, sweetcorn and gravy were wafting through the orphanage. The building was warm, as Mrs Trinklebury had arranged for oil to be delivered, and the boiler was now running full pelt.

Molly and Rocky gave all the children bubble bath and shampoo, and brand-new soft towels which Molly had bought at the airport.

By eight o'clock, everyone was washed, dry and wearing something new, chosen from Molly's suitcases. Even Gordon, Roger and Craig found T-shirts that they liked.

The dining-room tables were laid, sparkling with glasses and lit with candles. And the fire blazed.

Supper was the best Molly had ever had. Not the best food, although it was good, but best because it was fantastic to see everyone again, even Hazel and her old gang. And how different they were now. They were shadows of their former selves and very quiet as they ate and drank. The smaller children on the other hand got chattier and noisier as the evening went by, making Mrs Trinklebury, and even Nockman, laugh.

Then Gerry piped up, 'So, Mrs Trinklebury . . . Are you and Mr Nockman going to be our mum and dad now?' and Mrs Trinklebury and Nockman both blushed.

Molly and Rocky gave everyone the presents that they'd bought at the airport. Cameras and Walkmans for Hazel and Cynthia, radio-controlled cars and planes for Gordon, Roger and Craig and teddies and walkie-talkies for Gemma, Gerry, Ruby and Jinx. Gerry also got a stuffed mouse. Everyone was given a tiny TV set each and a huge bag of sweets. Mrs Trinklebury loved the perfume and the necklace they bought her and Mr Nockman liked his new suit.

After the present-giving, Gemma asked Molly to do her song-and-dance routine again. 'You know, the one you did at the talent show.'

Molly smiled and shook her head.

'I'm sorry to disappoint you, Gemma, but the thing is, I've given all of that up. Did you like it?'

'Yes, you were *brilliant*!' remembered Gemma.

'I was, wasn't I?' agreed Molly.

When the candles on the table were melted to the size of mushrooms, Mrs Trinklebury suddenly tapped the side of her glass with a fork. Everyone grew silent as shy Mrs Trinklebury stood up, coughed and bravely proceeded.

'Now as y-you all know, I'm a s-stutterer,' she began, smiling.

'But you're very nice,' said Gemma.

'Well, thank you, Gemma, and so are you. And stutter as I m-may, I'm going to t-talk to you all now about something th-that I haven't told anyone for years, but which I know I m-must tell you all. *This* is the right time to tell you. It's the right time, because

316

at last this building, our h-home, H-H-Hardwick H-House, has got hap-happiness inside it.

'M-Molly and Rocky, as you know, have asked me to c-come and live here and h-help take care of all of you. Which I h-hope is all right with you.'

Mrs Trinklebury took a deep breath.

'Before now, there was a lot of sadness in th-this building, and some of you probably felt that no one understood h-how it felt to be alone in the world. I d-don't think Miss Ad-Adderstone helped.

'I used to feel the s-sadness here when I came in to clean, and it almost broke my h-heart. Because, well, deep down, I know what it feels to be alone too. Because, well – and this is what I wanted to tell you – I am an orphan too.

'You may think I am a bit old and fat to be an orphan, but when I was a little girl, I had to go to an orphanage too. You s-see, my dad died when I was two, and then my mother got married again. Trouble was, her new husband had three children and then he had another two with my m-mum and, well, there were just too many children and my poor mum couldn't cope. One of us had to g-g-go. And the one that went was me.

'Now, that never seemed fair to me. And for a long time, I hated those other children for pushing me out. B-because they did, you know. They were like their dad. He was a b-brute of a man and they were brutish too. And they held on and kicked, and I was the one who g-g-got pushed out. I was more timid than them, you see.

'Then, one day, I heard a song that seemed to be written for me. Some of you know it.' Mrs Trinklebury smiled at Molly and Rocky. 'But for you others, I'll sing it now. It goes like this.' Mrs Trinklebury's quaky voice filled the dining room.

*'Forgive, little birds, that brown cuckoo*
*For pushing you out of your nests.*
*It's what mamma cuckoo taught it to do*
*She taught it that pushing is best.'*

Molly looked around, wondering if Hazel and the bigger children would be making faces after hearing the lullaby. But they weren't. They were sitting still, listening intently. Except for Gordon, who was still eating.

'That song taught me a lot,' said Mrs Trinklebury. 'It made me realize that I mustn't hate those children who pushed me out of the nest, because they were only being how their d-dad had taught them to be. So I forgave them. And from that moment onwards, life was better because I didn't h-hate them any more.

'Now, we all have stories of how we're here, and prob-probably some of you feel angry with whoever it is who's left you here. But you must try and remember that they were like that because that's how they were taught to be. You m-must try to feel sorry for them and forgive them.

'And because mother c-cuckoos teach their babies bad habits, and because what you learn as a ch-child you will pass on to people around you, from now on, this house is going to be a house of happiness.

'From this evening on, every single one of us is going to consider other people's feelings.' She turned to the small children. 'We don't need n-nastiness, do we? What's nastiness? A nasty b-bug. And we don't want to spread it about, do we?'

'No,' agreed Gerry, 'we don't.'

'So,' concluded Mrs Trinklebury, 'if it's all right with all of you, I want to change the name of this b-building, so that from now on, it's a place of joy. From now on, I propose this building should be known as Happiness House.'

Everyone stared at her.

'Are you agreed then?' she asked. 'If you are, r-raise your glasses.'

Everyone raised their glasses of Qube. Nockman raised his the highest. Cynthia flicked a piece of bread at Craig.

'To Happiness House,' Mrs Trinklebury toasted.

'To Happiness House,' everyone agreed.

And in the distance, they all heard the sound of the cuckoo clock chiming ten.

'Now,' finished Mrs Trinklebury, 'I think it's time for bed . . .'

'But first of all,' Nockman interrupted her, 'I would like to do a few little tricks.'

Molly gulped. She had a feeling that Nockman was about to misbehave. But over the next half hour, Molly saw a new side of him that surprised her. Nockman was in his element as he thrilled everyone with a fantastic array of card tricks, finding cards behind people's ears and under their chairs. He showed them how to cheat at poker, and Molly noticed Gordon's eyes lighting up as he watched Nockman in action. She'd have to keep an eye on those two, she thought. Gordon's fascination with Nockman could lead to trouble.

After his card tricks, Nockman showed off his amazing sleight of hand. He took a purse from Mrs

Trinklebury's cardigan pocket without her noticing, and a packet of sweets from under Hazel's arm. Everyone clapped and thought he was one of the nicest men they'd ever met. Little did Molly and everyone know that actually Nockman *had* misbehaved. He had stolen a camera from Hazel, a lolly from Ruby, five pounds from Gordon's top pocket and Mrs Trinklebury's front-door key, and had stuffed all these things into the front of his shirt. There they lay, below his diamond-eyed scorpion which nestled comfortably amongst the hairs on his chest.

By eleven, everyone had gone to bed. Only Molly and Rocky still sat in chairs by the crackling fire, wide awake. Petula lay happily at their feet, sucking a stone.

'What a day,' sighed Rocky. 'Mind you, I'm not tired because by New York time, it's only six in the evening.'

'Yup, we've got jet lag,' agreed Molly, staring into the fire. 'It was great today,' she said, 'and, actually, it's lovely here when it's warm.'

'Mmmn, so different from when Adderstone was in charge.'

'Trouble is,' said Molly frowning, 'that oil for the boiler was *so* expensive. Two hundred and fifty pounds! Mrs Trinklebury gave me the bill.' Molly reached into her fleece's zipper pocket and pulled out her envelope of money. 'If we keep buying oil and if we start spending money on other things, like redecorating the bedrooms and buying new furniture, soon we may not be able to *afford* heating or Mrs Trinklebury or good food. And we did promise we weren't going to use our hypnosis any more. Maybe we were idiots to say we'd go straight, because, Rocky, I don't really see how we're going to manage.'

Petula looked up, sucking her stone, sensing that Molly was worried.

'Well,' said Rocky, 'we'll just have to try and make ends meet. Things aren't going to be always perfect, Molly, but they'll be much better than before, and any problems that we have, we'll work them out.'

'Mmmnn,' nodded Molly.

Petula cocked her head to one side and wondered how she could cheer Molly up. She hated it when Molly was worried. She thought of her usual trick, that normally worked. Molly liked it when Petula gave her one of her sucking stones.

So, Petula affectionately scratched Molly's leg with her front paw, dropped her stone at Molly's feet, and barked a friendly bark.

This time, however, to Petula's surprise, Molly reacted quite differently to Petula's present.

'Oh my giddy aunt! I can't *believe* it!' Molly said, gawping down at the floor. And Rocky, equally stunned, exclaimed, '*Jeepers*, Petula! Where did you get *that*?'

Petula smiled a doggy smile. She had to agree, that particular stone was a nice one; the hardest stone she'd ever sucked. She'd found it in Molly's anorak pocket when she was trying to get comfortable yesterday morning.

Molly picked up the massive diamond and turned to Rocky with her mouth open. 'It's the diamond that gangster was holding in the bank vault. I remember I put it in my pocket, but I forgot to put it with the other bank stuff. So it never got packed into a gnome . . .'

Rocky looked perplexed. 'But the TV report said that every last jewel had been returned to the bank.'

'Maybe this diamond wasn't on any list yet. I remember that gangster guy saying that he'd stolen it *that* day, from another crook.'

'Raooof! Raoooof!' barked Petula, as if to say. 'Take it. It's yours!'

Molly scrunched her velvety ears. 'What shall we do with it, Rocky?'

'I don't know,' said Rocky, stroking the hefty diamond. 'It would be very difficult, maybe impossible, to find out who it *originally* belonged to.' Then, a naughty grin spread across his face. 'You'd better put it in a safe place, Molly.'

# Chapter Thirty-Nine

That night, Molly and Rocky finally went to bed at two a.m.

At four o'clock in the morning, Molly woke up.

The full December moon was shining through the window, its beams drenching Molly's bed.

Molly felt strange. Her hands began to sweat, and then, as if something was calling her, she got out of bed, put on her dressing gown and slippers, and took the leather-bound hypnotism book from under her mattress.

As if in a dream, Molly found herself leaving the bedroom, descending the staircase, collecting a coat and stepping out into the frosty night.

The moon lit the way as she opened the orphanage gates, trod the icy road that led down the hill, and walked around the village, towards Briersville town.

Molly felt drawn. Pulled. And she didn't mind the cold. Nor did she feel frightened. She simply felt she had to do something, although what exactly she didn't know. She found herself stopping finally at Briersville Library. She walked up its stone steps, past its old stone lions and into the library lobby. Across the way, in the reading room, she could see a light on. Molly knew she had to go there. She walked to the door and pushed.

There, sitting behind her desk, was the librarian.

'Ah,' she said, looking up, smiling. 'So you're back.' And looking out of the window at the full moon, she added, 'And perfectly punctually.'

When she said that, Molly suddenly emerged from her dream-like state. She felt as if she'd just woken up from a very good sleep. Her head was clear and everything around her looked extra-bright. There she was, in her dressing gown, coat and slippers, in the library reading room, with the hypnotism book under her arm. In a daze, she offered it to the librarian.

'Thank you, Molly. I hope it helped you,' said the librarian, taking off her spectacles.

Molly began to find her bearings. She looked at the librarian quizzically, wondering how she knew her name. Then she realized that the librarian must have seen her name scores of times when she had taken out books. But how did she know she was coming? Molly asked suspiciously, 'What did you mean when you said that I'd come back "perfectly punctually"? I can't remember making any arrangement with you.'

She thought back to how she'd first stolen the hypnotism book from the library. Had the librarian seen her? She felt embarrassed that she'd been caught red-handed. She'd wanted to put the hypnotism book back quietly to avoid all these feelings. But then she thought again. She was *sure* she'd smuggled the book away when the librarian wasn't looking. Yes, no one had seen Molly take it. So how did the woman know? Did they have cameras in the library? Suddenly Molly felt very muddled.

The librarian smiled. 'Oh, Molly, don't worry. Come and sit over here.' Molly sat down at the desk, in front of the librarian. And for the first time Molly looked at her properly.

She was a studious-looking woman, but now that she had taken her spectacles off, Molly saw she wasn't as old as she had seemed before. She wore her hair in an old-fashioned bun, and some of it was going grey, but her face didn't match it. Her face was young and smooth and as she smiled, her eyes lit up with kindness.

'You, Molly, probably thought I never noticed you, since I always had my nose stuck in a book or a file. But I did notice you. I noticed how you'd come in here so lonely and cold, and sit by the radiators. I had my eye on you for ages and I felt sorry for you. I wanted to help you. I had a feeling you would learn something, well, a lot really, from the hypnotism book. So, on that afternoon, when you came in here, all wet and bedraggled, I hypnotized you to find it. Do you remember waking up after a sleep on the floor?'

Molly nodded, her face frowning in disbelief.

'Well, that sleep was brought on by me. I hypnotized you when I said hello to you. And while you thought you were just sleeping, I, in fact was suggesting things to you. I hypnotized you to find the book. I thought that three weeks with it would be the right amount of time for you to have an adventure. So I asked you to bring it back on the night of the December full moon.'

'Perfectly punctually . . .' Molly said.

'That was the phrase that I said would wake you up from your full-moon walk. You weren't hypnotized to do anything else, by the way. Everything else that has happened to you was your *own* adventure.'

'Normally I'm so late for everything!' said Molly, although her next thought was that, actually, she hadn't been late for anything for weeks. 'But how come Nockman knew about the book?' asked Molly, trying to think straight.

'Oh, him. That liar. Well, a few days before, he called from the States, saying that he needed the book for important research work. He said he was a professor and that having the book for a while would help him enormously. He was very persuasive. I said he could *borrow* it. But then, he called back rather sneakily on my day off and spoke to one of the other librarians. He persuaded her to *sell* it to him. He sent the money in the express post, and when I came back the next day, she told me that he was actually coming over. At that point I'd started to smell a rat. And when I made my inquiries, I found that a Professor Nockman did not exist at the Chicago Museum. Not in any department. Before he'd set foot in this country, I knew he was a fraud. And also, by then, I'd been thinking about you. I wanted to lend it to you.' The librarian switched off the light on her desk. 'I'm sorry to have got you out of bed. It's ever so late, and I'm tired too. I've got to go home, and so have you.'

Molly was just starting to wake up, and questions were filling her head. 'I'm not dreaming, am I?' she asked.

'No,' laughed the librarian. 'But you should be. You should be in bed, fast asleep.'

'I'm not tired any more.'

'But I am. I really have to get home. I would love to talk to you properly though. So, as soon as you've got a moment, and if you feel like it, let's meet up for tea. You can tell me some of the adventures that you had, and I'll tell you some of mine.'

'You had adventures using hypnotism too?'

'Of course. Everyone who finds that they have the gift has adventures. I rarely use my skills now though. I use them sometimes, just to help people. I find that's best.'

'Like you helped me?'

'Did I? I'm so glad.'

For a moment, Molly was quiet as she thought of how much she'd changed over the last few weeks. She might still be unhappy if it weren't for the librarian. She'd learned so much because of her.

'Thank you,' she said very gratefully. 'Erm, sorry, I don't even know your name.'

'It's Lucy Logan,' said the kind-faced woman.

'Like the Doctor?' she gasped. 'Like the Doctor Logan who wrote the book?'

'He was my great-grandfather,' Lucy Logan replied, smiling again. 'But look, you've had enough surprises for tonight. You're going to find it difficult to get back to sleep. And I ought to lock up. So let's both go now and, Molly, you really are more than welcome to come back and visit whenever you like, and I'll tell you all about my great-grandfather and we can talk about hypnotism. All right?'

Molly nodded and got up from the table.

As she left the library, Lucy Logan waved. 'And Happy Christmas, Molly, if I don't see you before then!'

'Happy Christmas,' said Molly, dizzy from the night's revelations.

Molly walked back home, under the December moon. Every so often, she shook her head as she thought of an episode in the past few weeks, reliving exciting or scary moments and seeing how chance had been on her side. She marvelled at how things had unfolded.

As she padded up the country road, thick, soft snowflakes started to fall, and the ground underfoot became whiter and gently crunchy. Trees above the hedgerow by the road seemed to beckon Molly onwards.

Molly saw the Briersville billboard, lit up in the distance. The Qube people in the swimming costumes looked as though their shiny teeth would be chattering now. And Molly thought how funny it was that only three weeks ago she'd thought these people were wonderful and she'd longed to be like them. Now, she couldn't care less about their Qube life. She had her own life to live, and it was far more interesting and meaningful to her than theirs.

Snow filled the air, swirling about Molly, muffling noises so that her walk was extra quiet and private. She felt truly excited about her life for the first time ever. She liked being Molly Moon, even though she wasn't perfect.

The hypnotism book had taught her that she had the power to learn anything, as long as she tried. Six months ago, if someone had told her she could be a great hypnotist, she wouldn't have believed them because she believed she was rotten at everything. Molly couldn't wait to try all sorts of other things now. One sport she'd decided to take up was cross-country running, just to see if she could get better at it. And Molly had made up her mind to really learn how to tap dance. Not to become a hugely famous tap dancer, but just to become good enough to really enjoy it. Molly didn't care about fame now, either. She just wanted to enjoy her life, and help other people enjoy theirs.

Now, there were only five days to go until Christmas! Molly had been so busy, she'd clean forgotten. She smiled. This was going to be the *best* Christmas *ever*.

Molly breathed in the fresh cold night air and grinned at the still, sleeping countryside. Tonight, life was almost too exciting. What had she thought when she'd first found the hypnotism book? That the possibilities it could bring were endless? Tonight Molly felt that was certainly true about her life. From the top of her head to the tips of her toes. Life felt completely magical. And once again, Molly thought how happy she was to be ordinary, plain old Molly Moon.

Ahead, the road shone like a silver ribbon in the moonlight, all the way home to Happiness House.

Three thousand miles away, four thousand feet up in the sky over the Italian Alps, a plane was doing a loop-the-loop. In its cockpit sat two women; one muscly, the other scrawny. The pilot had a mad glint in her eye, and no teeth. Her teeth were swinging below her chin on a string, like a pendant. The strong woman beside her was wearing a T-shirt that had the words, 'YOU BETTER LOVE ITALY OR ELSE . . .' written across the front of it.

As the plane looped the loop again, the bruiser got up. 'Fancy una pasta molto, molto bene, Agnes?'

'Mmmnnn, yes, but look, Edna, not spicy. I mean it this time, Edna . . . Not *too* spicy.'

The End

# About the Author

Georgia Byng was born in London and grew up in a large, noisy family in the Hampshire countryside. She now lives in a house in London full of art, flowers, curiosities and books, with her children Lucas and Sky, their two dogs Jet and Buster, and a tarantula called Hades (and there used to be a hibernating Canadian frog in the fridge). Her grown-up daughter, Tiger, lives nearby.

Georgia's bestselling debut novel, *Molly Moon's Incredible Book of Hypnotism*, won the Salford, the Stockton and the Sheffield Children's Book Awards. It has been translated into thirty-six languages, and the five other books in the series have firmly established Molly as a favourite with readers around the world. Georgia co-wrote the movie adaptation of *Molly Moon and the Incredible Book of Hypnotism*, which features an all-star cast, including Raffey Cassidy, Celia Imrie, Emily Watson and Joan Collins.

For more information about the movie and the other books in the Molly Moon series, head to
**www.mollymoonsworld.com**

# Read the next two books in the hypnotic Molly Moon series